The man wore a black leather jacket.

He stood in the doorway, surveying the coffee shop. He exuded an impression of power and detachment, a kind of quiet, forceful masculinity that Laurel found surprisingly attractive. But she saw that, despite his good looks, the man's face had a cynical expression, and there was a bitter line to his mouth.

She watched as he came into the room, tensing automatically as she waited for him to notice and acknowledge her presence. But his eyes passed over her and moved on without pausing.

Laurel felt a brief, hurt surprise.

She told herself it was irrational to be upset at the way the man seemed to dismiss her. The whole idea of her charade was to blend in with the townspeople and become invisible. Her efforts had clearly been successful.

Or had they? Laurel was aware of those remarkable eyes flickering over her again. This time there was something—a glimmer of recognition? It lasted less than a second, then his glance turned cold and impersonal, and he looked away.

The waitress brought Laurel her food, but her appetite seemed to have vanished. Suddenly she needed to put as much distance as possible between herself and the stranger in the black leather jacket.

ABOUT THE AUTHOR

In *The Hiding Place*, Margot Dalton's fourteenth Superromance novel, readers get the opportunity to revisit the small town of Wolf Hill, Alberta, and meet again many of the characters from *The Secret Years*.

Margot has been writing for Harlequin since 1990. In addition to her Superromances, she has published seven titles for the Crystal Creek series and has contributed to a couple of the Harlequin anthologies. In February of this year, Margot's first mainstream title, *Tangled Lives*, was published by MIRA Books.

Books by Margot Dalton

HARLEQUIN SUPERROMANCE
558—ANOTHER WOMAN
576—ANGELS IN THE LIGHT
622—KIM & THE COWBOY
638—THE SECRET YEARS
664—MAN OF MY DREAMS

Margot Dalton
THE
HIDING PLACE

Harlequin Books

TORONTO • NEW YORK • LONDON
AMSTERDAM • PARIS • SYDNEY • HAMBURG
STOCKHOLM • ATHENS • TOKYO • MILAN
MADRID • WARSAW • BUDAPEST • AUCKLAND

ISBN 0-373-70693-6

THE HIDING PLACE

Copyright © 1996 by Margot Dalton.

This edition published by arrangement with Harlequin Books S.A.

® and TM are trademarks of the publisher. Trademarks indicated with
® are registered in the United States Patent and Trademark Office, the
Canadian Trade Marks Office and in other countries.

Printed in U.S.A.

THE
HIDING PLACE

CHAPTER ONE

THE APRIL MORNING was gray and cold. Freezing rain fell on Manhattan, pattering against the mounds of dirty snow piled at the curbs, washing into swollen storm drains. Traffic slowed to a crawl, and tempers frayed as drivers jostled for position in the crowded streets.

Outside a midtown hotel, a white-gloved doorman ventured from his post to hail a cab, then stowed a small pile of luggage into the trunk while a woman stood under the awning, waiting.

She was tall and slender, wearing a belted navy trench coat over beige flannel slacks and a white turtleneck. Her light brown, shoulder-length hair was pulled smoothly back from her face and tied with a red and navy scarf. Her gray eyes were framed by dark lashes, and her face had a look of composure that seemed to set her apart from the noisy activity surrounding her.

The doorman slammed the trunk, turned and nodded to her.

Laurel Atchison moved forward and handed him a couple of bills, climbed into the rear of the cab and settled back.

"La Guardia, please," she said to the driver, a stocky young man with curly black hair and thick glasses.

"Okay. Which airline?"

"Air Canada."

He laid an arm along the back of the seat and turned to glance at her. "You in a big hurry?" he asked.

Laurel shook her head. "My flight doesn't leave for about two hours. I like to get to the airport early. I'd much rather wait in an airport lounge than in my hotel room."

"That's good." He swung his cab into the traffic, weaving his way expertly among the crawling vehicles. "There's accidents all over the city. The streets are real icy."

She looked out the rain-smeared window at the lines of traffic. The driver braked and swore under his breath, glaring at a panel truck that had hemmed him in on the right. He slumped behind the wheel, tapping his fingers impatiently as he waited for the intersection to clear.

"Are those your children?" Laurel asked, looking at a plastic-covered photograph hanging from the dashboard. The picture showed a little dark-haired girl about four years old, sitting next to a fat solemn baby on a furry rug.

The driver glanced at her, startled. "Yeah," he said. "That's my Luisa and David. Great kids."

"They're very beautiful."

"Luisa's like her mama. She's already got a lot of musical talent."

The little girl wore a pink ruffled dress and held a small teddy bear. Laurel wondered what it would be like to have a couple of children like that, waiting for her at home.

"I'm working two jobs so I can save for their college education," the young man went on, pulling into the traffic again. "I drive cab in the daytime and work night shifts as a security guard in a warehouse over in Queens."

Laurel tried to imagine the life he described. Immediately she felt ashamed of her expensive leather shoes and shoulder bag, her briefcase fitted with a laptop computer and the soft woollen coat that had probably cost more than this man earned in a month of driving cab.

But the driver seemed untroubled by the contrast. He continued to chat happily about his wife and children as he drove toward the tollbooth.

"I don't plan for us to live this way forever," he told Laurel over the sound of the windshield wipers sweeping rhythmically at the sleet. "One of these days I'm gonna sell one of my screenplays, and then we'll be rolling in money."

"You're a writer?" she asked.

"I've written six screenplays," he said proudly. "I sent one to a big studio in Hollywood, and they told me it's under consideration."

"Good for you! That sounds really promising."

"Yeah, it is. They don't pay much for an option, but if I... Oh, *hell*,," he muttered, then gave Laurel an apologetic glance.

"What's the matter?"

"There's another big pileup at the tollboth, and I can't get out of this lane. It'll take a while to get through."

"That's all right," Laurel told him. "I've got plenty of time."

Again she felt a wave of embarrassment when she realized that for the driver, time was money. She leaned forward and handed him some money for the toll, resolving to tip him generously when they reached the airport.

"I *hate* this," he complained, staring at the cars that were immobilized around them. "I hate sitting in traffic."

"Since you're a screenwriter," Laurel said to distract him, "maybe you could help me solve a hypothetical problem about...about something I'm working on."

"Yeah?" He brightened, looking at her over his shoulder.

"Suppose you were writing a screenplay," Laurel began. "And one of your characters was in a...sort of awkward situation, and needed to get away for a while. Secretly, I mean. Where could a person go and not be found?"

"How long?"

"Just a month or two."

"Hmm." The driver frowned with professional interest, tapping his fingers on the wheel. "This screenplay, where's it taking place? What's your setting?"

Laurel hesitated. "It's...set in a big city on the West Coast. In Vancouver, actually."

"I don't know much about Canadians," the young man said.

"I think they're pretty much like everybody else," Laurel told him dryly.

"They play hockey all the time, and they're real polite, and they don't like guns. Right?"

"Right," Laurel agreed, smiling.

"So tell me more about this main character. Rich or poor?"

"Quite well-off," Laurel said after a brief hesitation. "Say...a managing partner in a big company, owns a large block of shares and a high-rise condo in the city, drives an expensive car, all the good stuff."

"How old is this guy?"

"Thirty-one," Laurel said, amused to note that as soon as he heard the description, the driver automatically assumed that her story character was a male.

But then, a lot of people made the same mistake . . .

"Married?"

"Pardon?"

"This guy in your story. Is he married? Divorced? Got any kids or responsibilities?"

"No kids or responsibilities," Laurel said with a touch of sadness. "Married once, a long time ago, and divorced for almost five years."

"Doesn't see the ex?"

"The ex is remarried, teaching college courses in England."

"Hmm," the driver said again, pulling through the tollbooth and heading onto the expressway to the airport. "And how come this guy needs to disappear?"

"It's a complicated situation," Laurel said, glancing out the window at the dark sky above the warehouses. "Somebody close to him is being investigated by the police, and if this person—the main character—if he were called to testify under oath, he might have to incriminate the other person."

"Why can't he just lie?"

Laurel shook her head. "He's not that kind of person."

"What's the other guy supposed to have done?"

"He's being accused of insider trading," Laurel said. "He's suspected of profiteering . . . That means placing some heavy stock orders based on secret government information that was passed to him illegally. It's a very serious charge."

"But he didn't do it?"

"It's all a misunderstanding. He did place the orders, but there was nothing illegal about it. He placed them for a friend in the government who can verify that the broker didn't know about any government contracts in advance."

"So what's his problem?"

"The timing of the transaction looks suspicious," Laurel said, frowning out the window again. "But I'm... But the central character of our screenplay knows his partner is innocent, and he's also the only one who knows exactly when the orders were placed. Without his testimony, there's no way for the police to get a conviction."

"So what's he going to do? He can't hide out forever, right? He's got this big high-powered job to do."

"He doesn't need to hide forever," Laurel said. "Just for a month or two, while this other person manages to round up the evidence that will clear him of wrongdoing."

"Hey, that's a real interesting plot, isn't it? I wish I'd thought of it."

"Yes," Laurel said softly. "It's really interesting."

"Now, this guy—he's got lots of money, right? He could go anywhere?"

"Anywhere," Laurel agreed. "He just needs to drop out of sight for a while."

"Is there a chance the police might be looking for him?"

"An excellent chance," she said. "That's the whole point of the story. The police want this person to testify at the preliminary hearing against his...his friend, you see. He's not under suspicion himself, but he has to avoid being served with the subpoena."

"Okay, I see the problem. But he can't leave the country. He couldn't use his passport, right? They'd be able to trace that."

"I guess they would."

"And he can't go to a holiday resort or anything, because he'd start to get pretty conspicuous after a few weeks if he was still hanging around."

"Yes, I've thought of that."

"No friends or relatives who could hide him out somewhere?"

"Not for that long. He thinks it would be for a month or two, but you see, it would all depend on how quickly this other person was able to gather the necessary evidence to clear himself."

The driver snapped his fingers. "I got it."

The airport came into view, looming out of the mist. Laurel sat erect and looked at the man's curly head with interest. "You know how to write the story?"

"Yeah. The guy goes to a little town, maybe out in the Midwest somewhere. That's the best way for him to disappear."

"In a little town?" she asked dubiously. "Wouldn't he be *really* conspicuous?"

"No. The thing is, nobody would expect a man like that to go to some one-horse town. He'd have to change his appearance—get rid of his expensive clothes and stuff. He wants to look like everybody else, right? So he puts on old clothes and gets a bad haircut, drifts into town looking for work. He gets a job doing janitorial work or something, rents a little basement suite, goes to the bar on Friday night. He becomes part of the community, and nobody notices him."

"I see," Laurel said thoughtfully. "You're saying the best way to hide something is to put it right out in full view, in a place where it looks the same as everything around it."

He pulled to a stop at the curb near the Air Canada terminal. "Hey, this could be a great story," he said. "When are you planning to write it?"

"Soon." Laurel cast him a rueful glance as she rummaged in her shoulder bag. "I think I'll probably be writing it very soon."

"Well, good luck. And remember, send that guy to a small town. It's a surefire plot."

"Thanks," Laurel said.

She climbed out of the cab and watched as he took her luggage from the back. Then she gave him the cab fare, took her suitcases and walked into the terminal, leaving him staring in amazement at the bills in his hand.

She had a pile of work in her briefcase, including a profile of market statistics she'd acquired during her trip to New York and a list of new company accounts to enter. Laurel found a quiet table in the airport's executive lounge and worked at her laptop computer until boarding time, occasionally sipping from a cup of lukewarm coffee.

But after she settled into her seat in the plane, she found it hard to get back to work. She watched the big plane lift off, rising far above the messy snarl of clouds and up into a world of blue sky and sunshine. Her seatmate, an elderly lady traveling West to visit her daughter, pulled up a blanket, adjusted her pillow and fell asleep at once, snoring gently.

Laurel reached into the briefcase for her computer, then reconsidered and took out a book she'd bought in the Vancouver airport before leaving on her business trip. The slim volume had promised light reading, but Laurel was fascinated by it.

The book was called *Wolf Hill Schoolmarm,* a published edition of an authentic century-old diary, apparently edited and offered for publication by descendants of a young teacher who'd worked in a one-room school on the Canadian prairie. The foreword, written by a woman called Katherine Cameron, told how the diary had been discovered in a cavity under the windowsill during the renovation of an old hotel in the small prairie town of Wolf Hill, Alberta.

"I hope that Ellen Livingston's story will touch other hearts as surely as it has transformed my own life," Mrs. Cameron wrote.

Laurel had at first dismissed this as excessively sentimental, but she found herself beguiled by the story's simple charm. Ellen Livingston, the young schoolteacher, had certainly been an interesting woman. Her lively descriptions of local characters, pioneer farming methods and social occasions brought the town of Wolf Hill to vivid life, along with its gallery of colorful occupants.

Thoughtfully, Laurel turned the pages back to the introduction, which read:

To this day, Wolf Hill remains largely unchanged. Those who live here are just as strong-minded, generous and eccentric as the townspeople of Ellen Livingston's day. Wolf Hill is, in fact, the quintessential small town. It is a place that shuns change, looks after its own and guards all those wholesome values so dear to the hearts of ordinary people.

Laurel felt a sudden quickening of interest. She took a pocket atlas from her briefcase and consulted it, then looked down at the little book again, holding it tightly in her hands as she gazed out the window at the sunlight glancing off the rosy sea of cloud beneath the airplane's wing.

THEY TOUCHED DOWN in Vancouver around midafternoon, and Laurel hailed a cab to take her across town to her office. The streets of Vancouver weren't ice-covered like those in New York, but they were just as wet. Rain fell in long sparkling needles that stabbed the ground and flattened on the pavement. Laurel asked the doorman of her building to take her luggage down to her car, which she'd left in the lower parking garage while she was away. Then she rode up to her office, a huge corner room with a sweeping view across the harbor to North Vancouver. Grouse Mountain loomed in the background, wreathed in clouds and lightly sprinkled with snow.

Laurel stashed her shoulder bag and overcoat in a closet and emptied her briefcase onto the desk. Her office was clean and orderly, with all the plants watered, books and ornaments dusted, files in order, mail opened and stacked neatly.

"Of course," she said aloud, addressing an open door at the side of the room, "I *do* have the best secretary in the world. It helps a lot."

"Hey, did I hear my employer's voice?"

Her secretary popped in through the door, carrying an armful of files and a folded newspaper.

Dennis Ames was a cheerful young man in his early twenties, medium height, with a square, pleasant face and an easygoing manner that belied his awesome efficiency. He wore corduroy slacks and knitted vests, had a seemingly endless procession of girlfriends, played hockey in his free time and kept Laurel's busy life in perfect order.

"Hi, Dennis," she said. "I brought you a gift from New York."

"No kidding?" He gave her a winsome smile. "Isn't that sexual harassment, if you start giving me presents?"

"Actually," Laurel said, digging into her briefcase, "speaking of harassment, I'm just softening you up for the kill. I need a date tonight, and I was hoping you might volunteer."

"First let me see the present. Then we'll decide how far I'm prepared to let this go."

She handed him a gift pack from the hotel boutique, which he opened to reveal a yellow T-shirt covered with dancing cows. Party Till The Cows Come Home, the logo read.

Dennis chuckled. "It's *definitely* me," he told her with pleasure. "Thanks, Laurel. Now, what's this about a date?"

"Wilmott and Abrams are having some kind of party tonight, and I should probably go. They're major clients."

"I have a prior engagement," he said promptly. "Why don't you find yourself a real boyfriend?"

"I don't have time. Bring your date along," Laurel pleaded. "Come on, Dennis. It won't take much of your evening. I just need to make an appearance. I'll pay you double overtime," she added.

"My date works till nine," Dennis protested, but he was looking more interested.

"Where does she work?"

He grinned. "She teaches aerobics at a gym downtown. This girl is really, really gorgeous."

"Oh, Dennis." Laurel shook her head sadly.

He held the T-shirt against his chest and admired himself in the mirror. "Is this party a sit-down-and-eat thing, or what?"

"It's just a lot of people standing around with drinks in their hands, shouting at each other."

"The kind you hate the most," Dennis said. "Is that why you don't want to go alone?"

"If I'm alone, Mort Schall will spend the whole evening trying to entice me into the library."

"Hey, you could do worse, Laurel. Mort's old, but very rich."

"Oh, I don't think it's my luscious young body he's interested in. Mort wants some insider tips on stock trading off new government contracts, and God knows, that's the last thing we should be—"

She fell abruptly silent, and her secretary became deeply interested in a snag on his thumbnail.

"Okay," he said at last, folding the T-shirt. "I'll meet you here right at seven. You can make your appearance at the party, and I'll still have time to pick up Jennifer."

"Thanks. You're a lifesaver," Laurel said gratefully. "Jennifer?" she added. "I thought that was old news."

"This is a brand-new Jennifer. Blond, this time."

"Dennis, Dennis." Laurel shook her head again and sorted idly through her mail. "Were you people busy around here while I was gone?"

"Nothing major. How's everything in New York?"

"The joint is jumping," Laurel told him. "Their markets are going through the roof. They still seem to be a little nervous about our national bond rating, though.''

''With good reason. Look, I finished up the Connors stuff, and there's a prospectus on your desk about that new Asian mutual fund. Oh, and the big guy is looking for you. He wants to see you the minute you come in. Emphasis on that. The *very* minute.''

Laurel smiled at her secretary. ''He probably needs advice on which tie to wear to his Shriners' banquet tonight.''

They laughed together, then sobered.

''Dennis...''

''Yeah, boss?''

''Dennis, if I were to take a little holiday sometime in the next few weeks, I wouldn't want you to worry. You know?''

''Hell, Laurel, if you took a holiday, I'd be overjoyed. I can't remember the last time you had one.''

''I mean,'' she went on, looking down at her desk, ''if I happened to do it sort of...unexpectedly. If I just dropped out of sight for a while and didn't tell you where I was going, I'd want you to realize that it was all planned in advance and I was just fine. Nothing to worry about.''

Dennis stood in the connecting doorway, holding his T-shirt and giving her an unhappy look. ''He's really in trouble, isn't he?''

Laurel turned away to pluck a dead leaf from the ficus plant near her window.

''It's so damned unfair,'' she murmured. ''He's the most honest, hardworking person in the world.''

''I know he is. But, Laurel, why can't he just...''

She waved her hand. ''It's best if we don't discuss it, Dennis. All I can do is thank you for your loyalty and tell you not to worry if I take a holiday sometime soon. And if anybody should ask,'' she concluded, crossing the room with a businesslike stride, "you don't know a thing about it. Okay?''

He hesitated, then nodded reluctantly. "I don't know a thing,'' he said. "Around here, I just water the plants and keep my eyes closed.''

He vanished through the door to the reception area, leaving Laurel alone in her office.

A few minutes later, she gathered an armful of files from her desk and headed down the hall to the office of her partner in the brokerage firm, the only person in the company whose position was senior to her own.

Laurel entered the lavish suite of rooms and tossed her files onto the desk.

A tall handsome man with graying hair stood near a leather couch. He was holding a golf club, and concentrating on hitting balls into an upended cup.

"Hi, Dad,'' Laurel said. "How are you?''

Stewart Atchison looked up in delight. "Laurie!'' He hurried over to embrace her, carrying the golf club. "Glad to see you, sweetheart. How was the trip?''

"It was wet and cold,'' Laurel said, hugging him back.

Her father was the only person who ever called her Laurie. Even though she adored him, Laurel had always disliked having her name shortened.

"We heard New York was completely socked in with fog and rain. Marta worried that your flight might be delayed.''

"There was no problem. How's Marta feeling?''

"She's blooming. Positively radiant.''

Stewart's wife was four years younger than his daughter, and massively pregnant with their first child.

Laurel wasn't altogether sure how she felt about the imminent arrival of this new little brother or sister, especially at a time when she seemed to be developing some strong maternal yearnings of her own. But she liked Marta, and made every effort to keep her reservations well-hidden.

Her father returned to his putting area and gripped the club, taking a few practice swings. Laurel sat in his swivel chair, rested her feet on the desk and leaned back, suddenly weary.

"You're still bending your right elbow too much, Dad."

He straightened his arm and putted the ball neatly into the cup, beaming with satisfaction. "Have you read the prospectus on the new Asian mutual fund, Laurie?"

"Not yet. I just got here a few minutes ago. Dennis left it on my desk, though. I'll get to it before I leave for the day."

"Good. Are you going to Wilmott's party tonight? Mort was asking if you'd be there."

"Yes, Dad." She sighed. "I'm going."

"Keep your ear to the ground, okay? If you can get Mort alone, find out what he's doing with his Latin American funds."

"I really hadn't intended to spend any time alone with Mort Schall," Laurel said dryly.

Her father gave her a sympathetic smile. "You look so tired. Maybe you shouldn't go. I can go to the party tonight, dear. It's just that Marta's been . . ."

"It's okay, Dad. I'll go. Dennis is coming with me."

"Good. I know Mort's a bore, but we could use a bit of an inside track on this one."

Laurel relented and smiled back. "Have you heard anything about... you know?" she asked after a brief silence.

He shook his head, tossed his golf club aside and sat on the couch. "I keep trying to get hold of Chet Landry, but he won't return my calls. I thought public servants were supposed to be accessible."

"Isn't he still in Japan?"

Stewart nodded. "He's with the government trade delegation. They won't be home until sometime next week, and that could be too late."

Laurel stared at him, her face draining of color. "Why?" she whispered. "Have they... has anybody approached you?"

Her father flexed his arm a couple of times, then frowned at the carpet. "Not yet. But it's in the wind. It's just a matter of time."

"Dad, what makes you think it's going to be that soon?"

He shook his head, then gave her a worried glance. "I wish I could get hold of Landry. He promised me he'd tell the truth about our deal, and then I'd be totally in the clear."

Laurel clenched her hands to keep them from shaking. "You should never have placed those orders for him," she whispered.

"I know that now. But I honestly thought the whole transaction was above board. I didn't know he was using inside information, Laurie."

"Oh, Dad..."

Stewart's boyish face took on a look of determined cheerfulness. He got up from the couch and crossed the room to drop a hand on Laurel's shoulder. "Maybe we're making a mountain out of a molehill, honey.

When Landry gets back, I'll pressure him into clearing up this whole thing, and there'll be no problem."

"But if he doesn't, we could lose our company, Dad! You could even go to jail!"

His jaw set. "I'm not going to jail when my wife's pregnant, just to take the rap for some crooked bureaucrat. Landry's got a lot to answer for."

"But if the police are ready to—"

Stewart turned and looked directly at his daughter. "They can't prove anything. You're the only one in the firm who knows when or how I placed the orders."

"And I won't be available to testify," Laurel said dully.

She toyed with an onyx penholder on her father's desk and stared out the window at the brooding clouds.

"It's only for a little while, sweetheart." Her father sat on the corner of the desk and leaned toward her earnestly. "Just until I can get my hands on that damn Landry and force him to tell the truth. You'll be home in no time."

"Maybe."

"Definitely. Come on, how can I run the company without you? Half our clients won't deal with anybody else."

Laurel looked up at him, trying to smile. "What if Marta has the baby while I'm gone? I'd hate to miss something like that."

"Don't you worry. I just won't allow it. The baby will have to wait till Auntie Laurie's back in town. Besides," he added, getting off the desk and moving past Laurel to stare out the window, "you won't be gone that long. We'll get this all straightened out, as soon as Landry comes home."

"I've decided where to go, Dad," Laurel said. "I was reading this book, a published edition of an old diary, and there's a little town in—"

"Don't tell me!" Stewart said hastily. He gave her an apologetic smile. "I don't want to hear about it, honey. You know how hard it is for me to tell a lie. When they ask me where you are, I want to be straight with them. I want to say that I have no idea where you've gone."

Laurel nodded and got to her feet. Stewart walked across the room again and held her briefly, dropping an awkward kiss on her cheek.

"God, I'm so proud of you," he whispered. "No man ever had a finer daughter, kiddo."

Laurel drew away and smiled at him. "I love you, too, Dad," she said, standing on tiptoe to press her face close to his.

As was the current fashion in the business world, Wilmott and Abrams had chosen to host their annual cocktail party at their downtown offices instead of at one of the owners' homes. Laurel and Dennis arrived late and blended into the crowd, edging their way to a corner of the room near the buffet table.

Laurel was wearing a simple black dress accented with heavy, ethnic-looking jewelry. She'd been too rushed to have her hair done, and had chosen instead to sweep it up into a French knot softened by a few tendrils around her face.

"Smashing," Dennis muttered, standing at her elbow in his customary sport coat and blue jeans. "Don't let old Mortie get anywhere near you, or he'll gobble you up."

Laurel punched his arm and looked at the buffet table. "Hey, a shrimp tree," she murmured. "And deviled eggs."

"Great. All the basic food groups. Fill up," he said. "I'll track down some beverages."

"Hurry back," Laurel told him. "Don't forget I'm paying you for protection."

He strolled away, returning in a few moments with two champagne glasses. Laurel stood near one of the windows, eating hungrily from her paper plate. Dennis handed her a glass and looked with concentrated attention at a leggy redhead in a group near the door.

"Don't you *dare*," Laurel muttered. "You have a date with Jennifer in less than two hours."

"I was just *looking*," he said with an injured air.

"Yeah, like a bird dog. I know that look. Dennis, these little sausage things are just great."

Dennis took one of the sausages. "How's the big boss?"

"He's fine," Laurel said absently.

"Really? No problems? Nothing I should know about, for instance?"

"Nothing major," Laurel said, suddenly serious. "If anybody asks you—"

"I'll tell them he seems a little nervous these days. Of course," Dennis added casually, "he's almost sixty years old and about to become a new daddy. That's enough to make a guy a little edgy."

"You're right," Laurel said, relieved. "Of course it is. Oh, no," she added, seeing a waitress approaching them, holding a cellular phone. "Do you suppose that's for me?"

"Probably. No doubt some client has developed a sudden urge to buy out the futures market in pork bellies, and he can't wait till morning to place his order."

Laurel took the phone and smiled her thanks to the waitress.

"Hello," she said into the mouthpiece.

She heard her father's voice and her body tensed. "Right away?" she whispered. *"Tonight?"*

She was silent for a few seconds, listening. Finally, she switched off the phone and placed it on the window ledge, then turned to Dennis.

"You're right, something's come up," she murmured. "I have to go home. I'll just take a cab back to the office and pick up my things, okay?"

"You're sure?" he asked.

"I'm sure. Thanks for everything. I'll see you . . . I'll see you soon," Laurel said. She hurried away to find her coat.

CHAPTER TWO

THE WOLF HILL bus depot was no more than a small section of an all-night service station, consisting of a counter for ticket sales, a scarred wooden bench and grubby washroom. A young man in grease-stained coveralls stood behind the counter examining a pile of cardboard boxes that had arrived on the bus along with Laurel, who was the only passenger to disembark at Wolf Hill.

No wonder, she thought bitterly, looking at her surroundings.

At ten o'clock on a cold spring night, Wolf Hill wasn't the cozy little town she'd pictured. Beyond the window, a full moon glistened on endless miles of barren prairie, dotted here and there with silvery patches of melting snow. The wind howled around the corners of the old building and sent bits of debris whirling across the deserted parking lot.

Laurel shifted uncomfortably on the bench, glancing down at her clothes. Acting on the New York cab-driver's advice, she'd gotten off the bus for a few hours in Calgary earlier in the day to buy a new wardrobe at a downtown thrift store. She now wore old blue jeans with a ragged hole in one knee, a sagging lace-trimmed blouse and a heavy plaid shirt that doubled as a jacket. The shirt had a torn collar and was missing most of its buttons.

The battered duffel bags at her feet contained similar items, along with an extra pair of cheap running shoes. Hidden at the very bottom were the pleated flannel slacks and Italian hand-knit sweater she'd been wearing when she started her journey.

Laurel felt miserably awkward and out of place in the shabby clothes. Worse, it seemed like forever since she'd bathed or washed her hair. In fact, she realized with bleary surprise, she hadn't bathed since leaving New York City.

That was only yesterday morning, but it felt like a century ago.

She was exhausted, frightened and terribly alone, and all of her natural confidence seemed to have deserted her.

The loutish young mechanic glanced over at her, leaning on the counter and idly swinging a wrench in his hand. Laurel looked back at him, surprised by the expression on his face.

"You can't sit here all night, you know," he said with some belligerence. "Loitering ain't allowed."

Laurel's cheeks flamed with humiliation.

It's these clothes, she thought. If she'd been well-groomed, wearing the slacks and sweater hidden in that duffel bag, the mechanic would probably be falling all over himself to treat her with respect. But her shabby blue jeans and old plaid shirt apparently gave him permission to be rude.

The unfairness of it was outrageous.

Laurel's original embarrassment gave way to a bracing flood of anger which drove away her weariness and, strangely enough, lifted her spirits. She was about to make a cutting remark in reply when she realized, almost too late, that she was *supposed* to look like a vagrant. The whole idea, after all, was to be meek and inconspicuous.

She bit her lip and took a deep breath.

"Is there a place around here where I can stay for the night?" she asked him. "I don't know much about this town."

"It's a real small town," he said with a shrug. "We got no homeless shelters or anything. Just a hotel down the street. Of course," he added with a leer, taking a closer look at her, "you can come home with me if you like. I got a little place over the feed store, and there's lots of room in my bed."

Laurel restrained herself with effort.

"I have some money," she murmured, keeping her head lowered. "I guess I'll get a room in the hotel. Can you tell me where it is?"

"You got money?" he asked with a skeptical look.

"A little," she said. "Enough to pay for my room till I can find some work."

Actually, Laurel had about fifty dollars in her cheap plastic handbag and another three thousand in cash, rolled neatly into one of her socks at the bottom of the largest duffel bag.

She had no idea how long she'd have to be away, or how much money would be required for this little adventure. But she knew that she wouldn't be able to write checks or use her credit cards, so she'd brought a good supply of cash.

"There's no decent jobs around here," the mechanic said. "It's a pretty slow town."

"I'm willing to do any kind of work." Laurel got to her feet and shouldered her bags. "As long as it's a job. Now, if you could just tell me where to find the hotel..."

"Hey, are you sure you wouldn't rather just come to my place?" he asked, coming out from behind the counter and moving closer to her.

Laurel's careful meekness deserted her. "I'd rather die a thousand deaths," she told him with icy coldness, lifting her chin and looking directly into his face. "Please tell me where the hotel is."

He backed away, clearly startled, and retreated uncertainly behind the counter. "It's up the street," he muttered with a jerk of his greasy thumb. "Two blocks west, right-hand side."

"Thank you."

"Wait," he called when she opened the door.

She paused, looking back at him.

"What's your name?"

Laurel hesitated, then pushed on the door again. "Laurie," she said, stepping out into the cold night wind. "Laurie Atkins."

UNLIKE THE TOWN of Wolf Hill, the hotel was a genuine delight, and looked much the way Ellen Livingston had described it in her diary. Laurel booked a modest room on the third floor and climbed the broad oak staircase, almost faint with weariness. Still, she wasn't too exhausted to appreciate the gleaming woodwork, the flowered wallpaper and chintz upholstery, the pleasant smell of floor wax and furniture polish.

She bathed in an antique cast-iron tub with heavy claw feet, washed and dried her hair and fell into bed with a sigh of bliss, curling up under a down-filled quilt that looked handmade.

But she couldn't sleep, even though her body ached with weariness. After a few minutes of staring anxiously at the ceiling, she got out of bed, switched on an antique lamp and rummaged in her duffel bag, planning to retrieve the sock with the money and find a better hiding place for it.

Now that she was so far away from home, she was very aware of how important her roll of cash was.

Laurel paused and looked around the room, wondering where she could safely hide three thousand dollars.

A hundred years ago, she recalled with a brief smile, Ellen Livingston had concealed her diary in the cavity under the windowsill. Amused, Laurel crossed the room and gave an experimental tug at the window frame, but it held fast.

"Sorry, Ellen," she murmured aloud. "No luck here, I'll just have to try something else."

She returned to her duffel bag and reached in to get the money, then felt a chill of alarm. She began to rummage frantically, finally upending the bag and its contents onto the brightly stitched quilt.

Her money was gone.

She sat on the bed and buried her face in her hands, trying to think where she could have lost the money.

Since leaving British Columbia, she'd been so careful with her luggage. Except for...

Too late, she realized that the bag containing the money had ridden all the way from British Columbia in the lower luggage compartment, being handled by baggage carriers at many stops.

Under usual circumstances, the loss of three thousand dollars wouldn't have a huge impact on her personal finances. She had a comfortable private fortune inherited from her wealthy mother who'd died when Laurel was fourteen. And her annual earnings from the brokerage firm were in the six-figure range, even during years when the markets were shaky. But these were not usual circumstances, and this particular sum of money had special significance, because there was no way to replace the missing funds.

Fearful of having her movements traced or her belongings searched, Laurel had left behind her driver's license and other forms of identification, locked in the safe in her Vancouver office. For the month or two that she needed to avoid being questioned while her father struggled to clear his name, she'd intended simply to be Laurie Atkins, a vagrant worker with few worldly goods.

But she'd counted on having sufficient money with her so that the charade would never become real enough to be scary.

Now Laurel *was* scared.

She opened her cracked plastic handbag, turning everything onto the quilt, even searching through the lining. It contained fifty-six dollars and some change.

Not enough to pay for two nights at the Wolf Hill Hotel, she realized in despair. If she didn't find a job right away, she was in real trouble. She could probably be charged with fraud for booking a room she wasn't able to pay for.

Of course, she could always wire her father and ask him to send money, but that was definitely a last resort. In fact, it was not really an option. Stewart's whole plan hinged on not knowing where his daughter was hiding. If the police subjected him to rigorous questioning, he needed to be able to reply honestly.

She could call Dennis, Laurel thought, brightening for a moment when she thought about her secretary's cheerful efficiency. Dennis would send her the money with no questions asked . . .

But, of course, that was also out of the question. She sagged on the bed, tightly gripping the handbag in her fingers.

Dennis, too, would be questioned about her whereabouts. It wasn't fair to make him lie to the police. He had to be able to say with complete sincerity that although his employer had recently mentioned the possibility of taking a holiday, he had no idea where she'd gone.

"Oh, Dad," Laurel whispered, staring at the quilt littered with her meager possessions. "Oh, Dad, you've really gone and done it this time. Why do you have to be so *nice?* Why can't you ever say no when people ask you for favors?"

Finally, numb with shock and too exhausted to think anymore, she tidied the room, stashed the old duffel bags under the bed and crawled beneath the covers. This time, mercifully, the darkness claimed her almost at once.

LAUREL WOKE from a deep sleep to a bewildering medley of sounds. She lay in her bed, puzzled, and gradually realized that there were several different sources of noise, both inside and outside the hotel.

Somebody seemed to be shouting down in the lobby, and a baby was howling somewhere in the building. A distant sound of hammering filled the air, accompanied by a clatter apparently related to the heating system. Most of the noise, however, came from outside. Laurel slipped from her bed, crossed the room to draw aside the curtain and was greeted by a remarkable sight.

A truck with a wooden rack dangling loose from the back stood in the middle of the dusty main street. A load of pigs had obviously escaped from the truck.

They milled about in the street, squealing noisily, their fat pink sides gleaming in the sunlight. A couple of men were trying to round up the animals but were hindered by passersby on the sidewalk who were watching with lively interest and offering advice.

"Grab his ears, Jim!"

"Get a lasso and rope that sucker!"

"Hey, bring a couple of them pigs over here, Allie. I'd like some bacon for my breakfast."

Laurel watched for a while, captivated. Finally, the last pig was corralled against a fence and herded back onto the truck. The drama apparently over, she let the curtain drop and looked around.

Her spirits plummeted when she saw the tattered blue jeans and shirt hanging over a chair, and remembered the missing cash. She dressed with reluctance and examined herself in the antique mirror.

Probably not a good idea to wear makeup, she decided. And she couldn't leave her hair hanging free, either. Now that she'd had a chance to clean up, her hair looked too glossy and expensively styled to go with the jeans and shirt, so she dragged it back from her face and tied it with one of the stained shoelaces from her second pair of running shoes. She frowned at her reflection, then went down the stairs to the coffee shop.

A pert young waitress arrived with an order pad. The girl had bright red hair, a slim figure and a wide, full mouth.

Laurel smiled at her, suddenly thinking about Dennis.

The waitress was just his type...

Laurel looked with longing at the fresh-fruit plate on the menu, but it was too expensive. Instead, she decided on the three-dollar special of ham, eggs and hash-browned potatoes, which seemed to be what everybody else was eating. The waitress wrote down the order and vanished, returning almost at once with a heavy mug of coffee.

Laurel sipped her coffee and gazed out the window at the main street, now empty of pigs, truck and townspeople. Wolf Hill was just as bleak in the light of day as it had seemed late at night. A cold wind howled among the buildings, carrying bits of paper and swirls of dust.

Apparently, it was always windy out here.

She shivered, and looked away from the window. Movement in the doorway caught her eye.

A man stood there in silence, surveying the coffee shop. He was tall and broad-shouldered, wearing a leather jacket, white shirt and blue jeans. He had thick brown hair, piercing hazel eyes and an aquiline nose. Overall, he exuded an impression of power and detachment, a kind of quiet, forceful masculinity that Laurel found surprisingly attractive in spite of his rugged appearance. But she noticed that despite his good looks, the man's face had a worn and cynical expression, and there was a bitter line to his mouth.

Laurel watched as he came into the room, tensing automatically as she waited for him to notice and acknowledge her presence. But his eyes slid over her and moved on without pausing.

Laurel felt a brief, hurt surprise.

Of course, the whole idea of her charade was to blend with the townspeople and become invisible, and her efforts had clearly been successful. It was irrational to be upset about the way this man seemed to dismiss her without a trace of interest.

Still, she didn't like the feeling.

He passed close to her on his way to a table near the back, and she had a confused impression of arrogant maleness, along with a pleasantly exciting scent of leather and shaving cream.

Laurel turned briefly to watch him sit down, then looked away quickly when those remarkable eyes flickered over her again with a cold, impersonal glance.

The waitress brought her a plate of food and she tried to eat it, but her appetite seemed to have vanished. She picked at the eggs, left the meat untouched and ate a few of the crisp potatoes.

The waitress, she noted, lingered near the handsome man's table and seemed to find a number of tasks—like cleaning out the pie case and restocking the shelves with chocolate bars—that brought her within his line of sight.

He seemed courteous enough when he spoke to the young woman. Laurel could hear the quiet timbre of his voice and the girl's eager laughter. She turned cautiously and tried to catch another glimpse of him, wondering what he would look like if he smiled.

But the stranger was deeply absorbed in a newspaper. His face in repose still looked grim and remote. Laurel turned away quickly, finished her coffee and got up to pay the bill, conscious once again of her vagabond appearance.

"Everything okay?" the waitress asked, punching buttons on the till.

Laurel looked at her, startled.

"Your breakfast. You didn't eat much of it. Hilda likes us to ask if people didn't like the food."

"Oh, it was fine. I'm just not very hungry this morning."

"Sure." The girl smiled. Her pretty face, lightly dusted with freckles, looked tired at close range, and there were dark blue smudges under her eyes. Laurel forgot her own troubles for a moment in a wave of sympathy. This girl had probably been working since before dawn, while Laurel was still sleeping cozily under her down-filled quilt.

Lots of people had difficult lives, she realized. All over the world, in big cities and small towns, in high-rise apartments and log cabins, people were struggling to survive, battling destitution with no cash in reserve.

They weren't attending glamorous cocktail parties in little black dresses, or having lunch with influential clients. They were driving cabs and getting up before sunrise to wait on tables.

"Isn't he a *doll?*" the girl whispered, leaning forward with a confiding glance.

"Who?" Laurel asked.

The waitress jerked her head toward the man in the leather jacket, who was still absorbed in his newspaper. "I think he must be a movie star or something," she murmured. "He's so gorgeous. And he's got that drop-dead sexy look, you know?"

Laurel nodded in perfect understanding. "Isn't he a local man?" she asked, also whispering.

The girl laughed aloud, then leaned forward again. "Local? *Him?* You gotta be kidding. Have you seen any of the locals?"

Laurel thought about the leering mechanic in his greasy coveralls. "Not many."

She hesitated, watching while the waitress counted out her change. Nervously, Laurel tried to calculate how many more meals she could afford. "Do you know of any jobs around here?" she asked.

"Doing what?"

"I don't know. Anything, I guess. I have to earn some money for bus fare."

"You could go down to the post office and see if there's any jobs on the bulletin board. That's where people usually advertise if they're looking for help."

"Thanks." Laurel smiled wanly and turned to leave.

Out in the lobby, a small squabble seemed to be taking place. A baby stroller sat near the office door, and a woman bent over the occupant of the stroller, working busily at the restraining straps.

She was small, blond and attractive, probably in her fifties but artfully made up to look younger. She was wearing high-heeled gold sandals, lime-green tights and a matching tunic dotted with seed pearls and gold beads, the kind of glitzy at-home wear that Laurel had never expected to see in Wolf Hill.

A younger woman, also blond but taller and more causally dressed, stood in the doorway to the office. She had an attractive, tanned face and an air of intelligence and humor that made Laurel think she would like to get to know the woman. At the moment, however, the younger woman seemed upset.

"Mom," she was saying wearily, "can't you just leave him alone? He'll fall asleep in a few minutes if you'll leave him in the stroller."

"Nonsense," the older woman said, lifting the baby and cradling him in her arms. "Our little sweetums doesn't want to sleep in Mummy's old stroller, does ums?" she crooned, nuzzling his downy head. "Our little sweetums wants to go upstairs with Grandma and have a nice bubbly bath, doesn't ums?"

The baby, who looked to be about six months old, nestled in his grandmother's embrace and beamed over a lime-green shoulder pad at Laurel, who smiled back. Lately, she'd found herself unusually interested in babies, and this one was truly beautiful. He was plump and healthy, with huge, sparkling dark eyes and an alert expression.

His smile faded, however, when the younger woman reached for him and tried to take him from his grandmother's arms.

"He doesn't need a bath at exactly ten o'clock every morning," the mother was saying. "I just have a few accounts left to go over, and then I'm taking him home. Please, Mom, leave him in the—"

The baby stiffened and began to howl, and Laurel recognized the full-throated roars that had wakened her earlier. The older woman gave her daughter a reproachful glance.

"Now see what Mummy's done," she said, cuddling the screaming child and rocking him up and down. "Sweetums is all upset, isn't ums? Don't worry, precious. Grandma will give ums his bubble bath. Baby will have his nice bath..."

She moved toward the stairs, still murmuring to the baby who hiccuped a couple of times, then began to smile again when he apparently realized he wasn't being put back in the stroller.

The young woman stood in the doorway, hands on hips, watching helplessly as her mother disappeared up the oak staircase. She exchanged a brief, rueful glance with Laurel, then turned and went into the office, closing the door firmly behind her.

Laurel edged a little closer to read the brass nameplate set into the gleaming wood. Kate Cameron, Manager, it said.

She looked at the name in surprise, realizing that the beleaguered young mother was the same woman who'd edited the schoolteacher's century-old diary.

Feeling somewhat cheered, Laurel left the lobby and headed down the street in search of the post office, which turned out to be a two-part business venture housed in an old frame building.

Half of the interior was given over to Margie's Beauty Shop, a bright place decorated with gingham curtains, plastic flowers and cute ornaments. The other half was labeled Wolf Hill Post Office, with a bank of numbered letter boxes and businesslike government signs that displayed postal codes, mailing rates and hours of pickup and delivery.

The two businesses were separated by a brick half-wall on which a row of china kittens pranced, slept and played with balls of string. Laurel moved to look at the bulletin board.

Two jobs were advertised. There was a position open for a general laborer at the Wolf Hill livestock auction yards, shoveling pens and doing other heavy work. Another job, stocking shelves and managing inventory and warehouse at the local hardware store, required previous experience.

No upper-level accounting positions, Laurel thought ruefully. No openings for licensed stockbrokers, financial analysts or investment counselors...

She felt another wave of concern about her father, and a brief touch of resentment, which she immediately quelled. None of this was his fault, after all. His only crime was being too trusting in his dealings with a government official.

Still, Laurel fretted, he should have known how risky it was to invest those particular funds the way he had.

If accusations of insider trading came to light, they wouldn't just taint the firm's reputation. They could also result in criminal charges being laid against her father.

Laurel shivered and clenched her hands, trying to imagine her handsome, debonair father living in prison, wearing a gray cotton uniform, carrying a tin plate and cup.

But those thoughts were ridiculous. Stewart wasn't going to prison. For one thing, he was innocent of any wrongdoing. And besides, nobody but Laurel could testify how those orders had been placed. As long as she stayed out of sight until her father had time to arrange the support of his government contacts, everything would be all right.

She shouldn't need to stay in Wolf Hill for more than a few weeks, a couple of months at the most. Her father had given his word, and he'd never once broken a promise to her.

At this moment, though, a few weeks in Wolf Hill looked interminable . . .

While Laurel was absorbed in her gloomy thoughts, a plump woman with shocking-red hair appeared in an alcove at the back of the beauty salon.

"Well, hi there," she said. "I didn't see you out here. Need some help?"

"Not really. I'm looking for a job."

"Not many jobs around here. You ever done any hairdressing? I could use a part-time girl."

Laurel shook her head. "I don't know a thing about hairdressing."

"Pity," the woman said sadly. "Girls these days, they really should get some kind of professional training, you know? If a girl can cut hair, she can always get a job."

"You're probably right," Laurel said, thinking to herself that she could certainly use a skill like that right now.

She turned to leave, conscious of the woman's bright eyes watching as she went back out into the morning sunshine.

BEHIND CURTAINS and through wooden shutters, other eyes were also watching Laurel's progress as she trudged along the quiet streets of Wolf Hill.

One pair of eyes belonged to Nellie Grossman, who leaned forward in her rocking chair and peered through a narrow opening in the front-room drapes.

"Two strangers in one day, Fluffy," she said to her cat, who watched her from the kitchen doorway. "There's this young woman who's not what she seems, and a tall handsome man in a leather jacket, and he's got secrets, too. Isn't that interesting, Fluffy? I wonder what's going on."

The cat yawned hugely, looking bored. His name had clearly been given at some very early stage in his life, because he'd long since outgrown any trace of fluffiness. He was now a big, sullen, gray tomcat. Most of his left ear was missing, and his left eye was permanently narrowed by a puckered band of scar tissue on his forehead.

His mistress examined him sadly, then leaned forward to lift the drape back another fraction of an inch.

"There's something odd about this young woman, Fluffy," she said, rocking gently in the chair. "She's mysterious. Look at the way she walks, like she's treading on marble floors. Look how she holds her head. She's a princess, Fluffy, dressed up like a pauper. Now, why would she be doing that?''

Nellie huddled in her chair and peered through the drapes until the woman vanished around a corner, her old plaid jacket flapping in the morning breeze.

The tall man in the leather jacket appeared soon afterward, striding along with his hands thrust deep in his pockets. Nellie watched closely as he passed, and wondered if perhaps he was following the woman. A half hour ago, when the young woman first went downtown, he'd come prowling along a few minutes behind her, just like this.

She examined him closely, trying to read his expression. He seemed unhappy, Nellie decided. Life hadn't been kind to him, and he was bitter about it. Good-looking though, she thought, opening the drapes a little wider and watching as he disappeared around the corner behind the woman.

Ben, Nellie's husband, had looked like that when he was young. He'd been tall and fair, with a proud stance, and a pair of shoulders that could fill a doorway. But Ben was never cold and withdrawn like this stranger. He'd been a big, happy, good-hearted man with a laugh so infectious that you had to smile along with him, just from the sheer happiness of being with him.

A few tears gathered in Nellie's eyes and trickled down her cheeks. She was eighty-three years old, and Ben had been dead now for almost ten years. But she still missed him every day, with an ache that never seemed to heal.

Fluffy came into the room and marched toward Nellie's chair. He sat for a moment on the braided rug at her feet, then leaped heavily into her lap and settled there, gazing with slitted eyes at a few starlings perched in a tree outside the window.

Nellie held him gratefully, brooding over the two strangers.

She didn't like to think about the man who reminded her of her dead husband. Besides, there was something disturbing, almost threatening about him. Instead, Nellie turned her thoughts to the young woman, who interested her a great deal more.

The woman looked to be in her late twenties, about the same age as Nellie's granddaughter, Stacy, who lived with her husband in faraway Toronto. But Stacy was a big, athletic girl with black hair that she kept clipped very short. And she was pregnant with her second baby, Nellie's great-grandchild, due in June.

Nellie knew about the baby from a brief note in Stacy's last Christmas card. This annual card with its dutiful, scribbled message was the only communication she ever received from her grandchild. She'd never seen the other baby, now almost four years old.

Busy, Nellie thought sadly. All the young people were so busy these days.

Her son, William, Stacy's father, was an insurance salesman in Regina who hadn't managed to pay a visit to his mother in almost three years. He called sometimes and even sent an occasional letter, but it wasn't the same as seeing him.

Nellie's other child, her daughter, Karen, had long ago moved to Ottawa with her second husband. Karen was an executive secretary who'd never had any children. She and her husband lived well, entertained and traveled lavishly. Nowadays, Karen maintained less contact with her mother than William did.

And the townspeople, Nellie's neighbors, were also too busy to visit. A few of them had dropped in from time to time after Ben died, just to make sure Nellie was all right, but gradually their lives settled back into normal patterns and they forgot all about the old lady living in the small white house behind its screen of lilacs.

Nellie was too shy to seek anybody out. She tended her garden, watched television, looked after Fluffy and ventured out every few days to buy her groceries, greeting her neighbors with quiet humor and inquiring courteously about their jobs and families. She did jigsaw puzzles that filled the whole dining-room table, cheered loudly for her favorite teams during televised baseball and hockey games and treated herself once a week to a special dinner of frozen pizza and chocolates.

But sometimes Nellie was so lonely, she wondered how she could go on living.

Fluffy shifted in her lap, looking restless. Nellie gripped him firmly to keep him from jumping to the floor.

"I wish you'd cuddle more," she told the cat wistfully. "It feels so nice when you stay with me like this and let me pat you, Fluffy. It feels so nice and cozy..."

The big tomcat glared at her with contempt, pulled away from her grasp and leaped onto the rug. He marched through the archway and into the tidy little kitchen.

Nellie gazed at the doorway where he'd vanished, her eyes faraway and lost in her thoughts.

She wished the young woman was her granddaughter, who'd come to town to pay Nellie a nice long visit.

It was just a foolish daydream, of course. This woman didn't look at all like Stacy, whose heavy fea-

tures smiled from a gold-framed photograph Nellie kept
on her sideboard.

The shabbily dressed girl who'd passed Nellie's window this morning was a different type altogether, slim
and graceful, with a delicate line of mouth and cheek
and a proud lift to her head. Nellie recalled how she'd
paused for a moment outside the gate, smiling wistfully up at the starlings in the leafless tree.

That engaging lopsided smile had lifted the young
woman's mouth on one side in a tentative, humorous
fashion that was utterly irresistible.

She's a sweet girl, but terribly worried, Nellie
thought. She's all alone just like me. I wish she would
come over to visit. We'll visit and chat, have tea. Then
she'll tell me what her problem is, and I'll give her a hug
and tell her not to worry. . .

Nellie heaved herself from the chair with sudden energy and hurried across the room. She was a tiny
woman, not much more than five feet tall, trim and neat
in her cotton housedress and gingham apron.

She took her best lace tablecloth from the sideboard
and spread it on the old oak dining table. Then she
lifted down her good china and set places for two. Nellie lined up the silver and the crystal with loving care as
she thought about the girl's pale face and lost, frightened look.

Fluffy came back into the room and sat by the table,
watching her.

"I want to be ready when she comes," Nellie told
him, her cheeks pink with excitement. "I'll make some
scones and put a kettle on, Fluffy. Won't it be nice to
have a visitor?"

The tomcat licked a paw and swiped it across his
whiskers, then got up and padded from the room,

heading for the bedroom where he liked to sleep on Nellie's quilt.

The old woman watched him leave. Her burst of energy faded, and her body sagged. At last she set down the cup and saucer she'd been holding, sank into a chair. "You're right, Fluffy," she said. "I'm just a ridiculous old woman."

LAUREL CLIMBED the steps to the hotel veranda and entered the lobby. She sat down on a green velvet chair in one corner, and began to leaf idly through a magazine. It was only midmorning, and the day stretched ahead of her like a vast, unending desert of time.

How on earth did people fill their days in a small town like this? Of course, she thought, most people had a home and a job.

She found herself bitterly regretting her decision, made so hastily on the strength of a book she'd been reading and a New York cabdriver's advice. No doubt it would have been more sensible to go to a resort. Even if she'd been dangerously conspicuous, staying all alone for a month or two in some luxurious place, at least there'd be a pool, some tennis courts and shopping malls to occupy her time.

She could leave, of course. Just because she'd made a mistake, she didn't have to stay here until . . .

With a sickening feeling of loss, Laurel remembered the stolen money and realized that she was trapped. She didn't have enough money to leave Wolf Hill. She barely had enough to eat. She certainly couldn't pay the hotel bill unless she found a job right away, and there seemed to be no work available that she could possibly do.

Maybe she could take a crash course in hairstyling, Laurel thought grimly.

The door opened, admitting a gust of wind and the tall man in the leather jacket. He strode into the lobby and looked around. His dark hazel eyes raked her once more with a cold, piercing glance. Laurel looked down at her magazine, feeling self-conscious.

Her cheeks warmed with embarrassment. They were alone in the oak-lined room and it seemed almost rude not to speak to him, but his manner was so intimidating. She couldn't remember when a man had ever made her feel like this, tongue-tied and awkward, as if she were a gawky adolescent.

It was because of the clothes, Laurel told herself. If she were well-dressed and properly groomed, she'd be her usual confident self. She probably wouldn't even notice this man, who was certainly no fashion plate himself.

She watched as he clattered up the stairs without giving her a second glance. Apparently, he was also a guest at the hotel.

Not a local man, the red-haired waitress had said. Laurel wondered about his occupation. He had the look of a hard-edged drifter. And his body had a taut, prowling, athletic appearance, as if he did something physical for a living.

Maybe he was a cowboy. After all, there were cowboys everywhere in this town, wearing boots and Stetsons, carrying rifles on racks in the back windows of their pickup trucks. But the stranger didn't have that look, either. There was something vaguely familiar about him, but she couldn't put her finger on where she'd seen him.

Maybe he was a . . .

"Well, there you are," a voice said comfortably. "I been looking all over for you, girl." Laurel glanced up, startled, to see a plump woman in a candy-striped apron standing in the entry to the hotel dining room. The woman had a frosting of silver curls, a round face and pair of blue eyes that were sharp with intelligence.

A man stood behind her, large and calm, wearing a plaid shirt and denim coveralls. Laurel recognized him as the man who'd been running the hotel desk last night when she checked in. He carried a folded newspaper in one hand and a large model airplane in the other.

"I'm Hilda Fairweather," the woman said. "And this here's my husband, Luther Barnes."

Laurel nodded. "My name is Laurie Atkins," she said.

Hilda looked her over with calm appraisal, then nodded as if satisfied. "I know. You'll prob'ly do," she said.

"I will?"

"I heard you want a job," Hilda said. "Well, I'm offering one."

"You're offering me a *job?*"

"If we can get along. Now, are you a real hard worker?"

"Yes, I am. I'm a very hard worker. Always have been."

"Don't quit till you're finished?"

Laurel thought of hours spent alone in her office, long after Dennis and the rest of the staff had gone home for the night. Hours in which she often finished placing clients' buy orders for the next day and watched the opening numbers from the European and Japanese stock exchanges coming up on the monitor in the small hours of the morning . . .

"That's right," Laurel said. "I don't usually quit till I'm finished."

"You don't mind hard, dirty work?"

Laurel shook her head.

"You know anything about working in a kitchen?" Hilda asked.

Back in Vancouver, Laurel's own kitchen was equipped with every modern convenience. Occasionally, when she had the time, she would prepare elaborate dinners for guests. Minted lamb was her specialty, with a tangy bouillabaisse and a luscious dessert cake made of layered chocolate, whipped cream flavored with Grand Marnier and sliced mandarin orange sections...

"Yes," she said, realizing that Hilda was watching her closely. "Yes, Ms. Fairweather, I've worked in a kitchen before."

"Well, it's nothing fancy to start," Hilda warned her. "You'll just be washing dishes, cleaning the fry grill, maybe doing some vegetable prep if we're real busy."

"Where?" Laurel asked.

"Here in the hotel. I run the coffee shop and the dining room," Hilda said proudly.

"I see," Laurel said, wondering what the job would pay.

"Four dollars an hour," Hilda said as if she could read Laurel's mind. "Seven till four, with an hour for lunch. You can eat free in the kitchen and Kate will give you a half rate on your room. Crystal will be your supervisor, but I'm *always* the boss," Hilda added with a dark warning glance.

"Who's Crystal?"

"Red-haired waitress, cute smile, figure like a movie star's?"

"I saw her this morning," Laurel said, wondering what it would be like to have that pert young girl in authority over her.

But she was hardly in a position to complain. After all, it was a paying job, and it wouldn't be for very long.

"Fine, then," Hilda said, bustling away through the lobby. "Tomorrow morning, seven o'clock in the coffee-shop kitchen. Bring me your social insurance number for the employment forms, okay?" she called over her shoulder.

Laurel's heart began to pound. She'd completely forgotten that a prospective employer would require her identification number. What if some nationwide computer network was already alerted to pick up that number?

"I had some things stolen from my luggage on the bus," she said awkwardly. "Almost all my cash is gone, and I don't have my social insurance card."

"I don't need the *card*," Hilda said, "as long as you can remember the number."

Laurel, who had an astonishing head for figures, could remember all kinds of numbers. Not only her own social insurance number but her mother's and father's, as well as the combination for the office safe, their computer security codes and telephone numbers for everybody she knew.

"Yes," she said to Hilda's vanishing form. "I think I can give it to you from memory."

In fact, she'd decided to use her mother's identification number. She'd be long gone before any bureaucrat found the mistake.

Even at four dollars an hour, Laurel calculated that she could probably save enough in less than a month to pay her hotel bill and bus fare back home. Especially if she ate most of her meals for free in the kitchen.

She became aware of Luther Barnes, who was still standing quietly in the doorway. He gave her a gentle smile.

"Hilda seems a little gruff sometimes," he said, "but she's a real sweet woman."

Laurel glanced at him in surprise. "I'm sure she is. Is that . . . is it yours?" she asked, gesturing at the model plane.

"I built it," he said with pride. "It flies by remote control. I was just taking it out to the empty field by the stockyards to run it through a trial flight."

Laurie smiled, touched by the look of boyish eagerness on his weathered face. "I'm sure it'll fly just fine," she told him.

They exchanged another smile. Then Laurel turned away to cross the lobby in the wake of her new employer, still feeling a little dazed by this unexpected turn of events.

CHAPTER THREE

THE OTHER NEWCOMER at the hotel, the one Laurel had noticed with such covert interest that first morning in the coffee shop, was a man named Jonas O'Neal.

On a warm spring afternoon, the day after Laurel started her job in the kitchen, Jonas ran lightly up the stairs to his room, shrugged off his leather jacket and stood looking around in silence.

His room was pleasant enough, with its old-fashioned wallpaper and furnishings and the antique china ewer and tray on a carved oak sideboard. Above the bed hung a sepia photograph of a young woman with an abundance of hair rolled onto the top of her head. She gazed out of the ornate frame with a sad, faraway look in her eyes.

"I really hate hotel rooms," Jonas told the woman in the picture. "Don't you? I've been in a thousand of them, and after a while they all look the same."

He moved closer to study her faded image, wondering what her life had been like.

Did she love her husband? Could such a sweet, tender woman enjoy being a pioneer wife out here on the prairie, or had the rigors of this existence been enough to destroy her spirit? Maybe the sadness in her eyes was from loneliness and despair, or maybe she'd lost a baby to some childhood illness . . .

Jonas turned away from the silent face, prowled restlessly over to the window and looked down, but nothing at all was happening in the main street of Wolf Hill. He watched the drowsy stillness for a few minutes, then came back to sit on the handmade quilt that covered his bed. Rummaging briefly in a duffel bag under the bed, he drew out a leather case, opened it and revealed several parts of a compact, high-powered rifle.

Jonas assembled the gun expertly, sighted down the barrel, took a cloth from inside the leather case and polished the weapon's gleaming surfaces. Then he took the rifle apart again and packed the pieces away, locked the case and restored it to the duffel bag, shoving the whole thing out of sight under the bed.

He lay back on the bed with his hands behind his head. The silence pressed at him, broken only by the monotonous sound of the wind sighing around the eaves of the old building.

"Damned wind never stops blowing," he said to the woman in the picture. "It could drive a man crazy, that wind. Did it make you feel that way, too?"

She looked down at him with those tragic, gentle eyes.

Jonas wondered if she'd been hanging up there for a hundred years, ever since the hotel was built. If so, she'd probably heard a lot of windstorms in her time...

He levered his long body off the bed, pulled his jacket on and left the room, clattering down the beautiful old oak staircase. In the lobby he hesitated for a moment, then walked down the hallway toward the back of the hotel and peered around an open doorway into the kitchen.

The woman was there, all right. She stood with her back to him, slumped over a big worktable with a pile of silverware that she was scrubbing in a tray, then polishing with a cloth.

Jonas grinned when he saw the blackened mess on her hands, the weary droop of her shoulders and the dogged way she kept picking up utensils and jamming them into the dirty water. Her hair was limp and untidy, with long strands that had escaped the shoelace and hung against her neck. The side of her face that he could see was covered with black smears, obviously from all the times she'd reached up with those filthy hands, trying to brush back the strands of hair.

Dead on her feet, he thought with grudging approval, but she still wouldn't quit. She'd probably keep working till she dropped.

Beside her on the floor, next to her shabby running shoes, were a couple of bushel baskets full of cuts of raw meat, partly thawed and oozing blood. A heavy-duty meat grinder was affixed to the edge of the table, above a big plastic container.

Jonas calculated that after the silverware was cleaned, the next job would be grinding up all that meat into hamburger. A nasty, messy job, he thought. She'd be covered with blood and bone chips before she was done.

Again he had to battle a conflicting set of emotions. It tickled him to watch her struggle, working at this ridiculous job and trying to fit in with her surroundings.

After what she'd done, the woman deserved to suffer a bit, he thought grimly.

Still, he couldn't deny her gallantry. Despite everything he knew about her, a part of Jonas was stunned with admiration over the way she was slogging at this awful job.

And she was pretty, too, under the shabbiness and soil. There was a delicacy about her, a stillness when she thought herself unobserved, like a mountain lake, tranquil and withdrawn, self-contained and beautiful. A man could sit near such a woman and lose himself in her eyes, her smile and that air of gentleness. Being with her, just sitting quietly next to her, holding her hand, would be a soothing, healing thing...

He shook himself abruptly, embarrassed by this wayward flight of fancy.

Jonas knew, all too well, that this woman wasn't what she seemed. In fact, she was all the things he held in contempt. And sitting anywhere close to her was absolutely the last thing Jonas O'Neal ever intended to do.

He moved silently away from the door, leaving her bent over the worktable, then faded down the hall into the lobby. For a moment, he hesitated, thinking about telephones.

There was a phone in his room, but it probably went through the hotel switchboard, if a little hotel like this even had such a thing. At any rate, the line wasn't guaranteed to be secure. In the hotel lobby, a modern pay phone had been installed in an antique wooden telephone booth in one corner. Jonas eyed the structure and decided against using it.

If this was going to take much longer, he really needed to get a place of his own. Jonas left the hotel and headed downtown, hands plunged deep in his pockets, wondering if there were any decent rental properties in Wolf Hill.

At last he found a pay phone in a glass booth near the hardware store. He entered the booth, dialed and waited impatiently, watching a couple of small boys dragging a black-and-white dog past the phone booth on a piece of twine.

"Tell him it's Jonas O'Neal," he told the woman who answered.

His boss came on the line, sounding brusque. "About time you called."

"I've been trying to get hold of you for three days," Jonas said.

"We've been busy at this end," was the brief reply. "It's really crazy around here this week."

Jonas held the phone to his ear and looked at the empty main street of Wolf Hill. Even the little boys and the dog had vanished around the weedy corner of the hardware store.

"It's not busy here," he said.

"So, what have you got, O'Neal? Are you still with her?"

"I'm with her. I saw her just a few minutes ago."

"Where's she staying?"

"It's a little town on the prairie, not far from Calgary. The town's called Wolf Hill, and she's staying in the Wolf Hill Hotel. So am I," he added with a wry smile. "The two of us are a major part of the client base at the moment. Most of the income seems to be generated by the bar, not the hotel guests."

"What's it like?"

"The hotel? It's pretty nice. The place is run by a local rancher's wife, name of Kate Cameron. Her husband's name is Nathan Cameron. They're a wealthy, powerful family around here, and she operates the hotel as a hobby. It's her own business."

"Any other long-term residents?"

"Just the Cameron woman's mother, Mamie Reeves."

"Is she living there?"

"Not exactly. It's more like an extended holiday, I think. I had coffee with Mamie yesterday so I could learn a few things. She's married to a military type who's in the Balkans, acting as adviser to the peace-keeping forces. Normally, they live in Vancouver."

"Will she be a problem? Are you concerned about her?"

Jonas grinned. "Oh, I don't think so. She's quite a woman, Mamie is. She's a real high-stepper, dresses like a movie star and spends money like water."

"That sounds like trouble. What if—"

"Mamie's fully occupied these days. She's busy driving her daughter crazy."

"How?"

"The Camerons have a baby, you see. Cute little guy about six months old. The mother wants to be stern with him, but Grandma keeps insisting on spoiling him rotten. It's kind of fun to watch the power struggle."

"Well, I'm happy to hear that you're being enter-tained, but that has nothing to do with our interests," the voice said curtly. "Can you tell me more about the town?"

Jonas squinted at his surroundings, looking at the deserted main street, the run-down businesses and the golden sprawl of prairie rolling off into an infinity of sky.

"It's…peaceful," he said at last. "How long do you expect me to stay?"

"As long as it takes. What's she doing with her-self?"

"She's got a job in the hotel kitchen. It's the damnedest thing you ever saw."

"What kind of job?"

"Dog work," Jonas said briefly. "Scrubbing, cleaning, dishwashing. She looks tired out of her mind. Last night I was in the lobby when she got off work and it was all she could do to climb the stairs. I wanted to pick the poor woman up and carry her to her room."

"Don't even think of it," his supervisor said coldly. "You're not allowed to get close to her. Your job is just to watch her."

"You think I don't know that?" Jonas said, annoyed. "How long?" he repeated.

"As long as it takes. You know the situation."

Jonas thought again about her weary body slumped over that worktable, the delicate line of her shoulders, her slender neck stained black from the dirty silverware.

"Look," he began, "why can't I just grab her and bring her in? Why wait around and go through a whole damned charade? This could take weeks, and be hard on everybody. To say nothing of the expenses involved."

"How long and costly it might be is none of your business. You know what has to be done."

"But she's—"

"Why do you feel so much sympathy for her, anyhow, O'Neal? I thought you'd be happy to watch her struggle a bit."

"I may not agree with what she's done, but watching a woman suffer isn't exactly my idea of a good time. Besides, she's ..."

"Keep watching her," the voice interrupted. "Don't give yourself away, and don't let her out of your sight. We don't want somebody else getting to her first. She could be in real danger, you know."

"I'm going to be a little conspicuous, hanging around this town for weeks if it takes her that long to give up and head for home."

"Then do what she's doing."

"What do you mean?"

"Just what I said. Get a job."

Jonas held the receiver away from his ear and looked at it in disbelief. "A *job?* Here?"

"You're a big strong guy, O'Neal. You've had lots of specialized training. You could probably get yourself a job, couldn't you?"

Jonas smiled without humor. "I doubt that a lot of jobs around here require the kind of specialized training I've got."

"Then find something ordinary. Just keep an eye on that woman, notify us of her every move and don't let her leave Wolf Hill. All right?"

"Sure," Jonas said, shifting restlessly in the cramped booth.

"And, listen, O'Neal . . ."

"Yes?"

"Don't let her get hurt. We're counting on you for this. You understand?"

Again Jonas thought about her quiet gray eyes, her air of stillness and grace, the gentle sweetness of her mouth.

"Sure," he said briefly. "She won't get hurt."

He hung up the phone before there was time for a reply, let himself out of the phone booth and wandered through the gathering dusk, back to the hotel.

LAUREL TRUDGED down the street toward the post office, carrying a pile of bills and letters that Hilda had sent her to mail. Taking out the mail each morning was supposed to be Crystal's job, but the young waitress hadn't turned up for work again today, and Laurel was doing almost all the kitchen work while Hilda waited on tables in the coffee shop. Actually, the morning trip to the post office was a relief, a chance to get out of the grease and steam for a few minutes and breathe some fresh air. Unfortunately, Laurel was too exhausted to appreciate the warm spring sunshine or the pleasant scent of rain-dampened prairie and wet sage.

After three days at her new job, her whole body sagged with weariness. Her shoulders ached, her back was sore from bending over the sink and her hands were scraped raw and covered with small cuts and burns.

She looked up blearily at the houses as she passed, standing silent and withdrawn, surrounded by leafless hedges and dull brown lawns. Laurel wondered who lived behind the darkened windows, and whether anybody else in all the world felt as miserable as she did on this sunny April morning.

It was too hard, she thought, fighting back tears. Nobody could be expected to work this hard, no matter how urgent things were.

Tonight she'd call her father and explain that her situation was impossible. She'd ask him to wire her some money, enough to let her go to some pleasant resort in Florida or California where she could wait in comfort while Stewart settled his affairs.

He wouldn't even need to know where she went after she left Wolf Hill . . .

She passed a little white house sitting behind a screen of lilacs, and saw a curtain lift away from one of the windows. Laurel found herself looking directly into a woman's face.

They gazed at each other, startled. The woman looked small, frail and very old, with a crown of fluffy white hair and a bright-eyed, alert expression. Perhaps it was her imagination, but Laurel thought she saw both interest and compassion in the old woman's gaze.

She hesitated in the street, fighting a ridiculous urge to go through the wire gate and walk up to the door. She wanted to knock and be admitted to that cozy little doll house. She wanted to sink into a chair, lay her head on the table and pour out all her weary frustration and loneliness to somebody who would listen and be sympathetic.

Just then, the curtain dropped hastily and concealed the old woman's face. Laurel turned away, embarrassed by her overwrought emotions, and continued her trip to the post office.

Margie was busy in the beauty salon, applying a malodorous permanent wave to a middle-aged woman in a pink plastic shawl. Laurel nodded in response to their greeting, then dropped her mail into the slot, fumbled in her pocket for the key and emptied the little silver box. She tucked the bundle of mail under her arm and turned to leave, almost colliding with a man in the small vestibule.

It was the tall stranger from the hotel.

Laurel stepped away abruptly, her heart racing, and waited for him to move so she could open the door. But he stood blocking the entry, looking down at her with an enigmatic expression.

Laurel stared back at him, feeling another unsettling wave of adolescent awkwardness. At close range, the man was even more impressive than she'd thought. His tall body seemed to fill the vestibule with masculine presence and a sense of controlled power. His strange golden eyes were dark in the shadows, but the bitter line of his mouth softened almost imperceptibly when he looked at her.

Again Laurel wondered how he'd look if he smiled. But that thought was replaced almost at once by painful embarrassment over her own ragtag appearance, her torn, stained jeans and reddened hands and the T-shirt that had a few splatters of gravy on the front.

"Good morning," he said. "I didn't think they let you out for walks."

His voice was surprising, deep and relaxed, with a humorous edge that annoyed her.

"I'm getting the mail," she said coldly. "I do it every morning."

Not that it's any of your business, her manner implied.

"Among other things. I guess you're working pretty hard in that kitchen, aren't you?"

He moved past her and scanned the bulletin board on the wall. While Laurel watched in astonishment, he reached out and removed one of the job notices, the one requesting warehouse and clerking help at the local hardware store.

"This job," he told her, pocketing the notice, "isn't available anymore."

"Why not?" she asked, her anger fading into uncertainty once again. There was something so unsettling about the man.

"Because," he said, moving closer and staring at her intently, "they just hired me."

For the first time, she saw him smile. Deep creases appeared in his cheeks, and his hazel eyes sparkled. Laurel looked away quickly, her heart pounding. Then his words registered and she looked up at him in surprise.

"You're going to work at the hardware store?"

"Why not? If you can work in a kitchen, I can work in a hardware store. Right?"

There was a mocking edge to his words, as if he could read her thoughts. Laurel hesitated. "What do you mean?"

"Nothing." He held the door open for her with detached courtesy and stepped onto the street behind her. "Just that women aren't the only ones who can work hard, I guess. We're starting our jobs at pretty much the same time, so we'll see which of us can last the longest, okay?"

Laurel's back stiffened when she heard the teasing note in his voice. She thought about her plan to call her father and demand an escape, and wondered again if this strange man could somehow read her mind.

Silently, she turned away and started back toward the hotel while he took a few steps in the opposite direction, heading downtown.

"Hey," he called.

Laurel paused and turned around. "Yes?"

"What's your name?"

Again she felt like telling him that nothing about her life was any of his business. But she didn't want to overreact, or give him any idea that he was so upsetting to her.

"Laurie Atkins," she said coldly.

"I'm Jonas O'Neal."

He paused with his hands in the pockets of his leather jacket, looking at her. He was bareheaded, and his thick brown hair lifted and stirred in the morning breeze.

"You'd better hurry back to the hotel, Laurie Atkins," he added with another of those rare, luminous smiles.

"Why?" she asked suspiciously, seeing the mocking light in his eyes.

"Because some farmer just delivered a dozen chickens to the back door," Jonas said, his grin widening. "And I believe you're the one who's going to pluck and clean them."

CHAPTER FOUR

JONAS TRUDGED DOWN the street, hands thrust deep in his pockets, thinking about the woman's pale face and big grey eyes, her self-deprecating smile.

"Oh, *hell*," he muttered aloud.

He turned and stared moodily at her vanishing shape, watching as she hurried toward the hotel. She rounded a corner, her tattered jeans and old plaid jacket fading from sight behind a leafless bank of caragana hedge at the corner. Jonas continued to stand alone in brooding silence, gazing fixedly at the place where she'd disappeared.

"She's a real mystery," a voice said beside him. "Isn't she?"

Startled, Jonas glanced down to see a tiny woman standing near him on the sidewalk. She had a soft wrinkled face and a crown of snow-white hair. The old woman wore a pair of red cotton slacks and a turquoise ski jacket zippered warmly to her chin. She was holding on to the handle of a brightly painted red wagon.

"I beg your pardon?" he asked courteously.

She eyed him with suspicion. "You're watching her, aren't you? You've been watching her ever since she came here."

He tensed and glanced cautiously around, but they were alone on the dusty street.

"I've never met the woman before," he said. "Why? Do you know her?"

The little old lady shook her head. "No," she said sadly. "But I'd love to meet her. I can tell she's a princess."

Jonas hid his surprise. "How do you know? She doesn't dress like a princess."

The woman glared at him. "Clothes don't make a princess. That young woman is noble and beautiful, and you know it. Don't you?"

"What's your wagon for?" he asked, ignoring her question.

"I'm going down to Harold Baines's general store to pick up my groceries. They're too heavy to carry, I need a lot of things this time."

"Why?" Jonas asked, falling into step beside her as she headed toward the cluster of stores along the town's main street.

She glanced up at him, then looked away quickly, muttering something he couldn't hear over the clatter of the wagon's wheels.

"Pardon?" he said, leaning toward her. "I didn't catch what you said."

"I said, I might be having company. I might be having somebody special coming over soon for tea, somebody who's never visited me before, and I need a lot of things for baking."

Her wistfulness sent a jolt of sympathy through Jonas.

"Who?" he asked, taking the handle from her and pulling the wagon along behind them.

"Somebody who's new in town."

"That lady in the plaid jacket?" he guessed shrewdly. "Do you think she might be coming to visit you?"

The old woman looked away. "Maybe," she whispered, her voice so low that Jonas had to bend closer to hear. "After all, the poor girl doesn't know anybody. She could use a friend. Maybe she'll come visit me."

He straightened, his face carefully expressionless. "What's your name?" he asked at last. "I'm Jonas O'Neal."

"I'm Nellie Grossman. I live back there." The old woman waved a hand vaguely in the opposite direction. "Here's the store," she added.

"If you like, I can help you take your groceries home," Jonas volunteered. "I don't have anything else to do right now."

She hesitated. "Are you sure that's not a bother?"

"It's fine. Nellie, is it okay to leave this wagon outside while we pick up your things?"

"Of course," she said in surprise. "Why not?"

"Where I come from, if you leave something on the street, it's gone in ten seconds."

"That must be awful," she said. "Just awful. Not being able to trust people."

"I doubt that it's much different wherever you go," he said, trying to keep the bitterness out of his voice. "There aren't many people in this world who you can really trust."

Nellie regarded him in silence for a moment, then moved into the store, consulting a shopping list written in a cramped and careful hand.

Once again his heart ached with sympathy as he helped her select the meager items. A tiny pot of strawberry jam, a couple of frozen dinners, a few tea bags, three apples and a couple of bananas, all were examined with judicious care before they were dropped into the basket.

Harold Baines, the proprietor, greeted Nellie at the checkout counter and added up her purchases, while Jonas waited near the door.

"Need any help with this stuff, Nellie?" the grocer asked.

Nellie shook her head. "This young man is helping me," she said, nodding toward Jonas.

Baines gave him an interested glance. "You're the new guy who's working for Clarence Krantz over at the hardware, right?"

"That's right," Jonas said, marveling at the speed with which news seemed to travel in this small town.

The grocer studied him briefly, then turned back to Nellie. "Nellie, I'm sorry, but your prescription won't be ready for a while," he said. "I'm still waiting for the truck to come down from Calgary."

Her face creased with disappointment. "I need my pills, Harold. I'm all out."

"I know you do. I'll see if I can drop them off for you. But I'm really busy so you may have to come back later on this afternoon."

She shook her head, then watched gratefully while Jonas hefted the sack of groceries and took them outside. "I'll carry them," he told her. "You can pull the wagon, all right?"

She trundled along beside him with her empty wagon. Jonas glanced down at her curly white head and felt another stirring of gentleness, a feeling that was somehow all mixed up with his troubled thoughts of that other mysterious woman with her sweet gray eyes and rueful smile.

LAUREL STOOD in the kitchen, hands on hips, staring unhappily at a row of naked, headless chickens on the big worktable. There were twelve of them, mostly plucked but still bristling with pinfeathers, their scaly yellow claws dangling from plump drumsticks.

Hilda passed by with a load of glasses from the dishwasher.

"You'll need to get all them pinfeathers off," she said. "I can't abide pinfeathers."

"I know," Laurel said wearily. "I dipped the chickens in a pail of boiling water like you told me, and most of the..." She paused and took a deep breath, rubbing her sleeve across her forehead. "Most of the feathers came off, except for those little ones. They're more like hairs than feathers."

"What you do, you turn the gas real low on the stove, then hold the bird over the flame just for a few seconds. Turn it quick so it singes lightly all over. The heat will burn off them little feathers just as slick as can be."

Laurel continued to brood over the row of chickens while Hilda bustled out toward the doorway.

"Look, Laurie," she said, "I have to go to the bank, and then I got a dentist appointment. I told Crystal to come over from the dining room and help you clean them birds. You can wrap them in plastic and put them in the big fridge, okay? And when you're finished, you can take the rest of the afternoon off. Things are pretty slow today."

"Thanks a lot," Laurel said, but her irony was lost on her employer who had already vanished into the hotel lobby.

She took another deep breath, turned the gas ring onto its lowest setting and began to singe the birds as she'd been instructed, fascinated in spite of herself to discover that Hilda had been right, as usual. The stubborn little feathers seemed to melt away in the heat, leaving the birds smooth and gleaming.

Crystal wandered in, carrying a cup of tea and a couple of saltines which she nibbled moodily. Laurel glanced at the young waitress, who seemed somewhat out of sorts these days.

Her face was pale so that the freckles stood out in sharp relief, and her eyes were darkly ringed with blue shadows. She seemed worried and preoccupied. Even her flirtation with the local cowboys and truck drivers had lost its sparkle.

Laurel suspected that her fellow employee was troubled about something, but a few days on the job with Crystal had dulled any traces of sympathy she might have felt. Laurel was doing much more than her share of work in the hotel kitchen, filling in constantly for the other girl while Hilda wasn't looking. At times, she was strongly tempted to complain about the injustice, and only her stubborn pride prevented her from telling Hilda what was going on.

"This is awful," Crystal muttered, wrinkling her nose at the smell of wet and burning feathers. "Laurie, you shouldn't really singe them till after they're cleaned," she added.

"I didn't know," Laurel said. "Come on," she added, gesturing at the sharp knives in a wooden block on the table. "Hilda said you'd help me clean these things, and then I can have the rest of the day off. I'm practically dead on my feet, Crystal."

The girl's face turned even whiter against the fiery red of her hair. She sank into a chair and stared at the chickens.

"I can't," she muttered, covering her face with her hands. "Oh, no. I can't clean those chickens. Please . . . I'll do anything else."

Laurel curbed her impatience with an effort. "I can't do this myself," she said. "Crystal, I've never cleaned a chicken in my life. I wouldn't even know where to start."

"You have to cut the feet off right here, at the drumstick joint." Crystal pointed with a trembling hand. "And you pull the crop out of the breast cavity, yank the neck off and make a slit here below the breastbone, along the—"

She stopped speaking abruptly, gave Laurel a glance of mute appeal, then jumped to her feet and ran toward the door, holding her hand up to her mouth.

"Crystal," Laurel said. "Come back here! We need to get this done."

"I'll be in the dining room," Crystal said in a muffled voice, from the doorway. "I'm sorry. Please don't tell Hilda about this, okay?"

Laurel looked at the girl's sagging form and felt her anger dissipate. Crystal did really look awful. But there was no way Laurel could manage on her own. "Crystal, go get a drink of water or something. I'm sorry, but I need your help."

"Please, Laurie," the girl whispered. "I'm really tired right now. I feel just awful. Please don't tell Hilda."

Her face contorted and she fled, leaving Laurel alone with the row of naked pink chickens.

Grimly, she rinsed out Crystal's teacup and slammed it into the cupboard. Then she took the sharpest knife and began to slice off the feet as she'd been instructed, trying with fierce concentration to locate the center of the drumstick joint and make a neat cut. Her technique improved with each bird, and the last ones looked quite professional.

Laurel examined them with cold satisfaction, gathered the scaly yellow claws and dumped them into a huge plastic sack that already bulged with wet feathers. She gripped the knife and studied the row of chickens, her uncertainty returning. Frowning, she tried to remember exactly what Crystal had said.

Something about the neck, and then a slit in the...

Laurel closed her eyes, almost faint with fatigue.

This was impossible. Nobody could endure this. She'd made a real effort, but there were limits. She couldn't possibly...

"Having some problems?" a voice inquired.

Laurel opened her eyes and looked up, then stiffened.

Jonas O'Neal lounged in the doorway, carrying an armful of bags and packages. His face was expressionless, but his eyes were alight with sardonic humor as he glanced at Laurel, then at the row of naked birds.

Her cheeks reddened and she looked away hastily, the knife dangling in her hand. To her horror, she found herself battling a flood of tears. On top of everything else, she simply couldn't endure the humiliation of being laughed at by this hard-faced stranger.

"Why is this so funny to you?" she asked, struggling to keep her voice steady. "Why do take such pleasure in watching me struggle? I don't even know you. Tell me, are you just generally sadistic, or do you have some personal reason for enjoying my problems?"

"Don't be so dramatic," he said mildly, depositing his packages on a chair and moving over to stand next to her. In spite of her anger and weariness, Laurel was once again sharply conscious of his nearness.

There was something dangerously attractive about the man, but it was entirely a physical thing. And, Laurel told herself, she was a grown-up woman, hardly the sort to be seduced by a physical attraction. After all, this man was probably more Crystal's type than hers. Besides, he was...

She watched in amazement as he reached into the neck cavity of the nearest bird and pulled out a small, lumpy sack, displaying it on the palm of his hand.

"See that?" he said in a mild instructive tone, like a college lecturer. "That's the crop. It comes out easily, but you have to be careful not to break it because it's full of wet grain, and it can make a real mess."

She nodded, feeling numb, and leaned forward to watch as he took a sheet of paper toweling, wrapped it around the bony neck and gave a sharp yank.

"That's the neck," he said, laying it aside. "You'd better save it, because they probably use it to make gravy or something. Now," he went on in that same neutral tone, "you make a slit here below the breastbone..." He took a knife from the block and made a neat, professional cut. "And then you reach inside to get the giblets and both pieces of liver. The gall bladder's attached to the liver so you have to be careful. If it's punctured, it makes the meat bitter."

Once she was accustomed to the ripe smell and the blood that smeared on his hands, Laurel found herself fascinated by what he was doing. She leaned forward as he worked over the birds, and studied the growing array of chicken innards piled on the mat of toweling.

"Look," she said in amazement. "Those are eggs, right?"

Jonas held up the glistening, soft-shelled little objects. "The big ones are almost ready. Those others are just forming. She was a pretty good laying hen, this one. A pity they had to butcher her."

Laurel nodded, looking down at the table. "What are those?"

"The lungs. And this..." He removed a bluish, oval-shaped organ which he slit open with a knife. "This is the gizzard," he said, displaying its corrugated interior.

"What are those shiny things?"

"Little stones, bits of rock and glass that the bird picks up to help grind its food."

Laurel gazed in astonishment at the glittering stones. "They look like jewels."

"They get really well polished over time. Sometimes there *are* jewels in the gizzard," he added with one of those rare, fleeting smiles that transformed his hard face. "This is where people find diamond rings and such. Birds will peck at anything shiny."

"Diamond rings?" She looked up at him with cautious skepticism.

He shrugged. "It's been known to happen. Once, when I was a kid—"

He fell silent abruptly and went on with his task. Laurel watched, amazed by the surgical precision of his movements. "Are you a doctor?" she said.

"A doctor?" He raised an eyebrow and gave her the familiar sardonic look, his warmth fading. "Now, why would you ask something like that?"

She flushed and looked down quickly. "I just... wondered. You're so good at this."

"I grew up on a farm."

"I see," she said, her cheeks still uncomfortably warm.

"I'm not a doctor. I've got a job in the hardware store. And you work in a kitchen. Why would either of us be anything but what we seem?"

Laurel ignored the pointed question, and busied herself by gathering the smelly mass of paper toweling and shoving it into the plastic sack.

"Why?" he asked again, following her across the room with more scraps.

"I don't know." She kept her voice deliberately cold to hide her confusion.

"Do you think I'm an imposter?" he asked, moving close to her and rinsing his hands. Again she was conscious of his body, his overwhelming maleness and the sense of danger that was somehow a part of him.

"I don't know," she said, reaching for a chicken to hold under the stream of cold water. "To tell the truth, I don't really think about you at all."

He gave her an intent look, his golden eyes dark and thoughtful. Then he turned aside abruptly and gathered his packages from the chair.

"Next time you have to clean a brace of chickens," he said, grinning at her, "you'll know how to do it all by yourself. You're acquiring all kinds of valuable career skills, Ms Atkins. Right?"

Laurel stiffened, wondering if he'd placed deliberate emphasis on her false surname, or if she'd just imagined it. For a few moments after he was gone she stood in silence, looking at the empty doorway.

Who was he?

Certainly not the itinerant worker he was pretending to be. Despite his protests, Jonas O'Neal didn't belong among the dusty shelves of the local hardware store, any more than she belonged in this kitchen. The man had a cynical, big-city air about him. In fact, he looked more like a . . .

She shivered with sudden dread. Jonas O'Neal looked like a plainclothes policeman. He had that powerful, prowling walk, a cold watchful look and an unmistakable air of authority. And, she recalled with mounting alarm, he'd arrived in Wolf Hill practically the same time she had, and nobody seemed to know what he was doing here.

She shook her head and turned to grab another chicken, running the water furiously over its plump body.

She was just being paranoid. If the man were a policeman assigned to follow her, he certainly wouldn't get a job in Wolf Hill and settle down to spend an indefinite period of time in this little town. Nor would he hang around and needle her about being an imposter. He'd simply serve her with the subpoena and leave, and then she'd be legally required to go back to Vancouver and testify about Stewart Atchison's illegal trades.

Laurel stared out the window, thinking about her father. Her heart constricted when she recalled his gentle face, his kindly smile and endearing clumsiness. Everybody loved Stewart, from the board members to the boy in the mail room, and there wasn't a person in the company who hadn't benefited from his generosity at one time or another.

When his young wife had announced her pregnancy just before Christmas, Stewart had been like a boy again. His excitement had filled the whole office with sunlight.

Laurel swallowed hard and went on rinsing chickens, her shoulders stiffening with resolve. No matter how difficult this job got, she would continue to do her part. The weariness and loneliness were worthwhile if they gave her father time to clear his name and remove the threat that hung over all of them.

And as for Jonas O'Neal, she thought grimly, the best thing was to avoid the man. His presence in town had nothing to do with her. No doubt he was in hiding, too, and probably for a more sinister reason than hers. The less she had to do with him, the better off she'd be.

Laurel went to the pantry to take out a roll of plastic bags, then paused and moved back toward the table.

A small white sack lay on the chair where Jonas had deposited his packages. She looked at it uncertainly, then glanced at the doorway where he'd disappeared. The last thing she wanted was to go up to his room, knock on the door and be confronted once again by his sardonic smile and those piercing hazel eyes.

She wiped her hands on her apron and lifted the paper sack. It carried the logo of the local general store and pharmacy, and had a prescription-drug receipt stapled to the top. Beneath the receipt, in a firm dark hand, somebody had written, "Nellie Grossman's pills. She needs them no later than four o'clock!"

Laurel glanced at her watch. It was almost three-thirty. She looked at the address on the receipt and realized that Nellie Grossman, whoever she was, lived only a few blocks from the hotel. Obviously she wasn't well enough to pick up her own prescription, so she must really need her pills.

But why was Jonas O'Neal carrying deliveries for the local pharmacy? He'd taken a job at the hardware store, hadn't he?

Anyhow, none of this was her concern. Laurel set the package on the chair and went on cleaning and wrapping the chickens, trying to ignore the handwritten message that seemed to shout across the room at her.

NELLIE BUSTLED around her sunny little house, carrying things back and forth between the kitchen and the dining room. She'd fallen into the habit of setting two places at her dining table every afternoon, like a little girl playing tea party. It was fun to bring out the best china and silverware, unused for so many years. She loved to steep a pot of tea and plan good things to eat. And today, she'd found a pussy willow in bloom in the backyard and picked a spray to put in the center of the table, along with a few early tulips that were growing along the south wall of the garden.

She hummed under her breath, picturing the princess girl at the opposite side of the table, sipping her tea and glancing up with that grave look and endearing lopsided smile.

Nellie knew, of course, that all of this was only play-acting. The princess girl would never come to visit, and Nellie would wind up drinking her tea alone just as she did every day.

Sometimes, if Fluffy happened to be in an unusually expansive mood, she could coax him to sit in the opposite chair for a little while. But the big tomcat always got bored after a few minutes and leaped to the floor again, leaving her lonelier than ever.

Nellie paused by the window, battling a sudden wave of unhappiness. This familiar misery was like an enemy that had to be fought all the time with energy and cunning. If she gave in, the loneliness would roll over her head and drown her. She had to concentrate on the good things that happened each day, like the branch of

pussy willows and the strange young man who'd volunteered to carry her groceries.

Nellie lifted the curtain and looked thoughtfully out
at her lilac hedge, where a drift of fresh green buds were
beginning to lighten the stark outline of the branches.

He was such a handsome young man, but sad and
bitter. Nellie couldn't understand what troubled him,
and she worried over his stealthy interest in the princess girl. Still, the two of them had brought a new diversion into her life. Speculating about them made her
feel younger, less alone.

She frowned and turned away from the window,
thinking about her pills. Soon she'd have to go to the
pharmacy to pick them up, and she wouldn't be home
when the girl came by for tea.

The doorbell rang, interrupting her thoughts and
startling her. She exchanged a glance with Fluffy, who
stiffened alertly and stared at the door.

Nellie's doorbell hardly ever rang. Sometimes, the
Brownies came around, selling cookies. But that wasn't
in the spring, was it? And, she thought wildly, there
were a few neighborhood children at Halloween, but of
course that was in the fall. Occasionally, a traveling
salesman used to ring the bell, but the town council had
passed a bylaw forbidding door-to-door sales, so now
Nellie didn't even have that source of company.

The doorbell rang again, unnaturally loud in the silence.

Nellie pressed a hand to her mouth, looked at Fluffy
for courage, and moved haltingly toward the door. She
opened it a crack and peered out, then opened the door
farther and stood bewildered, blinking in the dazzle of
afternoon sunlight that slanted across the entry porch.

CHAPTER FIVE

LAUREL LOOKED DOWN at the little woman, distressed by the look of alarm on her wrinkled face. Nellie Grossman seemed dazed and uncertain, almost ready to faint.

"Are you...are you Nellie?" Laurel asked. "I found this..." She paused. "Somebody left this prescription in the hotel kitchen, and I thought I should bring it over for you. Are you all right?" she added when Nellie seemed unable to answer. "Can I get you anything?"

"I'm fine," the woman said at last. "I just...I wasn't expecting..."

"I'm sorry if I startled you." Laurel continued to hold out the prescription, which the other woman seemed too confused to notice.

"Thank you," Nellie murmured at last, reaching for the paper sack. "That was...it was real nice of you to bring it over."

"You're welcome." Laurel turned to leave, but Nellie grasped the sleeve of Laurel's plaid jacket. She looked at the woman in surprise, then down at the veined old hand that gripped her jacket.

"Don't go," Nellie said abruptly, then shifted on her feet and looked awkward. "I mean," she added, "maybe you'd like to come in for..." She paused, taking a deep breath. "For a cup of tea or something, since you came all this way."

Laurel glanced down the street, where the upper floor of the hotel was clearly visible above the trees. She smiled and shook her head politely. "No, thank you," she said. "I really should be getting back. I still have work to do."

But when she saw the wistful look on the old woman's face, she hesitated, then fell silent.

A big gray tomcat appeared in the doorway and sat looking up at them with cold insolence, his tail twitching. Over Nellie's shoulder, Laurel could see a tidy room, a small television set and braided oval rug, a padded rocking chair and a wealth of crocheted doilies and afghans. It all looked so cozy and inviting, like the grandmother's house in the storybook pictures she'd loved as a child. She wavered, suddenly aware of a delicious scent that wafted out through the door, something warm and spicy and rich.

"That smells so good," she said impulsively. "What is it?"

"A banana-nut loaf," Nellie said. "It's ready to come out of the oven in a few minutes. Come and have a slice while it's still warm."

Laurel nodded and stepped into the little house. Nellie closed the door and Laurel was wrapped in silence and peace.

"This is so nice," she said, moving toward the plump flowered sofa.

Her body felt suddenly overcome with weariness. Laurel sank onto the couch and was enfolded in a soft, floating kind of warmth. Sighing, she closed her eyes, resting her head against one of the crocheted antimacassars.

"Poor girl," Nellie murmured, pausing beside the couch and touching Laurel's hair gently. "You're just worn-out, aren't you?"

Laurel glanced up at her, trying to smile. "I guess I'm not used to working so hard," she said.

"What's your name, dear?" Nellie asked, still looking down at her intently.

Laurel found herself battling an absurd desire to tell this strange little woman the truth about herself. "Laurie," she said at last, watching as the cat leaped up beside her and settled on the afghan, kneading his paws luxuriously in the bright wool. "My name is Laurie Atkins."

Nellie bustled into the kitchen. "What brings you to Wolf Hill, Laurie?" she called from the other room.

Laurel got up, disturbing the cat who glared at her, then closed his eyes again. She moved toward the kitchen door and watched as Nellie took a pair of embroidered pot holders and removed a crusty brown loaf from the oven, turning it out onto a rack.

Beside Laurel was an oak dining table, beautifully set for two, with tulips and pussy willows as a centerpiece.

"But you're expecting somebody," she said with a pang of disappointment. "I shouldn't stay, Nellie. Really, I only came to bring the—"

Nellie gripped the loaf pan, turning to her in alarm. "It's all right," she said. "Really it is, Laurie. I'm not expecting anybody."

"But..." Laurel gave the table another bewildered glance. "But there are two places set."

Nellie waved a hand in dismissal, her wrinkled cheeks suddenly pink. "Oh, that doesn't mean anything," she said. "It seems like...somebody's always dropping by, so I usually set an extra place just to be prepared. I never know who'll be stopping in to visit. But I'm not expecting anybody in particular today."

Laurel nodded uncertainly. "I see. Can I help with anything?"

"Certainly not," Nellie said firmly. "Not when you're worn to the bone from working in that kitchen. You just sit down and let somebody wait on you for a change. Fluffy!" she added. "You bad cat, move over and give Laurie some room on the couch."

Laurel smiled at the surly tomcat who was now sprawled lazily on his back, his white belly exposed and his paws dangling. He seemed, indeed, to occupy most of the couch.

"Just pick him up and move him over," Nellie said. "He won't mind."

Fluffy opened one eye and gave Laurel a warning look as she approached the couch. She hesitated, wondering what to do, but he sighed and rolled over, curling into a ball and resting his chin moodily on his paws.

"Nice kitty," Laurel murmured, settling down next to him and stroking his sleek head, scratching gently around his ears.

He made an odd rumbling sound, like a race car starting. Laurel realized after a moment that he was purring.

"Nice kitty," she said again, smiling as she nestled into the soft depths of the couch. "Nice, nice kitty."

Fluffy edged closer to her, looking positively cordial. Laurel closed her eyes, bathed in warmth and comfort, and felt a rich contentment stealing through her body.

"What brings you to Wolf Hill, Laurie?" the old woman repeated, carrying a huge flowered teapot into the room and setting it on the table.

Laurel opened her eyes and looked up, her tension returning.

"It's all right," Nellie said with a gentle smile. "I know you have secrets, but I won't tell."

"Secrets?" Laurel asked cautiously. "What do you mean?"

"Well, for one thing, you're not a girl who should be working in a kitchen," Nellie said matter-of-factly, pausing on her way back to the other room. "You're a princess. I could tell the first time I saw you. I know there must be some good reason why you're here, but if you can't tell me, that's all right."

"It's just..." Laurel stumbled. "I needed to get away for a while, and I didn't know what to..."

Nellie nodded, as if she understood. "What made you pick Wolf Hill? Do you know somebody in town?"

"Not a soul. I just...I was reading a book about Wolf Hill. The schoolteacher's old diary that was recently published, you know? And it all seemed so...nice," she concluded, feeling shy and awkward. "I wanted to see the town, that's all."

Nellie looked at her shrewdly for a moment, then gestured toward the dining table. "Everything's ready," she said. "Come and sit down."

Laurel got up and moved toward the table. In addition to the banana loaf, there was an assortment of cookies and biscuits. All at once she realized that she was ravenously hungry.

"This looks delicious," she said, seating herself opposite Nellie, who presided over the teapot. "Thank you for having me, Nellie. You've gone to so much trouble."

"It's no trouble. Cream and sugar?" Nellie poured tea into a dainty flowered cup.

"Just a little sugar, please." Laurel looked longingly at the warm slices of banana loaf, and a small crystal bowl of butter that stood nearby. "You know, it's been years since I've tasted a fresh banana loaf."

"This was my mother's recipe. She was in the diary, you know," Nellie commented, heaping slices of the loaf onto a plate and handing it to Laurel.

Laurel looked up in astonishment. "Your mother? In Ellen Livingston's diary?"

Nellie nodded placidly. "My mother was Karen Mueller."

"For heaven's sake!" Laurel exclaimed in delight. "Really? Karen was your mother? The one who helped Ellen with the little children all the time?"

"As a matter of fact, I was named for Ellen Livingston." Nellie offered the plate of cookies. "But my father started calling me Nellie when I was just a baby, and the name's stuck with me to this day."

Laurel was intrigued. "So, who was your father, Nellie?" she asked at last. "Who did Karen marry?"

"Steven Oates. I believe he's mentioned in the diary, too, isn't he?"

"Oh, yes! Karen met him at the first school Christmas concert. They danced together all evening, and she was so excited."

"I remember Mama telling me about that night. They married about four years later, when my mother was nineteen. I was their second child, and the only girl. I had five brothers."

"Has your family lived here ever since?"

Nellie shook her head. "Most of them went to the city. And," she added, "two of my brothers were killed in the war."

"But the Muellers were a big family, weren't they? You must still have lots of relatives around here."

"Not anymore. There's my nephew Carl, who's the local plumber, and a few of the Oates relatives on my father's side, but most of the young people don't even know the family connections anymore."

Laurel nodded, trying to remember the names from the diary. "So you married . . . who? It must have been Luke Grossman."

Nellie laughed. "No, it certainly wasn't. I married Luke's oldest son, Ben Grossman. Luke was my father-in-law," she added, her smile fading. "And a nasty, selfish man he was, too."

"Ellen never liked him very much, did she?" Laurel paused to chew and swallow a mouthful of banana loaf. "Nellie, this is absolutely the most delicious thing I've ever tasted."

"Eat lots of it," Nellie said placidly. "I'll never be able to finish it by myself."

Laurel glanced at her hostess, wondering about all those people who kept dropping in unexpectedly to visit Nellie. Wouldn't they make short work of a fresh banana loaf?

But Nellie was still preoccupied with her memories. "I believe Ellen said in her diary that Luke Grossman was a bit of a lout, didn't she, Laurie?"

Laurel nodded, helping herself to a shortbread cookie. "And he was the oldest student in the school, too. I think Ellen was actually a little afraid of him."

"He was a hard, violent man," Nellie said. "My Ben was afraid of him, and Ben was a lot bigger and stronger than poor Ellen."

"What happened to him? Luke, I mean."

"He died in the thirties, a few years before the war. Not long after Ben and I were married, in fact. It was an accident on the farm."

"What kind of accident?" Laurel asked.

"One of the bulls killed him. Knocked him into a corral fence and then trampled him in the dirt. It was hours before Ben and I found his body."

"Oh, Nellie, that must have been terrible."

Nellie shrugged and leaned forward to check on Laurel's cup. "Those were terrible years. I can still remember," she added with a faraway look, "how hard we had to work, and how little we got for it. There was no money anywhere."

"That was during the depression, right?"

The old woman nodded. "You know, I used to wonder what happened to all the money," she said. "It was like all the money in the world just dried up and turned to dust. It seemed to vanish off the face of the earth. Nobody had anything in those years."

"Actually," Laurel said, buttering another piece of banana loaf, "the gold standard came under attack and world currencies were devalued sharply after the stock-market crash in 1929. It wasn't that all the money disappeared, Nellie. It was just that the traders had so little confidence. The markets slowed and people weren't willing to—"

She fell abruptly silent, conscious of Nellie's eyes resting on her with bright speculation.

Laurel cleared her throat. "Nellie," she began after an awkward silence. "Please don't..."

The little woman reached over and patted her hand gently. "No need to worry, dear. I told you before, your secrets are safe with me. I won't tell anybody a single thing about you."

Laurel nodded, feeling a flood of gratitude and warmth for this charming woman.

Nellie sipped her tea and returned to the former topic as casually as if they had never strayed into dangerous waters.

"When our first child was born...that's my son, William," she added, "Ben and I had to go out and pick up bones on the prairie so we could afford to buy vitamin drops for him. We sold bones by the truckload for about fifty cents a load."

"Buffalo bones?" Laurel asked.

Nellie chuckled. "Goodness, no. There weren't many buffalo bones left on the prairie by that time. Just the remains of poor starving cattle that were bleached by the sunlight, anything we could find to keep body and soul together. And we were some of the lucky ones," she added. "We lived on the Grossman farm and had animals and a garden. At least we could eat."

"But most of the crops failed in the thirties, didn't they?"

"Year after year. The rain didn't come, and the fields turned to dust and blew away. If we ever managed to grow a little crop, the grasshoppers would come and eat it, or prairie fires would gobble it up. Nothing seemed to work. They were such terrible years," Nellie repeated.

"But, you know," she went on thoughtfully, "we weren't that unhappy, when I come to think about it. We were all in the same boat, for one thing. And folks knew how to be friendly in those years. None of us had any money for entertainment, so we got together and had dances or community picnics, or just played cards. I remember when other young couples would come over to the farm with their children, and we'd make popcorn and then we'd all sit around the kitchen table for hours doing a jigsaw puzzle.''

"That sounds like fun," Laurel said wistfully. "People don't do things like that anymore."

"In some ways it was fun," Nellie agreed. "But," she added with a reminiscent smile, "my goodness, we got tired of plucking and eating chickens! Sometimes I thought we'd all turn into chickens. I kept looking for my babies to sprout feathers."

Laurel laughed. "Guess what, Nellie? I plucked and cleaned a dozen chickens this afternoon," she said. "For the first time in my life."

"No!" Nellie breathed. "Does Hilda Fairweather make you do things like that?"

"Hilda's a pretty stern employer," Laurel said, "but she's also fair. At least," she added with a touch of bitterness, "she's as fair as it's possible for her to be, considering she doesn't know everything that's been going on in her kitchen."

"What do you mean, Laurie?"

Laurel sighed and told Nellie about her troubles with her co-worker, and the problem of having to do Crystal's work as well as her own. "It was so awful today," she said. "Those chickens were absolutely the last straw. Crystal was supposed to come in and help me, but she took one look at them and said she couldn't. She claimed she was sick, and went running back to the dining room."

"The poor girl," Nellie said placidly. "Likely she's pregnant."

"Pregnant!" Laurel stared at her little hostess. "What makes you say that?"

"Well, I've cleaned many a chicken in my day," Nellie said. "Not many things make me squeamish, I can tell you. But when I was pregnant, I couldn't abide the smell or the mess. It made my stomach heave just to think about it. Poor Ben, he always had to pluck and clean the chickens for a month or two, until the morning sickness passed."

Laurel was stunned into silence. She thought about Crystal's pale face and blue-smudged eyes, the girl's listlessness and the distant, worried look on her face these days.

"Oh, my," she said slowly. "I never even considered that possibility. I don't think there's a man in Crystal's life just now. She was going out with a truck driver from Montana, but they broke up and she hasn't seen him for over a month."

"So she might have a few things to worry about besides waiting on tables," Nellie suggested.

Laurel gave the older woman a thoughtful look. "I guess everybody has things to worry about, don't they, Nellie? Sometimes we get so wrapped up in our own problems, we forget that other people can be suffering just as much."

"That's the truth. When you've lived as long as I have," Nellie said calmly, "you'll come to understand that no matter what you're going through, somebody else is likely feeling a whole lot worse. Have some more tea, dear."

Laurel nodded absently, still thinking about Crystal's unhappy face. And Kate Cameron's look of weary despair when her mother interfered with the care of that little dark-eyed baby. And Jonas O'Neal with his hard features and bitter, withdrawn look, and his rare, shining smile . . .

"So," Nellie was saying, "did you have to clean all those chickens without any help? Poor Laurie, that wouldn't be an easy job for anybody."

"I... actually, I had some help," Laurel said, and hastened to take a sip of tea, looking down at her cup so Nellie wouldn't see the color that suddenly warmed her cheeks.

But Nellie was far too alert to be fooled. She gave Laurel an interested glance. "You did? Who helped you?"

"It was nothing much, really," Laurel said, still concentrating on her cup. She ran her finger around the dainty gold swirls on the handle. "That man who's staying at the hotel... his name's Jonas?"

She glanced shyly at Nellie, who gave her an encouraging smile.

"Well," Laurel went on, "he happened to be passing by the kitchen, and he... he stopped for a few minutes and showed me what to do."

"Jonas O'Neal knows how to clean chickens?"

"Like a professional. He says he grew up on a farm."

"Now, isn't that strange?" Nellie murmured. "He looks like a city fellow to me."

"Why?" Laurel asked.

"I'm not sure. He just has that real hard look, you know? Like a man who's seen bad things and learned how to take care of himself."

Laurel nodded with perfect understanding, feeling a little involuntary shiver when she thought about the man's air of powerful masculinity and the threatening edge to his speech and manner.

"He has the most beautiful eyes," she said abruptly, startled by her own words. "They're like dark melted gold, and you wouldn't believe how long and thick his eyelashes are. And his mouth is shaped so..."

She fell silent, appalled by a sudden fiery storm of sexual desire that roared through her body and left her feeling limp and shaken.

Just then, Fluffy appeared next to her chair and Laurel bent to pat him and hand him a bite of cookie, grateful for the diversion.

To Laurel's relief, Nellie dropped the topic of Jonas O'Neal and began telling her delightful stories about the early days in Wolf Hill, and the ancestors of some of the people Laurel had met during her work at the hotel.

They talked for more than an hour, until the sun dropped low in the west and slanted faintly through the frosting of delicate green on the lilac hedge.

"Look how late it's getting! I should go," Laurel said at last, getting reluctantly to her feet. "Thank you so much for the tea, Nellie."

The little woman began to gather the cups and plates. "It was a pleasure," she said. "It was a real pleasure, Laurie."

Laurel started toward the door, then glanced around at the silent house, the gray cat and the rocking chair, the table with its brave centerpiece of tulips and pussy willows.

"Nellie," she said. Fluffy came and pressed close to her, looking hopefully up at the doorknob.

"Yes, dear?"

Laurel hesitated. "I was just thinking," she said casually, bending to stroke the cat so she could avoid Nellie's sharp eyes. "I know you have people coming to visit all the time and I'm sure they must keep you busy, but I was wondering if you'd mind if I came again sometime," Laurel said awkwardly. "Just to visit and talk for a bit, if it's not too much trouble. I've enjoyed this so much."

Nellie's hands tightened on the plate. "Nothing," she said simply, "could ever make me happier."

Laurel smiled at her. "I usually have to work in the afternoon," she said, "but the evenings are kind of lonely, especially now that the days are getting longer. I just go for walks or sit in my hotel room. Would it be all right if I stopped by some evening for another visit?"

"Tomorrow?" Nellie asked hopefully.

Laurel smiled. "I don't know about that. I'd have to check with Hilda and see how late I'm working. But soon," she promised. "I'll be back soon."

She let Fluffy out into the yard, waved goodbye to Nellie and started down the walk. As she went out the little gate and headed back to the hotel, she was conscious of a new lightness in her step, a sense of happiness and optimism that she hadn't felt for a long time.

A WEEK PASSED, then another. The kitchen work was still grueling, but Laurel found herself more able to cope as time went by. Some days, she even had a couple of free moments in the course of her work, times when she was able to sit down at the table and enjoy a cup of coffee.

On a balmy evening in early May, just as the supper rush was ending, she finished washing the last of the pots in the deep metal sink, put them on the rack and drained the water, then sat down at the worktable where an array of salad fixings were set out. She began to slice lettuce and tomatoes, looking up when Crystal came into the room.

The waitress carried an order pad and an armful of empty plates which she dropped on the table, then grimaced at Hilda's back. The cook stood over the fry grill with a spatula, busily frying hamburger patties.

"How many more salads will we need?" Laurel asked. "Should I make up about a dozen?"

Crystal sank into the opposite chair and rested her chin on her hands, gazing out the window at the hotel's backyard.

"Crystal!" Hilda called sharply from her corner. "Laurie just asked you a question."

Crystal pulled herself together with an obvious effort and glanced at Laurel. "What?" she said.

"I wondered how many more people will still be coming. Are there many in the booths?"

"There's hardly anybody left. Kate and Nathan stopped by to have supper with Luther, and Mamie's with them. Oh, and the hunk just came in a few minutes ago."

Laurel picked up a cucumber and began peeling it with great care.

"Who's the hunk?" Hilda asked.

"You know," Crystal said, staring moodily out the window again. "That gorgeous man who's been working over at the hardware store. I thought he moved out of the hotel last week."

"He did," Hilda said, flipping hamburger patties. "Clarence rented him a couple of rooms over the hardware store, but he still comes here for his supper. He's a nice boy," she added. "I like him."

"Jonas O'Neal?" Laurel forgot her usual caution and looked up in disbelief. "You think Jonas O'Neal is a *nice boy?*"

"Why not?" Hilda asked mildly. "What do you think he is?"

Laurel avoided her employer's scrutiny. "I think he looks like a . . . a bouncer, or some kind of professional thug," she muttered. "Certainly not the sort of person you'd describe as *nice*. Or a boy, for that matter," she said.

Hilda chuckled. "You girls are just upset with him because he doesn't fall all over himself to flirt with you."

Laurel and Crystal exchanged a glance.

Crystal reached over to pick up an illustrated leaflet from a pile in one corner of the table. "What's this?" she asked, flipping through it. "It looks like knitting patterns or something."

"They belong to Nellie Grossman," Laurel said. "I'm going over to her house later when I get off work, and I have to take those books back to her."

"Now, why would Nellie Grossman be giving you books of knitting patterns?" Hilda asked. She stacked the cooked patties at the side of the grill and peered into a bubbling vat of French fries.

"She's teaching me to knit. I'm looking for a sweater pattern I like, and on the weekend we're going down to the general store to buy the yarn."

Crystal sighed and closed her eyes, leaning back in the chair. Laurel glanced in concern at her white face and drooping body.

"Come on, Crystal," Hilda said, stacking food on plates. "Here's the three burger deluxes you ordered. Hurry up, girl. We can't keep the customers waiting, right?"

Crystal moaned under her breath and gripped the edge of the table, preparing to get up. Impulsively, Laurel reached out and touched the girl's arm. "I'll take them," she murmured. "You stay here and get the salads ready, all right?"

Crystal gave her a look of pure gratitude. "Are you sure, Laurie?" she asked. "There's a few other orders you'll need to take, too. I haven't waited on Kate and Nathan yet."

"Of course. What should I do?"

"Just ask them what they want and write it down. Thanks so much," Crystal said fervently. "I don't think I could walk another step. Oh," she added as Laurel moved toward the door, "the burger plates go to the three kids over by the jukebox. And the hunk needs to give his order, too. He usually just has the special, no matter what it is."

Laurel paused nervously, her heart sinking. She took off her grimy apron and hung it over the back of a chair, then wiped her hands on her ragged jeans and touched her hair. Hilda cast her a wry glance.

"So, what's going on here?" the cook asked. "You giving yourself a promotion, Laurie Atkins? Turning yourself into a waitress right under my nose?"

"Crystal's really tired," Laurel said. "She's been on her feet all afternoon, and the supper crowd's just about finished. I can take a couple of orders for her, can't I?"

Hilda waved her hand casually. "Okay. Make sure you get the facts straight, okay?" She grinned. "The boss is out there, you know. Besides, I don't want Luther sending his steak back to the kitchen because it ain't cooked right or something."

Laurel smiled, knowing how firmly Luther Barnes was under his wife's thumb. Hilda and Luther had only been married for a couple of years, and the burly handyman still looked at his wife with an expression of startled adoration, as if completely dazzled by his own good fortune.

Laurel picked up the plates of food and moved toward the door, suddenly not at all sure that she wanted to begin her career as a waitress at this particular moment.

In the coffee shop, the teenagers received their hamburgers with loud appreciation and began at once to smother the fries in ketchup.

Laurel smiled at them, then moved toward a large table near the windows where Kate and Nathan Cameron sat with Luther Barnes and Mamie Reeves, Kate's mother. The baby was in a high chair next to his grandmother, with a cushion wedged firmly beside him to keep his small body from slipping out of the shiny wooden seat. He held a spoon in his fat hand and beat it insistently on his high-chair tray, laughing at the noisy clatter.

"Joshua, stop that," Kate muttered, trying to take the spoon from him. "You're bothering the other people. Come on, give Mommy the spoon."

His forehead knitted and he began to whimper, bouncing defiantly as he clutched the spoon.

"Let him keep the spoon, Kate. He's not bothering anybody," Mamie said to her daughter.

Kate cast a wry glance at Laurel, who stood nearby with her order pad. "What do you think, Laurie? Isn't this a pretty annoying uproar?"

Little Joshua begun to shout along with the rhythm of his spoon, making his father wince.

Mamie cuddled the baby tenderly and stroked his hair while Laurel looked down at the group, conscious of the tension behind Kate's smile.

In another world, she thought, Kate Cameron might well have been her friend. They had a lot in common, according to the kitchen gossip she'd heard. They were about the same age, probably with a similar educational background. Most important, they were both women who'd achieved success in tough, demanding businesses usually dominated by men.

But there was no way Laurel Atchison and Kate Cameron were ever going to be friends. Not while Kate owned this hotel and Laurel was working in the kitchen, washing dishes.

"I don't think it's annoying," she said at last, studying her notepad. "Are you ready to order?"

Nathan Cameron reached over and wrested the spoon from his son's plump hand. Joshua gazed at his father in blank surprise, then began to howl. Mamie unstrapped the baby from the high chair and gathered him onto her lap, giving Nathan a cold glance.

"Where's Crystal?" Kate asked over this new uproar.

"She's not feeing well," Laurel said briefly, conscious of Jonas O'Neal watching from his table in the corner.

Kate studied the menu while Mamie cuddled the baby and whispered to him soothingly.

"I think I'll have the seafood salad and garlic toast," Kate said at last.

Laurel wrote down the order, then turned to the others. Nathan wanted prime rib, and Luther ordered a filet, well-done, with mushrooms.

Mamie, as usual, had her own ideas.

"Baby and I will share a hot turkey sandwich," she told Laurel, bouncing the child gently in her arms.

"Lots of gravy on the mashed potatoes," she added. "Jay-Jay *loves* gravy. Don't you, sweetums?"

"I don't want him to have the potatoes and gravy from the kitchen, Mom," Kate said. "They're too rich for him, and far too salty. I have some mashed carrots in the diaper bag."

"Mashed carrots!" Mamie scoffed, kissing the baby's cheek loudly and making him giggle. "As if our darling wants dull old mashed carrots. He wants some of Grandma's nice tasty potatoes, doesn't he?"

Kate exchanged an eloquent despairing glance with her husband, who seemed on the verge of saying something, but checked himself when Kate placed a warning hand on his arm.

"I'll have a glass of milk, please," she said to Laurel. "Mom prefers tea, and I guess the men will have coffee, won't you?"

She looked at Luther and Nathan, who both nodded.

"Anything else?" Laurel asked, writing busily on the notepad.

Everyone indicated that they'd ordered all they wanted so Laurel moved over to the corner where Jonas O'Neal sat alone.

She took a deep breath and nerved herself to speak, trying to sound as casual as if she served his dinner every day.

"Have you decided what you want?" she asked.

He gave her one of those rare, boyish smiles that utterly transformed his face. "You know," he murmured, "I think I have."

Laurel glanced down at him with sudden misgiving, but he was studying the menu. His smile had faded like a summer sun obscured by clouds, and he looked as withdrawn and remote as ever.

"What's the special?" he asked.

"Breaded veal cutlets."

"Okay. Baked and ranch."

Laurel gave him a puzzled glance.

"Potato and salad dressing."

Her cheeks warmed under his direct gaze. "Of course," she muttered, writing busily.

"And coffee. Decaf, please," he added. "I'm having trouble sleeping these nights."

Again she was conscious of his eyes resting on her with quiet intensity.

"How about you?" he asked when she turned to leave.

"I beg your pardon?"

"Are you having any trouble sleeping, Laurel?"

She was tempted to tell him it was none of his business, but she didn't want him to see how much he was able to upset her.

"Not really," she said with forced casualness. "When you work as hard as I do all day, you tend to sleep pretty well at night."

He gave her one of his rare smiles, his golden eyes dark and unfathomable.

Laurel started to walk away, but he reached out to grasp her arm. She shivered at the feeling of his hand on her bare skin, and was distressed by another jolt of sexual desire.

It was so completely irrational, the feeling this man aroused in her. Jonas O'Neal wasn't in any way the kind of man she found attractive. He was hard-edged and blunt, coldly cynical almost to the point of rudeness, and they'd never even had a pleasant conversation.

She didn't like him, and she didn't trust him. But there were times when she wanted, almost desperately, to feel his arms around her, his mouth on hers. She wanted to stroke his hard muscles and press her face into the curling mat of chest hair that she sometimes glimpsed at the collar of his—

"Let me go!" she said abruptly. "I have work to do."

He dropped his hand and she rubbed the place where he'd gripped her arm. "I just wanted to ask," he said mildly, "if congratulations are in order." He waved his hand at the notepad. "You seem to have been promoted from kitchen drudge to waitress. That's a pretty impressive accomplishment, right?"

She felt a sudden flood of anger. "Look, just leave me alone, all right?" she whispered furiously, leaning toward him. "I don't know who you are, or why you find it so enjoyable to insult me all the time, but I want you to leave me alone."

"Why? Do you enjoy being alone, Laurel?"

"I certainly prefer it to being in the company of people I can't stand."

Laurel hurried back to the kitchen, conscious of the man watching her. She burst through the swinging doors and paused, her heart still beating fast with anger.

Crystal drooped over the table, slicing tomatoes in listless fashion. Hilda glanced at Laurel with mild interest.

"You look upset, Laurie. Anything the matter?"

Laurel shook her head and dropped into a chair. She seized a knife and began to peel mushrooms with quick jerky movements. "It's just your friend, Mr. Jonas O'Neal. *You* might think he's a nice boy, Hilda, but I happen to think he's the rudest, most insulting person I've ever—''

"Do you have their orders?'' Hilda interrupted calmly. "Or did you spend all your time out there fighting with the customers?''

Laurel sighed and handed over the notepad.

"What was that awful noise a minute ago?'' Hilda asked, moving to the refrigerator to take out a plate of sliced crabmeat.

"Kate's baby was pounding a spoon on his high chair and yelling. Kate's mother wouldn't let her do anything about it, so Nathan had to take over. Mamie can't bear to see that baby disciplined.''

Hilda shook her head sadly and tossed a steak onto the grill. "There's going to be some real problems with that woman unless Kate gets tougher with her,'' she predicted.

Laurel concentrated on lifting a delicate strip of peel from the mushroom in her hand. "I've noticed there seems to be a lot of conflict over the baby.''

"He's Kate's baby,'' Hilda said. "Kate should be the boss. If I had a baby, I sure wouldn't let anybody tell me how to raise him.''

Laurel glanced at Crystal, wondering how the young waitress was reacting to all this talk of babies. But Crystal kept her face carefully hidden and went on slicing tomatoes.

"Makes you wonder, don't it?'' Hilda commented from her grill.

"What?'' Laurel asked.

"How much grown-ups should let their parents push them around. Nobody else could treat Kate the way Mamie does. Not another person in the whole world.''

Laurel was silent, thinking about Hilda's words.

There wasn't anyone in the world who could exact this kind of sacrifice of her, either, except her father. Nobody else could make her give up her luxurious home and come to live in a remote prairie town, work in a hotel kitchen, wear these grubby clothes, even change her name...

Suddenly, she gripped the knife and stared at the wall in horror.

Not a soul in this town knew her real name. They all addressed her as Laurie Atkins. But a moment ago, out there in the coffee shop, Jonas O'Neal had called her Laurel.

CHAPTER SIX

THE SUN WAS WARM for early May. It lay in golden ripples on the fields around the town and shimmered through the frosting of pale green leaves on trees and hedges. By midmorning, the sky was piled with fluffy white clouds like drifts of popcorn. Meadowlarks nested and sang in the tall prairie grass, while bees hummed drowsily among the new growth of wildflowers.

Jonas was working in the yard behind the hardware store, unloading heavy cartons of asphalt shingles from a truck and stacking them in a covered area next to the store. He was bare-headed and naked to the waist, his denim work shirt tossed onto the truck's tailgate.

He straightened and drew a gloved hand across his forehead, then paused to smile at a shaggy black-and-white dog of indeterminate breed that watched him from the shade of the truck.

"Hi, Blackie," he said. "I didn't see you down there. Did you find that plate of meat I set out for you this morning?"

Blackie wagged his tail and licked his chops, managing to indicate with those two simple gestures that he had indeed found the meal, that it had been delicious and he deeply appreciated the gesture, and that further such contributions would not be ill received.

Jonas chuckled. "You've got a pretty good thing going here, you know that?" He reached for another carton and heaved it onto the stack. "Just hang around looking homeless and sad, and everybody gives you scraps. You don't have a soul to answer to, and you probably eat better than any dog in town. Right, Blackie? It's not such a bad scam."

At the mention of scams, his smile faded and he felt a stirring of uneasiness.

But his thoughts were interrupted by a new arrival. Aggie Krantz, his employer's wife, emerged from the rear entry of the hardware store and marched toward him across the dusty yard. She held a clipboard and looked especially purposeful, her silver hair glittering in the sunlight.

Blackie stiffened with alarm and shrank into the shadow of the truck, where one bright eye could be seen peering cautiously around the fender.

Jonas grinned at the woman and went on stacking cartons. "Hello, Mrs. Krantz," he said. "Nice morning, isn't it?"

Aggie nodded stiffly and looked down at her clipboard. Jonas was puzzled by her manner until he realized that Aggie was uncomfortable being so close to him when he had his shirt off. She obviously didn't like being confronted by that expanse of hairy, hard-muscled chest while she talked.

Suddenly, her eyes widened.

Jonas followed her glance and saw that she was peering at the white scar tissue on the hard flat expanse of his abdomen, starting near the bottom of his ribcage and running down beneath the waistband of his jeans. He reached for his shirt casually and pulled it on, resisting a wicked urge to unzip the jeans while he tucked in his shirttail.

There were, after all, limits to what people like Aggie could endure. And Jonas didn't really want to upset her.

Unlike many in the small town of Wolf Hill, Jonas was rather fond of his boss's wife. There was a steely, determined quality about the woman that he appreciated. Aggie Krantz was a person who got things done, no matter what obstacles were thrown at her.

For instance, if Jonas were in a plane crash somewhere deep in the wilderness and only a handful of people survived, and they all had to stay alive by their wits, he'd want somebody like Aggie to be part of the group. She was the kind of person you could depend on.

He thought wistfully about a few other people he'd want in that group, too. Involuntarily, his thoughts turned to the slender gray-eyed woman in the hotel kitchen. Jonas felt a familiar mixture of annoyance and reluctant admiration.

He'd been doing his best, in a cautious, discreet fashion, to needle the woman, hoping to frighten her into dropping this ridiculous charade. At the very least, Jonas wanted to force her into flight, or some other kind of move he could react to. But she seemed to have no idea of the grim realities of her situation and the danger she was in.

Watching her plod through her days, staying in this backwater town and working doggedly in the hotel kitchen, Jonas felt himself growing almost wild with impatience. If she didn't do something soon of her own accord, he was going to be forced into a course of action he might regret.

But he wasn't supposed to think that way. His assignment was simply to continue being patient and unobtrusive. He had to beat the woman at her own game, by working at this job and trying to outwait her, no matter how hard it got...

Jonas sighed, buttoned his shirt and looked at his visitor. "Anything I can help you with, Mrs. Krantz?"

Aggie peered suspiciously at the truck. "Did I see that mongrel dog out here a minute ago?"

Jonas glanced at the fender where a bright eye disappeared from view. A long plume of tail lay in the dust, carefully still.

"You mean Blackie?" Jonas asked innocently.

"I didn't think he had a name."

Jonas smiled, knowing that Blackie wasn't the purpose of Aggie's visit. People in this town never seemed to approach any topic head-on. They always started an encounter by mentioning something entirely different, introducing a few topics of harmless small talk. Then, after the niceties had been taken care of, they sneaked up on the subject they really wanted to discuss.

"Don't you like Blackie?" he asked, playing his part in the conversational game.

"That dog's a real nuisance," she said firmly. "Always slinking around and looking for handouts. Last week, he knocked over two garbage pails in the alley behind Margie's post office. I'd like to get my hands on him. That dog should be properly controlled and trained to behave."

Jonas grinned. If Aggie had her way, Blackie would not only be captured and rehabilitated, he'd probably be bathed and forced to go to school, then sent out to find gainful employment.

His quirky imagination supplied him with a sudden image of Blackie sitting gravely at a desk among primary-school students, raising a paw to volunteer an answer. Jonas laughed out loud, then looked abashed when Aggie gave him a suspicious glance from behind her steel-framed spectacles.

"Sorry," he said contritely. "I just thought of something funny." He gave a casual glance at the clipboard. "Is there something I can help you with, Mrs. Krantz?" he repeated. "I really should get back to work. Clarence wants me to finish unloading the truck before lunch."

"I need a coach," Aggie said, finally abandoning the preliminaries and diving into the real purpose of her visit.

Jonas looked at her blankly. "You do? What kind of coach?"

"Baseball," Aggie said.

"You want to play *baseball?*" he asked in astonishment.

She actually smiled, a rearrangement of her severe features so brief and fleeting, it was almost imperceptible. "Of course not," she said. "I'm talking about Little League. Particularly ages seven through twelve. We desperately need a coach. Unless we can find a couple of volunteers, many of the smaller children will have no baseball this year."

Jonas began to feel apprehensive. "Look, Mrs. Krantz," he said, "I'd really like to help out, if that's what you're asking, but I don't know how long I'm going to be in town. I can't commit to anything when I—"

"You don't know how long you'll be here?" She gave him a suspicious glance. "I'm sure Clarence wouldn't have hired you for this job if he'd expected you to disappear at a moment's notice."

His feeling of discomfort increased. "I never made any promises when Clarence hired me. I said I'd be a good worker and stay with the job as long as I could. That's all.''

''Well, fine,'' Aggie said placidly. ''That's good enough for me.'' She began to scribble something on her clipboard.

''What are you writing?'' Jonas asked in alarm.

''I'm putting your name down to coach ages eight and nine. We call them Tiny Mites.''

''Tiny Mites,'' Jonas echoed with growing helplessness. ''Just out of idle curiosity, what if I didn't know anything about baseball?''

Aggie shrugged, clearly beginning to lose interest in him now that she'd achieved her purpose. ''The Tiny Mite coach last year was Gail Baines, Harold's wife, and she kept saying 'periods' instead of 'innings.' When the little boys were naughty, she made them take time-outs behind the backstop.''

Jonas nodded, trying not to smile. ''I see,'' he said gravely. ''So the new coach doesn't exactly have big shoes to fill, is that what you're saying?''

Aggie was all-business once more, the sunlight flashing on her glasses as she turned away. ''You can pick up your roster of players down at the town hall on Friday morning. You'll be expected to hold two practices a week, at your convenience, of course, until the competitive season begins.''

''There's a competitive season?'' he asked disbelievingly. ''With eight-year-olds?''

''The Tiny Mite league is a long-standing tradition, and very hotly contested,'' Aggie said calmly. ''Several of the local towns and farming communities are part of the same league. Harold Baines at the general store will sponsor your team and supply matching T-shirts. Oh, and you'll need an assistant," she added. "I'm leaving it up to you to choose your own help."

"An assistant? What for?"

Aggie shrugged. "Supervision of practices if you're not able to attend, schedule adjustments, general help with the players..."

"Holding hands and wiping noses," Jonas suggested.

Aggie turned to go, not dignifying this with a reply. Jonas grinned and reached for another carton.

"Aha!" Aggie shouted, and wheeled back to face the truck.

Startled, Jonas glanced up in time to see a blur of black and white streaking across the yard and through a hole in the fence.

He gave Aggie a look of soulful innocence. "I'll be damned," he said in wonder. "That dog must have been right here all the time."

Aggie glared at him for a moment then turned toward the store. "By the way, Jonas," she asked over her shoulder, "do you have any idea who you might choose as your assistant?"

Jonas tugged at one of his gloves. "As a matter of fact," he said, "I think I know exactly the right person for the job, Mrs. Krantz." With that, he turned back to his work, a smile tugging at the corners of his mouth.

LAUREL STOOD at the sink, peeling potatoes from a fifty-pound burlap sack and dropping them into a barrel of cold salted water. At the worktable nearby, Crystal lifted potatoes from the barrel and ran them through an electric slicer, producing mountains of sleek white French fries.

Laurel paused to brush her arm over her forehead, pushing back a strand of hair that kept falling into her eyes.

If she had to stay here much longer, it probably wouldn't be a bad idea to go to Margie's and have her hair cut. Something short and breezy, easy to look after...

Her hand tightened briefly on the peeler, and she looked out at the barren, weedy yard behind the hotel.

This situation grew more bizarre with every passing day. At first, Laurel had found it difficult to believe that she was really living in Wolf Hill, Alberta, working in a hotel kitchen for less than five hundred dollars a month. In those early days, she kept expecting to wake up and find that it was all a bad dream.

Now, just a few weeks later, she sometimes found herself behaving as if she might be stuck here forever.

But that, of course, was simply ridiculous. Her stay in Wolf Hill was only temporary. She would be leaving any day now. After all, Laurel Atchison had an important job and a position to fill. She had a condo in the city, a wide circle of clients who depended on her, employees to supervise and portfolios to manage. Her reality lay far from this dusty small town.

The problem was that she'd become so isolated from her real life. Since that night at the cocktail party when she'd taken her father's urgent call, Laurel hadn't spoken to a single person that she knew. She'd gone home and packed immediately, left Vancouver under cover of darkness and come straight out to the prairie.

For all she knew, their brokerage firm could have been dissolved by now. Her father might be hospitalized, she thought gloomily. What if his financial worries had driven him to a stroke or heart attack, and she wouldn't even know? Or perhaps Marta had fallen down the stairs and gone into premature labor, and then Stewart had...

Laurel took a deep breath and returned to the sack of potatoes, her hands shaking.

Tonight, she decided.

She'd phone her father tonight and find out what was going on. Stewart had begged her not to make contact for at least a month, but this enforced isolation was impossible to endure. Besides, it was almost a month since she'd left, and she simply had to find out what was happening.

"Laurie?" Crystal said behind her.

Laurel turned to give her co-worker an absent smile. "Sorry," she said. "Were you asking me something? I guess I was daydreaming."

Crystal fitted another potato into the slicer and yanked the handle, watching the French fries slide into a plastic bowl.

"I just wondered what you'd do if—"

Just then, Hilda bustled into the kitchen, carrying an armful of napkin holders from the dining room. "These all need to be filled before suppertime," she announced, depositing them on the table with a noisy clatter. "Luther promised to do the napkin holders and fill the salt and pepper shakers today, and where is the man? Off flying that silly toy airplane of his. Worse than a kid," she said, but the fondness in her eyes belied her words.

"It's a beautiful plane." Laurel watched as a long curl of brown peel fell into the sink. "No wonder he's proud of it. Look, Crystal," she added. "I'll bet you fifty cents that I can do this whole potato without breaking the peel."

Hilda lifted her hands in despair. "Another one who's acting like a kid. It must be spring fever or something. I never saw such a bunch of silly, addleheaded people."

She trotted out of the kitchen again, leaving the two younger women smiling at the doorway. After a moment, they both returned to their work.

Crystal took a deep breath and lifted another potato. "I have this...this cousin," she said, keeping her face carefully lowered.

Laurel glanced at the girl, then turned back to the sink. "What about her?"

"Well, she's...I guess she's sort of...pregnant."

"Sort of pregnant?" Laurel repeated, trying to sound casual. "Is that possible? I mean, people either are or they aren't, right?"

"I guess so." Crystal got up to run more cold water over the French fries, then shook them into a big plastic bag and deposited them in the fridge, positioning her empty bowl under the slicer again. "Anyway," she added after an awkward silence, "she doesn't know what to do. My cousin, I mean. She's...really worried."

Laurel forced herself to go on working impassively. "What about the baby's father? Doesn't he take any responsibility?"

"Oh, him," Crystal said bitterly. "He's long gone. He keeps saying," she added, her voice shaking, "that it's not even his kid, but that's just a big lie. I was...my cousin was crazy about him. She never even looked at anybody else while they were together."

Crystal sniffled and seemed to be concentrating hard on her task, while Laurel gazed carefully out the window. "So he won't help at all?"

"Not a chance."

"Does your cousin want to keep the baby?" Laurel asked gently.

"What else can she do?"

"Well, she could have the baby and give it up for adoption, or—"

Crystal shook her head vehemently. "My cousin couldn't stand that. Losing her own baby, I mean. She just couldn't stand it, Laurie."

"Then she has to go through with the pregnancy and plan how she's going to look after the baby, doesn't she? There's no other choice, really."

"I guess not," Crystal said, sounding miserable. "But she's...I think she's really scared, Laurie. My cousin, I mean. She doesn't know how she's going to—"

She fell abruptly silent. Laurel turned around, following the girl's gaze, and saw Jonas O'Neal lounging in the doorway.

"It's almost lunchtime, ladies," he said mildly. "The coffee shop's starting to fill up."

Crystal got to her feet and headed for the door, grabbing her notepad as she went. Hilda passed her in the doorway, bustling toward the fry grill with a stack of hamburger patties in her hands, and Laurel went to the fridge to get out a tray of prepared salads.

Jonas strolled into the kitchen and paused for a moment by the sink, then started peeling potatoes and tossing them into the bucket.

"Look, that's my job," Laurel said curtly. "I'll get back to it as soon as I have a few of the lunch plates made up."

"For goodness' sake, Laurie, don't discourage the man if he wants to work," Hilda said from her grill. "I can use a few extra hands around here. Especially," she added with a meaningful glance over her shoulder, "since everybody seems to be going crazy these days."

Crystal whirled back into the kitchen and paused by the grill to confer with Hilda over the lunch orders. Jonas wiped his hands on a towel and moved to stand next to Laurel. He stood so close that she was sharply conscious of his nearness and the warm, pleasant scent of sunshine and dusty maleness that clung to his denim shirt and jeans.

"I volunteered you for a job this morning," he said with a meaningful glance at her. "I hope you're properly grateful."

"A job? What on earth are you talking about?"

"Coaching Little League baseball. I'm the head coach and you'll be my assistant. We're in charge of the General Store Tiny Mites. We both get nifty yellow T-shirts, by the way."

She frowned. "What are you talking about? Baseball? I've never—"

"Never played baseball?" he asked with a teasing grin. "Not once in your whole life?"

"Of course I've played baseball!" she said vehemently, arranging lettuce and tomato slices onto a plate. "As a matter of fact, I was..."

She stopped talking, conscious of his eyes resting on her with amused speculation. "What?" he asked softly. "What were you, Laurel?"

"Never mind. I'm sorry, but I can't help you," she added stiffly, wishing he would move away and give her more room. She felt hot and short of breath, as if the big room had somehow shrunk into a space so tiny it couldn't comfortably hold both of them.

"Why not?" To her relief, he went back to the sink and started peeling potatoes again.

"Because I don't know..." Laurel lowered her voice and glanced nervously at Hilda, who was busy flipping hamburgers. "I don't know how long I'll be here. Maybe just a few more days."

He raised an eyebrow. "No kidding," he murmured. "Where are you going? Got a better job somewhere?"

"Not really," Laurel said nervously. "I just...Hilda knew that I was only planning to stay here until I could earn enough money to...to go to the city and see if I could..."

"What?" he prompted when she fell silent. "Let me guess. You'll keep on drifting, find another kitchen to work in, maybe get promoted to waiting tables full-time. Is that your major ambition, Laurel?"

"Why do you keep calling me that?" she muttered tensely.

"What?"

"Laurel. You've been saying it for days. I want to know why."

He held the peeler in his hand with sudden wariness. "It's your name, isn't it?"

"Everybody here calls me Laurie."

He turned back to the sink, his face impassive. Laurel shivered, inexplicably frightened, and fidgeted with the salad plates.

"So?" he asked over his shoulder. "Laurie's just a nickname, right? I assumed it was short for Laurel."

"It could be short for Lorraine, or Lauretta, or any number of other names," Laurel said, wondering why she couldn't just drop the subject. "I'm curious why you picked Laurel, that's all."

"Maybe it suits you," he said. "Or maybe I just like the name. Okay?"

She nodded, battling a ridiculous urge to turn and run, out of the building, out of this town, away from this dangerous man, standing by the sink with his hands full of potato peels and watching her.

"So," he said at last, "what's your answer, Laurel?"

"What about?"

"Baseball. Tiny Mites."

"Whatever," Laurel said wearily. "But only on a day-to-day basis. I certainly can't make any kind of long-term commitment."

He seemed about to comment, but Laurel turned away to concentrate on the salad plates, her heart racing.

This settled it, she thought desperately. She had to contact her father tonight and make plans to escape from this town. If she didn't get away soon, she was sure something dreadful was going to happen, and she was powerless to prevent it.

"THIS ONE has raglan sleeves," Nellie said, indicating a knitting pattern. "They're easier than set-in sleeves, especially for a beginner."

Laurel sat cross-legged on the couch with Fluffy sprawled in her lap. By now, she was as comfortable in Nellie's little house as if it were her own home, and came to visit as often as she could.

Fluffy closed his eyes, resting his chin on her arm while Laurel nibbled at a fresh brownie, oozing nuts and marshmallow.

"Do you think so?" she asked, casting a dubious glance at the picture. "It looks so complicated. There's all that detailing along the sleeve."

"That's just a slip stitch at the end of each row," Nellie said. "Nothing to it."

Laurel looked at her hostess with genuine admiration. "You know so many things, Nellie. You have skills I could never dream of learning."

Nellie raised her head. "Skills? Like what?"

Laurel took another bite and waved her hand expansively. "Everything," she said when she was able to talk again. "You can cook so well, sew anything, knit and crochet and embroider. You know how to churn butter and make sausage and render lard for soap. I'll bet you could teach an entire college course on how to be self-sufficient."

"Oh, go on," Nellie protested, but her face glowed with pleasure.

"Really," Laurel said. "I can't believe how talented you are."

"My generation had to know a lot of things," Nellie said calmly, leafing through the pattern book. "When my children were little, we didn't have store-bought food and clothes. I made everything we wore, and canned or baked or grew everything we ate."

"It sounds like such a hard life."

"In a way it was," Nellie said with a wistful smile. "But in a funny kind of way, it was a lot easier than modern times. The family was together all the time, you see. We didn't have to worry about finding baby-sitters while we held down two or three jobs, or buying and looking after a lot of expensive things, or keeping our little ones safe from traffic and kidnappers."

"Where are your children now?" Laurel asked. "I keep forgetting. There's the son in Regina, right?"

Nellie nodded. "That's my son, William. Stacy's father," she added, gesturing at the framed picture of her granddaughter.

"And you have a daughter, too, don't you?"

"Yes, that's Karen. She lives in Ottawa with her husband. Look at this one, Laurie. Do you like the high neck?"

Laurel glanced at the picture. "As long as the yarn isn't too heavy. Otherwise, it might be pretty hot to wear, don't you think?"

Nellie paged through the book again, and Laurel stroked the cat until he purred in lazy bliss.

"Do you see them very often?" she asked after a moment.

"Who?" Nellie asked, glancing over the top of her little gold-framed reading glasses.

"Your family."

Nellie shrugged and looked away. "They're all busy with their own lives," she said, her voice carefully neutral. "They phone all the time, but you can't blame them if they don't have a lot of time to travel all the way out here."

Laurel thought about how, if she had a mother or a grandmother as sweet as Nellie, she'd make every effort to visit and keep in touch. She wondered how people could take their family ties so lightly. Her thoughts turned to her own father and how much she loved him. There was no way she could ever turn her back on him. Which was why she was here in Wolf Hill.

Again, she found herself battling a desire to tell Nellie the truth about her situation and ask for advice.

They were growing so close, Laurel felt uncomfortable when she deceived Nellie about herself and her life.

But then she remembered Jonas O'Neal standing in the kitchen, watching her, with that faint air of menace that often seemed to edge his words. And she recalled, as well, that it was Jonas's doing that she and Nellie had made contact in the first place. Had he deliberately left Nellie's medication behind that day?

Laurel gave herself a little shake and ran her fingernail softly over the cat's white abdomen, making him squirm with pleasure.

"You were right about something else," she said abruptly.

"What's that, dear?"

"Crystal. I think she's pregnant, all right."

Nellie looked up. "Really? Did she tell you?"

"Not in so many words." Laurel recounted their lunchtime conversation about the cousin and her problem.

"Poor girl," Nellie commented.

"At first I didn't like Crystal," Laurel said. "But now I'm beginning to feel really fond of her. I resented the way she pushed so much work onto me, but after you told me she might be pregnant, I started looking at things differently. And now she must be feeling better, because she's actually doing more than her share these days."

"I've heard that she's a nice girl, even though she looks like a movie star."

"We've been talking a lot lately, Crystal and I. She's really a good person. But," Laurel added with a frown, "she seems so worried and unhappy."

"In my day, it was a shame for a girl to be pregnant without a man. Nowadays, it's more of a financial worry than anything else."

"You're right," Laurel said. "I wonder how on earth she's going to manage, looking after a baby with just a waitressing job."

"Well, thousands of other women are doing the very same thing."

"I know." Laurel gazed out the window at the mellow spring twilight. "I've been very lucky and protected. I always had so much, and I didn't..."

Her face warmed with discomfort, but Nellie merely gave her a thoughtful glance and then went back to her knitting book.

"Nellie," Laurel said.

"Yes, dear?"

Laurel put Fluffy gently out of her lap and got to her feet, wandering across the cozy room to look out the window.

"Pretend you could have anything in the world," she said at last, turning back to look at the little woman in the rocker. "Any treat you could think of. What would it be?"

"To have my whole family living nearby," Nellie said promptly.

Laurel came back and hugged her. "Besides that, I mean. What would be your fantasy?"

"I'm not sure." Nellie pondered for a moment. "I guess I'd like a trip."

"Really? Where?"

"Not far," Nellie said. "Just to the city. To Calgary, or maybe Vancouver. I'd like to have an evening on the town," she added placidly.

"No kidding. An evening on the town?" Laurel smiled at her.

"I'd like to dress up in a pretty new dress and go out to a fancy restaurant. Then I'd like to go to a stage show, some wonderful musical like *Phantom of the Opera*, and have champagne afterward. That's my dream," the old woman confided shyly. "I know that it'll never happen in my lifetime, but I still have lots of fun thinking about it."

Laurel's throat tightened with emotion.

Back in that glamorous, distant world that was her real life, it would have been so easy to make Nellie's fantasy into a reality. She pictured herself sending Nellie a beautiful dress, coming by in a limousine to pick her up and drive her to the airport, escorting her to a fine restaurant and then to one of the magnificent theaters in downtown Vancouver.

"Someday, Nellie," she murmured, crossing the room and bending impulsively to hug the woman. "I promise, someday I'm going to make that dream come true."

Nellie returned her hug. "But, Laurie," she said simply, "you make me so happy just by coming to see me. It's the nicest thing you could ever do for me."

"Oh, Nellie." Laurel turned away to hide the tears that blurred her eyes.

"So," Nellie asked after a moment, her voice casual and matter-of-fact, "have you seen any more of that mysterious young man?"

"Who?" Laurel asked, sitting on the couch and pulling the cat into her lap again.

"The handsome one who helped me with my groceries. Jonas. Wasn't that his name?"

"He's not around as much as he used to be. He moved out of the hotel to a suite of rooms above the hardware store."

"So you don't see him anymore?"

"Oh, yes, I see him," Laurel said briefly. "He comes over to the hotel to eat his lunch and dinner almost every day."

"I see." Nellie picked up a skein of wool and began rolling it into a ball.

"In fact, just today he was telling me," Laurel went on reluctantly, "that he's signed up both of us to coach Little League baseball this spring. I'm supposed to be his assistant, whatever that means."

"I see. Aggie Krantz got to him, did she? After all," Nellie added thoughtfully, "Aggie is his boss's wife. Pretty hard for him to say no."

"I can understand that," Laurel said, getting up again and pacing the little room. "But I don't know why he had to get *me* involved."

"Baseball is lots of fun," Nellie said. "Especially with those little boys and girls."

"But I can't be a coach!" Laurel said. "I don't even know how long I'm going to..."

She saw Nellie's face fall and crossed the room to stand next to the little woman.

"We'll still be friends, Nellie," Laurel said, kneeling by the rocker. "Even if I have to go away, I'll call you all the time and come to visit you whenever I can. I promise. You've been so nice to me."

Nellie smiled and patted Laurel's hair. "Don't worry, dear," she murmured. "These visits from you have been like a wonderful gift. If you have to go away, I'll be happy whenever I remember all the things we talked about, and the things we did."

Laurel hugged her once more and nestled close, burying her face against Nellie's soft pink sweater.

"And," Nellie went on, patting the younger woman's back, "maybe I've got an ally now."

Laurel sat back on her heels. "Ally? What do you mean?"

"This young man," Nellie said with a smile. "He seems to be trying hard to keep you in Wolf Hill. Maybe between the two of us, we can hang on to you for a while."

Again, Laurel resisted the urge to tell Nellie who she was and what she was doing in the little prairie town.

Soon, she promised herself. After she'd spoken with her father and learned what was going on, she'd come back and tell Nellie the truth. And then they'd make plans to take Nellie out to Vancouver for a holiday, and let her have a glamorous evening on the town.

Laurel smiled, thinking how much fun it was going to be. Maybe Hilda and Crystal could come along with Nellie and have a holiday from their kitchen work. Laurel would take them all to a beautiful restaurant and encourage them to order the most expensive thing on the menu.

And best of all, somebody else would be waiting on them...

Nellie watched her fondly. "When you smile like that, honey, you look like a little girl. Just as sweet as can be."

"Looks can be deceiving," Laurel said dryly, getting to her feet. "Come on, Nellie, let's go through all these books one more time. I want to find a knitting pattern so we can go shopping on my day off. Where did you say those raglan sleeves are?"

They were soon buried under masses of illustrated patterns, laughing as they tried to choose.

Then it was time for Nellie's hot apple cobbler with whipped cream, followed by a last cup of tea on the veranda in the fading light.

By the time Laurel left to go home, the night was like a stage set, and the prairie sky a rich canopy of black silk stitched with glittering sequins. Like a hushed chorus at the back of the stage, trees swayed and whispered in the misty darkness, their branches streaked brightly with silver.

Onstage, the Northern Lights flared in the sky above the town, sending down long fingers of gold rays to touch the prairie then leap up again. The light changed color from pink to green to mauve, shimmering and trembling in the evening wind.

Laurel paused in the street outside the hotel and watched the performance with a lump in her throat, feeling small and alone in the midst of such splendor. A great sadness flowed over her, bringing tears to her eyes. She felt an ache of yearning that she couldn't begin to understand, and was afraid to analyze too closely.

Still, she knew that her feelings didn't come from loneliness or homesickness. She wasn't longing for her familiar job and her luxurious apartment. What she wanted was something more nebulous and distant, something to do with the kind of memories that Nellie treasured, like a man's embrace and a little child in her arms, sweet and helpless . . .

She hugged her elbows, still brooding on the spectacular light show. At last she pulled herself away, mounted the veranda steps and went into the hotel, half expecting to encounter Jonas O'Neal in the lobby. He sometimes strolled across town in the evening to watch television at the hotel and read the magazines stacked on the big coffee table in the lobby.

But the lobby was as empty as the street outside. Laurel went upstairs, unlocked her room and washed her hands and face in the bathroom, looking at herself in the mirror for a long time. Finally, she sat on the bed, reached for the telephone and began to dial.

CHAPTER SEVEN

"HELLO? Hello, who is this?"

Laurel gripped the receiver, momentarily unable to find her voice.

Her father sounded just the same, vigorous and cheerful, with the jaunty lift at the end of his words that seemed to indicate he was delighted to hear from you.

Stewart Atchison had a gift for that sort of thing. Whenever he encountered anybody, even one of the office janitors in the hallway after hours, he gave the impression that this was the very person he'd been yearning to see, and nothing could please him more than a nice long chat.

What's more, he was absolutely sincere. Stewart really loved people. All people. He was such a nice man...

"Hello?" he said again, sounding concerned at the lengthening silence on the other end of the line. Laurel cleared her throat and dashed a hand over her eyes.

"Dad," she whispered. "It's me."

"Laurie! My God, where are you? Don't answer that," he said hastily. "It was just a reflex, honey. It's been hell for me, not knowing how you're doing or where to get hold of you."

"I know," she whispered. "I feel so isolated, Dad. It's like I've been wandering around on the moon."

"I hate this," he muttered. Laurel could hear the pain in his voice. "Sending you away, turning your life upside down . . . Nobody should have to go through this."

"It's hard for both of us," Laurel said. "In fact, the whole thing is probably worse for you and Marta than it is for me. I'm just lonely, that's all."

"I hate doing this to you, honey. But you know it's safer for both of us this way."

Laurel's heart sank. "Nothing's been resolved, then?"

"Come on, sweetheart," Stewart said. "You know how these government things work. Slow as molasses, while everybody's going crazy in the office. It's all up in the air."

"But . . ." Laurel twisted the phone cord, feeling mounting confusion. "Are they still looking for me? Is it safe for me to come home?"

"Not yet. The committee's started calling witnesses and you'd be the first on the list if you were here. As long as you're unavailable, they don't have a thing to go on."

"But, Dad . . ." Laurel swallowed hard and went on, "Isn't this . . . sort of illegal? I'm breaking the law by avoiding the inquiry, don't you think? At least the spirit, if not the letter, of the law," she amended.

"You've always been such a stickler for doing things right," he teased, sounding a little more cheerful.

"I don't think I've ever done anything consciously illegal in my whole life," Laurel said. "I can't run a red light at three in the morning, even when there isn't another car in sight. I'm a fanatically law-abiding person, Dad."

"Of course you are. And you're not breaking any law. You were never subpoenaed, so you're not doing anything wrong. You're taking a holiday at an undisclosed location. Actually, I've let the word get around that you've been a little under the weather. I told people you were suffering from a sort of clinical depression, and you needed a whole lot of time to recuperate without any contact from anybody.''

Laurel stared at the black expanse of sky framed between her flowered chintz drapes. "I wish you could have found some other excuse. That makes me sound pretty weak and cowardly, running away to hide from my problems.''

"Especially when all the problems are really mine, not yours?''

"I didn't mean that." She paused. "Have you talked to Chet Landry?''

"Good old Chet has hung me out to dry. He denies any knowledge of the orders we placed or the information he passed to me. None of it ever happened, according to him.''

"But, Dad," Laurel said in horror, "why would he do such a thing?''

"To save his own hide," Stewart said grimly. "His whole department was in it up to their necks, and Chet used me for cover. It's all a big game, honey. Save yourself and take no prisoners. I know I shouldn't ever have agreed to their plans, no matter how many government seals were on the letters. Thank God you're not here," he added. "Until I can find some other witnesses to clear my name, the only real protection I have is the fact that nobody else can testify how those orders were actually placed.''

Laurel felt a mounting chill of fear. "But I can hardly stay here forever, Dad. This little town where I'm living isn't—''

"Don't tell me!" he said. "Don't tell me anything about it. I really don't want to know where you are, honey," he added in a gentler tone. "This whole thing out here, it's a real mess right now. My only comfort is knowing you're safely out of the picture and I can be completely honest when they ask me if I know where you are."

"I see," Laurel said bleakly.

"The same with your secretary," he added. "They keep grilling poor young Dennis about where you are and whether you've called him."

"What does he say?"

"Nothing. He tells them you were tired and sick, talking all the time about going on a holiday, and then suddenly you left. End of story."

"Good for him." Laurel smiled wistfully, thinking about Dennis. "I miss him so much, Dad. I miss all of you. How's Marta?"

"Massive," Stewart said cheerfully. "It's hard to believe a woman can be that pregnant and still walk around."

"Maybe it's twins."

"Don't say that!" Stewart exclaimed in horror, making her laugh.

Laurel's father had always been able to make her laugh...

"How's Marta feeling about all these problems?" she asked.

"Fine," Stewart said, but he sounded a shade less confident.

"It must be so hard for her, getting ready to have her first baby and being forced to deal with this mess at the same time."

"It's damned hard," Stewart agreed. "I know it is, sweetheart, but Marta's a real fighter. Both my girls are fighters," he added fondly. "You know how much I love you, Laurie."

"I love you too, Dad." There was a brief silence. "When does the doctor expect the baby to be born? I hate the idea that I won't be there."

"He thinks it's not going to happen for a couple more weeks, at least. This could all be settled by then. I have an appointment with the finance minister a week from next Tuesday, and he's going to back me up."

"Dad!" Laurel said. "Really? Are you sure they'll support you?"

"They have to," Stewart said, his voice suddenly cold. "If they don't, I can certainly make things embarrassing for them. After all, Chet's their responsibility."

She sagged back against the pillows, limp with relief. "Thank God," she murmured. "That changes everything."

"So just tough it out for few more weeks, honey. But don't call me again unless you're in some kind of trouble," he added. "It's far too risky. For all I know, even this line could be tapped."

"How will I know when it's safe to come home?"

He hesitated. "Are you still in Canada?" he asked cautiously. "Don't tell me any details. Just say yes or no."

"Yes."

"Are you close to a newsstand where they carry the *Financial Post?*"

Laurel thought about the dusty rack of newspapers and magazines in Baines's General Store.

"I think so," she said.

"Good. When I've got things cleared up, I'll put a message in the Saturday edition under the personal notices. I'll address it to 'My Best Girl.' Okay?"

"Okay," Laurel said. "Just a few more weeks, right?"

"Well..." He hesitated. "Don't count on it absolutely, honey. You know how clumsy the process is. But I'm doing my best to speed things up."

"And if Marta has the baby..."

"I'll get word to you the same way."

"All right. Look, I have to tell you something, Dad. There's another thing I'm worried about."

"Yes?" he said with a rare touch of impatience.

Laurel could almost sense him glancing cautiously over his shoulder.

"Dad, at this place where I'm staying..."

"Don't tell me anything!"

"I'm not telling you anything. I just want you to know that there's a man here who's kind of... he's a little scary."

"Laurie?" he said, instantly alert. "What do you mean? Has somebody been threatening you?"

"Nothing like that. But I get the feeling he knows something about me. More than he's letting on."

"What kind of guy?"

"He's about my age. Quite handsome," Laurel said grudgingly, "in a hard-edged kind of way. Wears jeans and a leather jacket. Very polite," she added. "Don't get me wrong, he hasn't done anything specifically to frighten or threaten me. But it seems like more than a coincidence that he arrived here about the same time I did, and he—"

"Do you think he followed you?" Stewart asked, sounding alarmed.

"I don't know. At first he didn't even seem to notice me. But now, I often get the feeling he's watching me, sort of."

"Well, there you go," Stewart said with obvious relief. "No wonder he watches you. You're a fine-looking woman, sweetheart. Any man would watch you if he had the chance."

"You wouldn't say that if you could see the way I look right now," Laurel said, grimacing at her shabby clothes and chapped, reddened hands. "I'm working in a hotel kitchen, Dad. I wash dishes and peel potatoes for about ten hours a day. I've even learned how to pluck and clean chickens."

"Oh, Laurie," he murmured. "God, honey, I'm so sorry."

"Never mind about me," Laurel said. "Actually, in some ways I'm finding the experience quite interesting. It'll certainly be something to talk about when I get home. But I keep worrying that maybe this man is a policeman or a government investigator."

"Why? What does he do besides watch you?"

"Nothing sinister. He's got a job at the local hardware store. He unloads trucks and stacks cartons in the warehouse all day, and lives in a couple of little rooms above the store."

"Well, it sounds to me like you have nothing to worry about," Stewart said after a brief silence. "If he were on your trail, he certainly wouldn't go to all the trouble of getting a job and renting a place to stay. He'd confirm your identity, serve you with the subpoena and escort you back to Vancouver."

"I know," Laurel said. "I keep telling myself that, but..."

"But he keeps watching you," Stewart said with an indulgent chuckle. "And who can blame him? Don't worry, baby. And look...don't go falling in love with some local guy who works in a hardware store, okay? You're a spectacular woman, Laurie. Life surely holds something a lot more exciting for you than this kind of small-town dude."

"I have no idea," Laurel said dryly, "what life holds for me. I just wish I could get back to work."

"Well, I'm doing my very best. Sweetheart, I have to go. I'm afraid to talk any longer. Is there anything you need?"

"Would it matter?" Laurel asked. "How could you get anything to me without finding out where I am?"

"I guess I couldn't," her father admitted cheerfully. "But I'll still feel a lot better if you reassure me that you're fine."

"I'm fine," Laurel said, smiling in spite of herself. "Look, can you tell Dennis..."

"You know I can't tell him anything, Laurie. I can't let anybody know we've been in touch."

"I guess not," she said slowly. "Goodbye Dad. I love you. Hurry up and get your name cleared so I can come home."

"You bet I will, honey. Keep away from those handsome local guys."

"And you take care of that pregnant wife. I can't wait to see my little brother or sister."

"That's the spirit. Check the paper every Saturday, honey. You'll be hearing from me soon."

Then he was gone, and his familiar, well-loved voice was replaced by the impersonal buzz of the dial tone.

A FEW DAYS LATER, on a Wednesday evening, Laurel approached the vacant lot next to the stockyards where Luther Barnes liked to fly his remote-control aircraft whenever he could escape from Hilda's watchful eye.

Jonas was already there, looking boyish and handsome in a yellow T-shirt with the team name lettered on the back. He was surrounded by a clamorous group of small children in identical yellow shirts.

"Two sizes fit all," Jonas said when he saw her eyeing the flopping, baggy shirts. "Adult and kid. Where's yours, coach?"

"It's obviously the same size as yours. It hangs almost down to my knees."

He grinned, his face lighting briefly, but said nothing more about the missing T-shirt. "Do you have a glove?" he asked.

Laurel shook her head. "I looked at a few in the hardware store yesterday, but I can't afford to buy one. The cheapest glove cost fifty dollars. That's almost more than I can save in a month."

"I brought you a glove," Jonas said placidly. "It's on loan from the store."

He held out a neat little brown trapper with a deep pocket. Laurel slipped it on and smacked her fist into the glove experimentally, liking the feel of it.

"Go out in the field," Jonas instructed, hefting a couple of bats, "and shag some flies for us. You guys go with Laurie," he told a group who were absorbed in a lively wrestling match. "Come on, break it up! We're here to play ball, not kill each other."

The children disentangled themselves and rolled free, then rushed to gather up their caps and gloves. Laurel started out to the field with a growing sense of unreality, followed by a dozen yellow-clad urchins.

"What's your name?" she asked a skinny little fellow who trotted alongside. He had shaggy red-gold hair, a sea of freckles and a businesslike pair of miniature baseball cleats.

"Melanie," the child said, giving her a winsome gap-toothed smile.

"Oh," Laurel said, realizing her mistake.

"I'm Tyler," a boy said, pressing close to them.

"Wipe your nose," Melanie told him rudely. "You look like a baby."

The boy complied without embarrassment, then hitched his ball cap low over his eyes and took a position in the field near Laurel. He crouched tensely and extended his glove like a professional shortstop, although nobody had yet showed signs of approaching the batter's circle.

Melanie and Laurel exchanged a glance. "Boys," Melanie said, rolling her eyes eloquently. "They're so *dumb*."

"I'm not dumb!" Tyler shouted, still extending his gloved hand. "I'm just getting ready. Jonas told us a good fielder should always be ready for the ball."

"What ball?" Melanie asked.

Jonas stepped up to the plate, swinging a bat experimentally. He tossed a ball into the air, tapped it gently and sent it looping to the outfield, where it fell among a group of children who stood frozen and watched as the ball hit the ground, then scrambled wildly to recover it.

Laurel chuckled, thinking that perhaps coaching baseball was going to be a lot more fun than she'd expected.

She pulled down the peak of her cap to shade her eyes from the setting sun, and stole a glance at Jonas by the plate.

He looked more relaxed in this setting, with none of the hard, dangerous edge that had troubled her in most of their dealings. It was obvious that he liked children, and here in the mellow prairie evening, surrounded by his baggy-shirted team, he seemed almost boyish himself. For a while at least, the bitter line of his mouth eased and his face was warmer.

There was nothing wrong with his body, either, Laurel thought, admiring the way his biceps rippled and flexed as he swung the bat and his lean hips bent into the motion.

Again she wondered if Jonas O'Neal was a professional athlete, hiding out in this small town after doing something to ruin his career. He had that air of arrogant confidence, that easy grace of movement and a faraway, bitter look in his eyes as if he'd seen things other people couldn't dream of.

And his body was superb...

He knelt to give the bat to one of the children, holding the little boy within the circle of his arms as he showed the group how to grip and swing.

"Like this," she heard him say. "Nice and easy. Don't try to push the ball, just tap it and let the bat do the work. See?"

He swung again and the ball lifted high in an arc, sailing out over second base. Laurel trotted back a few steps, squinting into the sun as she tried to judge the trajectory.

"Your ball, Laurie!" she heard Melanie yell from somewhere behind her.

Laurel made a dive to the left, grabbed the ball before it hit the ground and came up running, tossing it neatly back to home plate.

"Nice catch," Jonas called. "Here's one for you, Tyler."

Tyler stiffened even more, closed his eyes and extended his glove. The ball drifted in his direction then bounced about three feet away while he watched, rigid with alarm.

"Now he'll cry," Melanie muttered scornfully. "He's such a baby."

Laurel went over to the little boy and knelt beside him, observing that Melanie had been right. Tears glistened in his eyes, and his nose was starting to run again. She took a tissue from her pocket and wiped his face, then hugged him.

"You have to watch the ball, Tyler," she murmured. "It's not enough just to be ready. You have to know where the ball's going and try to track it down. Come on, let's do it together, okay?"

He gave her a miserable, despairing glance and bobbed his head.

"Give us another one, Jonas," Laurel called. "Really high and light."

Jonas sent the ball up into the air, where it arced softly against the clouds and began spiraling down to them.

"See, Tyler," Laurel said, crouching beside him. "Watch the ball. Move over so you're right underneath it."

The child looked up in terror, then scuttled a few feet to his right and waited stiffly as the ball drifted toward the ground.

"Hold your glove out!" Laurel called. "Get ready, here it comes."

The ball dropped and landed in Tyler's glove with a satisfying thump. He looked down at it in amazement, then turned to Laurel, his tear-stained face breaking into a delighted grin.

"I caught it!" he shouted. "Hey, Melanie, look! I caught it!"

Laurel glanced at Jonas and saw him smiling. The sunlight glinted on his face and body, edging them brightly with gold. She smiled back at him, then turned away quickly, troubled by the way her heart was beating and her cheeks felt suddenly warm.

"Hey," Jonas called, looking beyond her into the field. "What's going on out there?"

Laurel followed his gaze and saw a half-dozen ball players squatting in a circle. They were staring at the ground, utterly oblivious to baseball practice.

"What is it?" she asked, trotting over to them.

"Gophers," a little boy said, beaming up at her over his shoulder. "They live down here."

Laurel looked at the ragged hole in the prairie sod, then at the excitement on the faces of the little boys. Jonas came up behind her, casually dropping an arm over her shoulders as they all examined the pitted ground.

"Gophers," Laurel told him.

He threw back his head and laughed heartily, giving her a warm hug.

"I think maybe we'll need to work a bit on concentration and competitive edge," he told her solemnly. "What about it, coach?"

Laurel nodded agreement. "Maybe you'd better stay out in the field for a while," she said, moving hastily away from him. "Melanie and I will go in and hit you some fly balls, all right?"

As Laurel had suspected, Melanie turned out to be a confident hitter with a smooth, surprisingly powerful swing for such a small girl. They spent half an hour driving balls toward the other players and watching as Jonas patiently instructed the boys in the art of fielding.

"This is going to be a pretty good team," Melanie said with satisfaction, tapping the bat against the dirt-crusted metal on her cleats. "Maybe we'll even win some games this year."

"Didn't you win any last year?"

Melanie rolled her eyes, an expression that she apparently used to convey a wide variety of emotions.

Laurel smiled at her. "Winning isn't everything, Melanie."

"Sure it isn't," the child said. "But it's *something*, right?"

Laurel thought this over. "Yes," she said. "Yes, it is."

"And boys need to know that girls are just as good as they are," Melanie said grimly, sending a hard fly into right field that made Jonas dive and scramble to come up with the ball.

Laurel chuckled and crouched behind the plate to trap the incoming ball, feeling suddenly happier than she'd been in weeks.

THE SUN DROPPED below the distant horizon and the wind freshened. Jonas gave the players a final pep talk, then dismissed the team, watching as the yellow T-shirts dispersed noisily on bicycles, on foot and in vans driven by parents and neighbors. Laurel and Jonas were the last to leave. She helped him gather up the balls and bats, the score sheets and bases and water jugs, and stash them in the trunk of his car.

He drove a gray Mercedes, at least fifteen years old but beautifully maintained. Laurel studied the car, thinking that it was as puzzling as everything else about this man.

Why didn't he drive a truck, like almost every other man in town? And if he'd been able to afford a Mercedes, why was he now reduced to working at the local hardware store, probably for a wage not much higher than hers?

She realized that he was watching her. Abruptly, she turned away and took her jacket from behind the backstop.

"Time to get home," she said. "I have to work an early shift tomorrow."

"You can't."

"Can't what? Go to work tomorrow?"

"You can't go home yet. You have to help me unload the supplies. It's part of your duty as assistant coach," he told her calmly.

Laurel hesitated, giving him a skeptical glance. "Who says?"

"I do. I'm the head coach, and I say you have to help. You can't expect me to look after all this stuff by myself, every time we have a practice."

Laurel wavered, wondering if he was teasing her again. "Where does it go?" she asked at last.

"I'm planning to store most of it in a shed at the back of the hardware store."

"All right," she said. "I'll help you unload it."

"Good. Hop in."

Laurel looked in alarm at the car, then at him. "I was planning to walk back into town. It's such a nice evening, and it's only a few blocks."

"Well, that doesn't make much sense," he observed cheerfully. "By the time you got there, I'd have all the stuff unloaded and put away. Come on, get in. What are you afraid of?"

"Nothing," Laurel said curtly, climbing into the passenger seat and looking around with reluctant curiosity.

The car was sleek and powerful, like its owner, and neat, not a single telltale object to give any clue about the man who drove it. There were no books or magazines in the side cases, no tapes or music disks on the seat, no extra clothes or hobby equipment tossed into the back. Nothing but gleaming chrome and softly polished leather, and that elusive, exciting scent of clean maleness that Laurel always associated with this man.

She settled back in the seat, looking out the side window.

"Do you like the car?" he asked.

"It's all right," she said in a noncommittal tone.

"Ever owned a Mercedes?" he said casually as he shifted into gear and headed onto the road.

She tensed and tried to laugh. "Yeah, right. Lots of dishwashers own expensive cars like this. Jonas," she added in alarm, "where are you going?"

"I want to show you something, so we're taking the scenic route," he said, bypassing the town and skimming out on a broad graveled road toward the setting sun.

"Stop the car!" she said angrily. "I don't want to go anywhere with you. I want to go home."

"Laurel, I just want to be friends. I really think you'll be interested in this. Can't we put aside all this constant suspicion?"

He pulled over to the edge of the road and got out, then strode around the car to open her door. She stayed inside and looked up at him. "Now what?"

"We're going for a little walk. Come on, put on your jacket."

WHILE SHE HESITATED, clearly wondering what to do, Jonas waited by the car and looked around.

The town had faded to a few distant shimmers of light on the horizon. The darkening prairie lay around them, bathed in mauve and blue shadow, and the wind was keen, touching his skin with fingers of ice.

He leaned over the door and smiled. "Please," he said gently. "Come for a walk with me. It's not far from here."

Laurel got out, zipped her jacket to her chin and started walking beside him. He carried a small flashlight that he played over the swaying tussocks of prairie grass.

"Somewhere right around here," he muttered. "Right in line with the fence, and a few feet to the..."

"What are you looking for?" she asked nervously.

Jonas looked at her. He could see her wondering how she'd managed to get herself in this position. Wandering around in the dark with this hard-faced stranger, alone on a deserted field that was miles from anywhere....

Suddenly, he was almost overcome by the urge to take her in his arms, cover her face with kisses, taste her skin and touch her breasts.

This was crazy, Jonas thought in despair. He didn't want to feel this way. He had a job to do, and it was getting harder all the time because of the conflicting emotions he felt for this woman.

If only she weren't so skillful at pretending to be something she wasn't. Here in the prairie twilight, she looked as innocent as the children they'd been playing with earlier. But there was nothing childlike about her curving body, or her utter desirability.

"Here it is!" he said abruptly, dropping to one knee so he wouldn't have to look at her face. "Come here, Laurel."

Reluctantly, she moved over to him, then knelt at his side.

Jonas directed the flashlight at something on the ground. It was a bird's nest, cunningly woven of soft prairie grasses and nestled in an indentation in the sod so neatly, it was all but invisible, even from a few feet away. Long grasses had been carefully woven overhead in the shape of a dainty arch, leaving an entrance at the side.

Laurel bent down to peer in through the entrance where Jonas shone the flashlight. Five small eggs glistened in the beam of light, white ovals speckled with brown and purple.

"Oh," she breathed, enchanted. "Oh, aren't they beautiful! Jonas, how did you ever find this nest? It's practically invisible."

"I was out walking yesterday and spotted the female tending the eggs. I marked it with some rocks so I'd be able to find it again."

"What kind of bird is it?"

"A western meadowlark. The same one that makes the pretty warbling call you hear all the time."

"But where's the mother now?" Laurel looked around in concern at the gathering darkness. "I hope we didn't frighten her away."

"Don't worry, she'll be nearby. She's probably out hunting insects, but she's surely keeping an eye on us, too."

"What if she abandons the eggs now that we've seen them?"

"She won't."

Jonas crouched beside her, conscious of her nearness. Her hair smelled as sweet as the wildflowers surrounding them, and her shoulder brushed against his as they peered at the eggs. Even this brief contact burned like a sweet fire. It took all the control he could muster to keep himself from grabbing her. He yearned to urge her slim body down onto the soft prairie grass and lie there with her...

Jonas got to his feet and reached for her hand to help her up.

"But," he added, feeling hollow and shaky with sexual need, "she might go away if we touch them. Songbirds can't abide the human scent on their eggs or nest."

"Can we...come back sometime?" Laurel asked shyly, releasing her hand. "I'd love to watch the eggs hatch, and see the babies."

He looked down at her wide gray eyes, the sweetness of her mouth and the delicate line of her jaw and temple. Involuntarily, he reached out and cupped her cheek. His hand curved to her face, stroked her hair, fingered one of those wayward strands that kept escaping from the lace at her neck.

She tensed, staring up at him, then pulled away and hurried back toward the car.

"It still gets really cold in the evening, doesn't it?" she said over her shoulder. "I keep forgetting how dry this place is. It's actually more like a desert climate, right? Hot in the daytime and really cold at night."

Jonas followed her silently, ignoring her nervous chatter. His whole body ached with frustration.

Back when he'd arrived in Wolf Hill, his assignment had been simple enough, merely tedious and time-consuming. Now it was all getting far too complicated. He'd certainly never expected to feel this way about the woman.

Jonas wasn't even certain what to do about her anymore. If she were finally goaded into heading back where she belonged, all kinds of problems waited for her. But if she got frightened and ran somewhere else, she could be in even greater danger.

Worst of all, he told himself with stark honesty, was the fact if she stayed in Wolf Hill, her greatest danger could be from him.

CHAPTER EIGHT

"YOU'VE NEVER SEEN a bird's nest before?" Jonas asked casually, concentrating on the graveled road in the headlights.

Laurel glanced over at his aquiline profile. He looked so cold and distant, much more like his old sardonic self. Yet, for a moment back there on the prairie, Jonas O'Neal had seemed almost on the verge of kissing her.

She gripped her hands in her lap. "Not close up like that unless they were in museums."

"So you grew up in the city?"

"Mostly," Laurel said cautiously, thinking about the luxurious acreage near Vancouver where they'd lived until her mother died. There'd been guest houses, stables and an equestrian ring, even servants' quarters below the main house.

But, she thought with a wistful smile, no meadowlark nests.

"What about your parents?"

"What about them?" she asked, her smile fading.

"What are they like? Where do they live? What kind of jobs do they have?"

"My mother died when I was fourteen," Laurel said briefly. "And I never see my father anymore. In fact, he doesn't even want to talk to me."

"No kidding?" Jonas gave her a quick glance, then pulled into the alley behind the hardware store. "Why not?"

Laurel shrugged, feeling increasingly awkward. "It's kind of complicated," she said. "One of those family things."

"I see." He parked near the shed and got out, pausing to greet a shaggy black-and-white dog that materialized from somewhere near the fence and capered around his ankles.

Laurel stepped from the car and bent to pat the dog, who dropped to the ground with his forelegs extended and his rump high in the air. His long tail rotated like a windmill, and his tongue lolled in a happy grin.

"Blackie, you devil," Jonas said. "I believe you're flirting."

Laurel tickled the dog's ears, making him sigh with bliss. "Is he yours?" she asked.

"He's a castaway." Jonas opened the trunk of the car. "Blackie's a derelict, just like you and me," he added, giving Laurel a level glance. "Nobody wants him, so he's struggling against cruel odds to make his own way in the world."

She turned aside and began to unpack baseball supplies from the trunk.

"Is that what you are, Jonas?" she asked, her voice deliberately light and casual. "A derelict?"

"Maybe not." He stacked the bases and carried them inside the shed. "More of a drifter, I guess."

"You don't look like a drifter." Laurel passed him with an armful of bats.

"What do I look like?"

She paused in the doorway, considering, then began to stack the bats along the wall of the shed.

"Laurel?" he asked when she came outside. "What do I look like?"

"I don't know. An athlete, a bank robber, a hired assassin . . ."

He chuckled with genuine amusement. "You make me sound like a pretty romantic figure. Especially for a small-town hardware clerk."

"Whatever you are," Laurel said calmly, "you're not a hardware clerk."

"I'm not?" He leaned against the car, his eyes sparkling in the dim glow of the yard light above the shed. "Then what am I doing in this town?"

"I don't know, Jonas." Laurel stood erect to look at him. "Why don't you tell me?"

"Why don't you tell me first?" he said softly. "Tell me what you're doing in Wolf Hill."

"I'm working at an honest job so I can earn enough money for bus fare. When I've got it, I'm leaving. And that's the whole story. No mystery at all."

"That's not what your friends say."

"What friends?"

He tossed a sack of baseballs into the corner, then closed and latched the shed door. "Nellie, for instance," he said.

Laurel tensed. "What about Nellie?"

"She told me you're a princess."

"Oh, for goodness' sake," Laurel said. "Nellie's so lonely, she'd think anybody who came to visit her was a princess."

Jonas gave her a keen glance. "But she told me that before she even met you."

"Then she wouldn't really have any idea about who I am, would she?"

He stepped closer and gripped her shoulders, looking down at her in silence. Suddenly, he reached out and unfastened the shoelace that held her hair back, pulling it free and letting her hair fall around her face.

"What are you doing?" she asked, raising a hand to stop him.

But he ignored her, lifting and fluffing her hair so it framed her face and lay softly on her neck and shoulders.

"I really need a haircut, don't I?" she said nervously, shifting under his intent gaze. "I'm going to get Margie to chop it all off one of these days. It's too hot when I'm working over the sink."

"It's beautiful. Why don't you ever let it hang free like this?"

"Because it gets in the way," she said, grabbing the lace from his hand.

He watched while she retied the mass of hair.

"Is that right? Or," he asked with an intent look, "is it because when your hair's down, you look too much like a princess?"

She turned away and started walking toward the gate with Blackie capering at her side.

"Where are you going?" Jonas asked, following her.

"Back to the hotel. It's late, and I'm tired."

"Don't go." He gripped her arm. "Come upstairs for a minute and help me with the player assignments."

"Upstairs?"

"Into my lair," he said with a wolfish grin, dropping his voice to a sinister growl and baring his teeth. "Are you brave enough, little girl?"

She laughed in spite of herself. "I'm certainly not afraid of *you,* Mr. Wolf. I'm just tired of being poked and prodded about things that are absolutely nobody's business but my own."

"I'll be good. I won't say another thing about princesses. All right?"

"Promise?"

"I promise."

She wavered. "What player assignments?"

"Well, we've had an evening to look these kids over and watch the way they field the ball. We have to start planning an outfield and an infield."

Laurel smiled. "Where can we put Tyler?"

"In charge of the water jug."

Jonas took her arm and led her toward a rickety staircase at the rear of the hardware store.

They climbed to the second floor while Blackie sat below in the moonlight, looking up at them wistfully.

Laurel waited as Jonas rummaged in his jacket pocket for a key. Her heart began to pound uncertainly and she felt some panicky misgivings when the door swung open. But Jonas calmly switched on the light, then ushered her inside and closed the door behind them.

His living quarters were so bleak and sparsely furnished that Laurel felt a treacherous rush of sympathy when she looked around. The apartment consisted of nothing more than a single room with a few bits of furniture. One corner contained a sink, hot plate and bar fridge, and across the room was a tiny alcove where she could see the edge of a bathtub.

Jonas had apparently arrived in town with little more than a suitcase full of clothes, because the place was empty of any kind of adornment. There were no books, no personal belongings, no cushions or throw rugs, and nothing on the walls but a faded hardware calendar almost fifteen years old.

Compared to this, Laurel's little room at the hotel was a haven of luxury.

"Not all that cozy, is it?" he said cheerfully, watching her reaction.

"What do you do in your spare time?" she asked. "There's not even a television set."

He shrugged. "I go for long walks on the prairie, talk with people over in the hotel bar, things like that."

"But it's so..."

"What?"

"Nothing. Where do you sleep?" she asked, wishing she could take back the words as she spoke.

He gave her a quick, meaningful glance and her cheeks warmed uncomfortably. But he didn't say anything, just strolled over and pulled aside one of the sofa cushions to reveal a pull-out mattress.

"I see," she said with forced casualness. "You should make friends with Nellie," she added, surveying the starkness of the little room. "She'd shower you with doilies and afghans and knitted cushions shaped like pussycats."

"I don't make friends that easily." He took a notebook from one of the tiny cupboards. "Come on, Laurel," he said, pulling out a chair at the cheap metal table. "Let's plan this team of ours."

Laurel sat next to him, watching while he made a neat sketch of a baseball diamond and began to write children's names at various positions.

He held out the pad and she studied it thoughtfully. "It's probably not a good idea to put Billy at first base," she said. "He's pretty fast. I think he'd be more of an asset in right field, chasing down flies."

"Good thinking." Jonas made a note on the pad. "Who's a reasonable prospect for catcher?"

"Well, it has to be somebody who isn't scared of the ball. That eliminates most of them."

"How about Melanie?" Jonas asked.

Laurel shook her head. "Melanie should be the pitcher. She's got a better arm than any of them."

"They'll all be furious," Jonas warned. "Those little boys are rabid chauvinists, you know. They won't think it's appropriate for a girl to be the pitcher."

"If she's the best," Laurel said firmly, "she should get the job."

Jonas smiled at her, his eyes crinkling. "You're absolutely right."

Laurel smiled back, disarmed by his warmth and the surprising pleasure of being with him in his barren little apartment.

Jonas got up and set the kettle to boil, then took out mugs and instant coffee. He rummaged in the cupboard and produced a cellophane pack of fig newtons, which he arranged on a cracked saucer.

"As you can see," he told her, taking a can of condensed milk from the fridge, "in addition to my skills at interior decoration, I'm also a suave and gracious host. Would you care for a little caviar with your fig newton, madam?"

"You know, I've never been all that fond of caviar," Laurel told him. The kettle began to whistle and she got up to fill the mugs with boiling water. "I think caviar is highly overrated," she added, dipping her spoon into the instant coffee. "Who wants to eat something that tastes like jam made from fish?"

Jonas gave her a thoughtful glance but said nothing. Laurel hurried to change the subject, her cheeks warming with embarrassment.

"Melanie thinks we've got a pretty good team," she said awkwardly. "And that we might even win a few games this year."

"We might." Jonas settled himself at the table and examined the player roster again. "If both the coaches stay around long enough to see the kids through the season."

Laurel was silent, stirring milk into her coffee and avoiding his eyes.

When they were finished their snack, he walked her back to the hotel, strolling along next to her in the silent prairie night, through streets that were dark and empty in the moonlight.

"Have you ever seen a town without street lamps?" he asked.

Laurel glanced at him. His hands were thrust deep into his jacket pockets, and the cold silver light glistened on the blunt planes of his face. The breeze lifted and stirred his hair, giving him a boyish look that was strangely at odds with his usual threatening, hard-edged manner.

"Not that I recall," she said casually. "I honestly didn't think places like this still existed."

"Why did you come here?" he asked. "I'm not prying," he added hastily. "I mean, why did you pick Wolf Hill of all the places in the world?"

"I read about it in a book," Laurel told him.

"In a *book?* This town?"

"You know Kate Cameron, the woman who owns the hotel?" Laurel asked.

"Tall blond lady, nice-looking, has a baby?"

"That's the one. Well, she found an old diary in the hotel when she was renovating. The diary was written by the town's very first schoolteacher, a woman named Ellen Livingston. Kate had the diary published, and when I read it, I thought Wolf Hill sounded like an...an interesting place to live for a little while," she concluded, feeling increasingly nervous.

But he didn't say anything, just nodded thoughtfully and paused in the shadows next to the hotel.

"Well, here you are," he said. "Safely home."

"Thanks, Jonas." Laurel turned to leave, but he took her arm, drawing her close to him.

"Please," Laurel murmured in alarm. "Please, don't..."

But it was too late for protest. She was in his arms, lost in the warmth and strength of his embrace, and then his mouth was on hers.

Laurel gasped at the sweetness of his kiss, and the disturbing power of her body's response.

It's been too long, she thought, savoring the taste of his mouth as it moved hungrily on hers. Far too long since somebody's held me like this. I'm lonely, that's all. This doesn't mean anything. I'm just so lonely...

He held her tightly, deepening his kiss. Finally, Laurel pulled away from him and stood close to the fence, rubbing her arms nervously.

"Laurel?" he asked.

She shook her head, not trusting her voice.

"Look," he began, "I'm sorry if I've upset you. It's just that you're so...so damned beautiful, and it's hard for me to keep my hands off you."

"You don't have to apologize," she murmured. "I'm a grown-up, Jonas. I'm not going to get all upset over a kiss. It doesn't mean that much, after all."

"Doesn't it?" He touched her cheek, turning her face so he could look at her. "Doesn't it mean anything to you, Laurel?"

She shook her head again, forcing herself to meet his eyes. "Nothing except that I'm lonely, and so are you, and it's making both of us act a little foolish."

"Why is this foolish?"

"Because you're a drifter, Jonas. You said so yourself. And I'm going to be gone as soon as I can get away. So let's not make any more of this than we should, all right?"

"What do you intend to do about it?"

"I intend to forget that it ever happened, and I think you should do the same."

Abruptly, she pulled away from his grasp and ran up the walk to the hotel, climbing the veranda steps and hurrying through the door to the lobby without a backward glance.

LAUREL WENT into the hotel kitchen early the next morning, expecting to find Crystal and Hilda busy with breakfast preparations. But only Kate Cameron was in the room, working at the table over a pile of account books.

She looked up quickly when Laurel came in, then smiled in obvious relief. "Hi, Laurie," she said. "I was hoping you weren't my mother."

Laurel came around the table and saw Kate's baby lying in a folding playpen near the sink. He held a blue plush rabbit in his hands, drowsily stroking its ears while his eyelids fluttered.

"He's almost asleep," Kate murmured. "As soon as he's safely gone, I'll carry him out and tuck him away in the crib in my office."

Laurel nodded and opened the fridge, reaching inside for one of the big flats of eggs. "Where is everybody?" she whispered.

"I don't know. I'm just in the kitchen to hide from my mother."

"Why?" Laurel carried the eggs to the table and took several loaves of bread from the pantry.

Kate sighed and pushed the books away, running a hand through her hair. "Mom wants to take Joshua to Calgary and get his picture taken again. He's probably the most photographed baby in North America," she said with a wan smile.

Laurel looked at the woman's tired face and gentle blue eyes. "If you don't want the baby to go to the city today, shouldn't you just say so?"

"You're right, of course, but it's not that easy. Not when you have a mother like mine."

"My father is pretty much the same kind of person. He'd run everybody's lives if he had the chance."

Kate looked at her with interest. "You never talk about your family, Laurie."

Laurel began to stack plates on the table and wrap silverware in paper napkins.

"So what do you do?" Kate asked. "Do you stand up to him?"

"I try," Laurel said. "But he's always so convinced he's doing everything for my own good. And I can't stand seeing him upset, so he can usually get me to knuckle under."

Kate nodded, looking down at her baby.

"I guess I'm not the best person to give advice," Laurel went on, "but I think when we're adults, we should try to be firm and take charge of our own lives. Otherwise, we're not going to be happy, and that's what our parents basically want for us, isn't it? That we'll be happy?''

Kate gave her a shrewd glance. "You know," she said thoughtfully, "you're a pretty interesting woman, aren't you?''

"Just a kitchen worker." Laurel held out her scarred work-hardened hands with a rueful smile. Kate took one of them and clasped it for a moment.

"Thanks, Laurie," she murmured. "You're absolutely right. It's time for me to take charge of my own family, even if my mother has to suffer a few growing pains in the process."

Hilda stamped into the kitchen at that moment, looking grim. "Well, this does it," she announced. "This is the last straw. Of all the..."

She caught sight of Kate at the table and stopped talking. Instead, she marched to the pantry and reached for her apron.

Kate leaned over to check on her sleeping baby, then gathered him up and carried him toward the door.

"I'll come back for the playpen and the account books," she whispered.

"Don't worry," Laurel told her. "I can put them away and bring them out for you later."

Kate smiled gratefully and vanished, leaving the other two alone.

Laurel glanced at her employer's angry face. "Hilda," she ventured, "is something the matter?"

"It's the last straw," Hilda repeated, cracking eggs into a bowl and stirring them furiously. "I've come to the end of my patience."

"With what?"

"With Crystal. I plan to fire her today."

Laurel looked up, her hands full of napkins. "Oh, no," she said. "Why?"

"She called Luther at the front desk a few minutes ago and said she can't come in this morning. She *knows* Thursday's a real busy day because of the livestock auction. But she expects you to do all the work again, all by yourself. I just won't have it."

"I can manage," Laurel insisted. "Really I can, Hilda. It's no problem. Once we get the breakfast rush over with, I can—"

"Now, aren't you a puzzle?" Hilda put down the bowl and looked at her directly. "You think I never noticed the way you've been working all this time while Crystal was sluffing off? And you were plenty upset about it, too, even though you never said anything. You practically wanted to kill the girl. Now I'm ready to fire her, and you're taking her side?"

"At first I thought she was being lazy and taking advantage of me," Laurel said. "But now I believe she's . . . she's really not feeling well. I wish you'd give her another chance."

"Well, you sure got a softer heart than I do. I'm tired of her behavior, and I don't want her in my kitchen."

"What if I go and see her?" Laurel pleaded. "I can run over there right now before breakfast starts, and see if I can get her to come to work."

"If you can get that girl in here this morning, ready to work, I might change my mind," Hilda said grudgingly. "Otherwise, you can tell her not to bother coming back except to pick up her check."

"I'll go right away." Laurel took off her apron and hung it in the pantry. "Where does she live?"

"In a little shack next to the general store, down by Margie's post office."

"Okay."

"Laurie?"

Laurel paused in the doorway.

"Take as much time as you need to talk some sense into the girl," Hilda said, looking down at her mixing bowl. "You can tell Luther to come in and give me a hand while you're gone. He's still at the front desk, but Kate can cover for him till you get back."

"All right. Thanks, Hilda." Laurel smiled. "You're not nearly as tough as you pretend to be, are you?"

But the cook was busy at the table again, beating her bowlful of eggs with a wooden spoon and adding clouds of seasoned pepper.

LAUREL WALKED BRISKLY along the street in the fresh coolness of early morning, delighted by the sights and scents of spring. Early lilacs and apple trees blossomed all around her, heavy with fragrance, and the damp prairie stretched out for endless miles around the little town in a rich, rolling carpet of green.

The day was so beautiful, she was almost able to forget the turmoil of her own life, until she rounded the corner by Nellie's house and saw the brick hardware store looming before her at the end of the street. The upper windows looked black and empty in the morning sunlight.

Laurel imagined Jonas getting ready for his day, shaving and dressing and making breakfast.

She thought of the evening before, the fun of their baseball practice and the surprising pleasure of being alone with him in his room.

And his kiss...

She rubbed her arms nervously and pushed the thoughts aside.

Just past the general store, she paused and looked at the ramshackle building on the adjoining lot, mostly screened by a ragged hedge of caragana covered with fresh new leaves. Laurel opened a sagging wire gate and started up the path, noting that the flower beds were freshly weeded and raked, and the lawn was neatly trimmed.

As Hilda had said, the house itself was little more than a shack, a tiny building covered with weathered brown shingles.

Laurel knocked on the front door and waited, feeling chilled in the shade of a spreading cottonwood by the cracked concrete step.

At last, she heard footsteps inside the house and the door opened.

"Laurie?" Crystal said, looking out at her blankly. "What are you doing here?"

"Hi, Crystal. I'm sorry to bother you so early in the morning, but it's really important. May I come in for a minute?"

The door opened wider and Laurel stepped inside. Crystal followed, wearing a blue nightshirt over a pair of tights that showed off her spectacular long legs. Her bright hair was an untidy cloud around her face, and her eyes were darkly shadowed.

"You look so tired," Laurel said with sympathy. "Have you been feeling sick again?"

Crystal nodded unhappily, sinking into a chair while Laurel sat opposite her on the couch. The girl tucked one foot under her and hugged a pillow, gazing at the opposite wall in silence.

"Crystal," Laurel began, "you really have to make an effort to come to work today. If you don't, Hilda says—"

"I'm pregnant," Crystal said abruptly. "It's me, you know. It's not my cousin at all."

"I was pretty sure of that," Laurel said.

Crystal looked up, her face white and drawn. Tears sparkled in her eyes. "Oh, Laurie," she whispered. "What am I going to do?"

"Well," Laurel said, trying to sound calm and businesslike, "the first thing you have to do is hang on to your job."

"Is Hilda really mad?"

"She's pretty upset. I think her patience is wearing thin."

"What can I do?"

"You can tell her the truth," Laurel said gently. "That would probably be a good beginning."

"I can't!" Crystal said. "I can't tell her! Laurie, promise you won't tell anybody."

"Look, you can't keep this a secret forever. Pretty soon, it's going to start showing, isn't it?"

"I guess so," Crystal muttered, still gripping the pillow tightly in her arms. "But I keep hoping I can figure something out. I just need a little time."

"Crystal . . ."

"If only I knew what to *do!*" the girl said in despair. "I wish I could think things through, but my mind keeps going around in circles and then I panic."

"Well, let's think about it," Laurel said. "What do you want to do?"

"About the baby?"

"No, about your life in general. What's your goal? Do you want to be a waitress forever?"

Crystal shook her head. "No way. Besides, if I want to keep my baby, I know I'll need a better job so I can look after it."

"What will you do?"

"I'd like to go back to school and get some training."

"In what?"

"Nursing," the girl said shyly. "I'd really love to work in a hospital. That's what I always wanted, but I sort of got sidetracked after high school."

"It might be hard to get the proper training when you have a new baby to look after."

"Everything's hard," Crystal said. "But lots of other people have managed to do it. I don't see why I can't, if I can just get things sorted out and start saving some money. There's assistance you can apply for if you're in serious job training."

"You've been thinking about this quite a lot, haven't you?"

Crystal sighed. "I haven't been doing anything else lately," she said. "I lie awake all night, thinking and worrying. I guess that's why I feel so tired and sick all the time."

"Well," Laurel said with sudden decision, "there has to be some way to work things out. In the meantime, I think you should quit worrying and concentrate on keeping your job until you've decided what to do."

Crystal nodded and got to her feet. "I feel a lot better now," she said, "just from telling somebody. I'll hurry and dress so I can walk back with you, if you don't mind waiting a minute."

"No problem."

Crystal smiled gratefully and walked into the other room.

While Laurel was waiting, she looked around, touched by the girl's brave attempts to decorate her shabby little rooms.

Crystal had done a surprisingly good job of making the place seem homey and appealing. There were plants on every windowsill and table, and a small aquarium filled with healthy goldfish and whimsical underwater scenery. Laurel fingered a bright afghan thrown over the sagging couch, looking at it with new awareness now that she was struggling with the intricacies of knitting.

"Who made this afghan?" she called. "The one on the couch that's all done in earth tones?"

"I did," Crystal shouted back over the sound of running water. "Don't look at the mistakes."

Laurel smiled and replaced the soft woollen covering on the sofa arm, thinking about the future.

Soon she'd be home in Vancouver, back at her job and in control of her finances again. Maybe she'd be able to help Crystal.

She stroked the afghan, thinking about possibilities. Laurel's family had a lot of contacts in the city, and Marta, her father's young wife, had worked on the hospital's administrative staff before her marriage. Surely one of them could come up with a job for Crystal, maybe even something in the medical field....

Crystal appeared in the doorway in her pink uniform. She was still pale but looked much more composed.

"Well, I'm all set," she said. "Laurie, you can't imagine how much better I feel, just from telling you. For the first time, I almost feel like things are going to work out."

"Of course things are going to work out" Laurel told her firmly. She followed Crystal out into the warm morning sunlight and waited while the girl locked the door. "I think everything's going to work out just fine."

CHAPTER NINE

A WEEK LATER, on Friday afternoon, Jonas parked his car near a high, isolated bluff overlooking the river, miles from town. He took a wooden tripod from the trunk, paced along the edge of the cliff and mounted the structure, driving the pointed legs firmly into the sod and attaching a paper target in the shape of a human torso.

When the target was secure, he retraced his steps, took the leather case from the back seat and assembled his high-powered rifle. Working with grim professionalism, he began to shoot at the paper torso from a prone position, then kneeling, standing and running as he refilled the ammunition clip. After almost an hour of practice, he went back and unfastened the paper, where dozens of holes were burned into the head and upper portion of the black outline.

Jonas studied the crude human figure, then gazed across the river into the soft clouds massed along the horizon.

The clouds were a lustrous, silvery gray. Like her eyes, Jonas thought. With every fiber of his being, he remembered the feel of her skin, the flowery scent of her hair, the taste of her kiss....

He groaned aloud, gripping his rifle.

How had the woman ever managed to get herself into this mess? How could anyone seem so absolutely sweet and good, and be just the opposite? More to the point, what was he going to do about these explosive, danger- ous feelings that he could hardly control any longer?

The best thing would be for him to dump the whole assignment. He wanted to pack up and move on to- night, get safely away without a word to anybody. But that was impossible.

She was the one who was on the run. And she had to make the next move, even if he forced her into it.

THAT SAME Friday evening, Jonas loaded the baseball equipment into the trunk of his car, pushing the bases over to leave room for the sack of lawn fertilizer he was planning to deliver at Nellie Grossman's house on the way to the ball diamond. Blackie sat near the corner of the shed, watching with a sad, melting gaze.

"No," Jonas told him. "You can't."

The dog's shaggy head drooped. He gave his tail a few mournful thumps, then peered up hopefully from under his forehead.

"No," Jonas said again, but with slightly less con- viction. "Why do you want to go, anyway? It's just a bare old pasture filled with little kids and gophers."

Blackie's eyes brightened and his tail began to thump faster.

"Two of your favorite things, right?" Jonas said dryly.

Blackie got to his feet and edged nearer, his tongue lolling. He whimpered piteously.

"All *right,*" Jonas said, exasperated. "Get in. But just this once, you hear?" he added fiercely. "I'm not about to start hauling around some dusty old mongrel everywhere I go."

Blackie scrambled happily into the passenger seat when Jonas held open the door. The dog sat erect, looking out the window as they pulled away from the hardware yard and drove off along the street.

Jonas parked in front of Nellie's house, shut off the engine and turned to Blackie who watched him with lively interest.

"You stay here, all right?" Jonas said. "I'll be right back."

Blackie coughed discreetly, then turned to examine the street again.

Jonas chuckled and went around the car to heft out the fifty-pound sack of fertilizer. He propped it easily on his shoulder, went up the walk and rang the door-bell.

Nellie appeared, smiling. "Oh, good," she said. "You brought it. Could you put it around back in the garage?"

"Sure thing. Lead the way."

Jonas followed as Nellie trotted through the back-yard and opened the door of a rickety, dirt-floored ga-rage that was empty except for some lawn and garden tools.

"Ben always had a car and a truck in here," Nellie said. "But I sold them after he died. What would I want with a car?"

Jonas dropped the sack in a corner on a sheet of cardboard, then looked down at her in the dusty light of the garage. Her face was soft with contentment, and her eyes sparkled.

"You're looking good, Nellie," he said. "Really chipper."

She beamed. "Well, thank you. I feel wonderful."

Jonas hesitated. "Nellie," he said awkwardly.

"Yes?" Nellie paused with her hand on the door and gave him a curious glance.

"She's not going to stay here forever, you know," he said gently. "Your princess girl, I mean. She's been keeping you company for a while, but she'll probably be moving on soon, and you'll be alone again. You have to be . . . careful," he concluded lamely.

The old woman's smile faded, but her eyes still looked happy and serene.

"You think I don't know that?" she asked. "When you get to be my age, you live for the moment. I've already told her so. If somebody puts a treasure in your hands, you don't throw it away because you might not be allowed to keep it forever. You enjoy it as long as you can, and after it's gone you can warm yourself with the memory of it."

Jonas nodded and followed her back to the front yard, thinking about her words.

He rejoined Blackie in the car and headed for the diamond, feeling a surge of anticipation at the thought of seeing Laurel.

But she wasn't there yet. On Friday evenings she often had to work a little later after the supper rush at the restaurant.

Most of the children, however, were already at the field, throwing a ball around the way he'd taught them and practicing their fielding. Jonas parked near the backstop and got out, holding the door for Blackie who clambered across the gearshift and tumbled onto the grass, then loped joyously into the vacant lot to join a group of boys who greeted him with ecstatic shouts.

Jonas grinned and began unpacking equipment. But he looked up in alarm when he heard his name being called.

"It's Tyler," Melanie shouted from first base. "He fell on a cactus."

"Oh, damn." Jonas tossed aside an armful of bats and reached for a small first-aid kit. He hurried out to the field where Tyler lay on his back, roaring at the top of his lungs and drumming his heels on the tufted grass.

Jonas knelt beside him, looking at the wicked spines bristling from the jeans on the little boy's lower leg. Children crowded around.

"Go away," Jonas told them. "Melanie, take them in, okay? Line them up and pitch to them. The guy who's just batted goes out in the field, and Blackie will help fetch balls."

The boys dispersed, yelling, and pelted toward the backstop to collect their bats. Jonas located a pair of tweezers in his medical kit and began gingerly removing the cactus spines.

"Ow!" Tyler screamed, writhing. "Ow, ow, *ow!*"

Jonas patted the little boy's shoulder and ruffled his hair, feeling a warm surge of sympathy. "I know it hurts, son," he said gently. "I still remember the first time I tangled with a cactus."

Tyler stopped yelling and swallowed hard. "You do?" he said.

Deftly, Jonas extracted a few more spines. "I was spending the summer at a dude ranch in Arizona with my cousins. I was about your age, and we were hiking up this rocky trail. I slipped and fell down the slope and put out my hands to break my fall. They went right into a big mass of prickly pear cactus."

Tyler listened, clearly fascinated, and wiped furtively at his tears. "Did you get lots of stickers?"

"Hundreds of them. My hands looked like pincushions. It took the doctor more than an hour to get all of them out. Afterward, my hands swelled up like two chunks of meat and had to be bandaged for more than a week. I couldn't do any of the neat stuff the other kids were doing.''

Tyler tensed and bit his lip as Jonas removed a particularly deep spine, but didn't yell. "Did you cry?" he asked.

"Sure I did," Jonas assured him. "I howled like crazy. It really hurt."

"Cactus hurts," Tyler said, his voice breaking. "It hurts a lot."

"I know it does," Jonas agreed gravely.

Just then, Blackie pelted by them in a blur of black and white to retrieve the ball. Jonas took advantage of the distraction to ease out the last of the spines, then lifted the boy's denim pant leg to dab some iodine on the sore places.

Tyler howled again at the sting, and Jonas gathered the little boy in his arms to soothe him.

"It's all over, son," he whispered as he held the child and cuddled him tenderly. "It's all done. I got every one of them. The hurting will go away now." Tyler's sobs subsided to whimpers and a couple of hiccups. Jonas looked over the little boy's head at the twilight glow of the sky, wondering how all this had happened.

How had his life suddenly become so complicated? He'd been in Wolf Hill less than two months, but in that time he'd somehow changed from a footloose loner to a man with a job, community involvement, even a bunch of little kids who looked up to him.

And worst of all, a woman creeping further and further into his heart . . .

Jonas shook his head and got up abruptly, setting Tyler down on the grass. "You're fine now," he said gruffly. "Go in and hit some balls with the other kids. And stay away from that cactus, okay?"

He looked up to see Laurel approaching from the direction of the hotel. Two little boys trotted at her side, holding their oversize baseball gloves and talking to her animatedly. On the gentle evening breeze, Jonas could hear the clear, sweet music of her laughter.

She wore a peaked cap pulled low over her eyes, and the baggy yellow team shirt with a pair of denim cut-offs that displayed her beautiful long legs. Even in this shapeless attire, she couldn't hide the graceful curves of her body. The sight of her brought a tightness to his throat, a sense of hungry urgency that was getting stronger all the time.

Jonas closed his eyes briefly, trying not to think about the body under that long yellow shirt. But the truth was, he spent quite a lot of time speculating about how Laurel would look without her clothes. He suspected that the rest of her was probably just as great as those legs. Her waist was slim, her breasts full and shapely under the loose cotton.

And when he'd held her and kissed her that night outside the hotel, she felt so perfect in his arms, so firm and curved and utterly desirable...

He swore under his breath and hurried toward the group of children at the backstop, trying to push the troubling sexual thoughts out of his mind.

Jonas knew that he had to hold on to the feelings that had brought him here. The cold, bitter anger, the cynical sense of isolation and the grim dedication he brought to his work—those were his only means of protection. If he began to let them slip, the world would close in on him again.

And this time he might not survive the encounter.

LAUREL PICKED UP the balls and bats after the practice. Jonas opened the trunk and loaded equipment while the children dispersed toward their homes, running and shouting noisily.

"They're so excited," Laurel said when the last yellow T-shirt vanished into the sunset.

"How about you?" he asked, passing her to toss the bases into the trunk. "Are you getting excited?"

"Actually, I'm getting scared," Laurel confessed. She knelt to pat Blackie, who licked her hand and gazed at her with adoration. "Tomorrow night will be our first real game, after all." She looked up at Jonas. "Do you think we're ready?"

"As ready as we'll ever be," he said briefly. "Why? Don't you think we're ready?"

He stood above her, holding the water jug. The setting sun was at his back, and his face was all hard planes and shadows. A small pulse throbbed near his temple, and she found herself suddenly longing to put her finger on it, to stand close to him and feel all the warm rhythms of his body.

Laurel returned her attention to Blackie.

"Well, we've certainly practiced hard," she said. "I guess you're right. We're as ready as we'll ever be."

"Time to stop practicing and start doing?" he suggested.

Laurel cast him a quick glance but he was holding the back door open for Blackie. He rounded the car and opened the passenger door.

"There's probably dog hair on the seat," he told her. "Do you mind?"

Laurel hesitated, looking at the car with sudden nervousness. "I can walk, Jonas. It's such a beautiful evening."

"Come on," he said curtly. "Don't argue all the time. I'm taking you over to my place for coffee."

She thought about his little apartment, the stark neatness of his room and the feeling of menace and excitement that seemed to heighten almost unbearably whenever they were alone. Again she looked into his face, and found his eyes resting on her with an intensity that took her breath away. Laurel struggled with herself and her urgent desire to turn and run, to put some distance between herself and this man. She was frightened of his hard-edged presence, and the cold, inexplicable anger that sometimes made his face look so dark. Most of all, she was terrified of the powerful sexual pull he seemed to exert.

Nowadays, that physical appeal extended far beyond their time together, pervading her entire life. Whether she was working in the kitchen, soaking in her bathtub or lying sleepless in her bed, she could feel him somewhere nearby. And she constantly hungered for his arms around her, his mouth on hers...

"Okay," she said recklessly, moving past him and climbing into the car. "I guess I can find time for one cup of coffee."

Blackie strained forward from the back seat to lick her ear, and Laurel gave the animal a rueful glance, reaching out to pat his shaggy head.

"You're a good dog," she whispered, nervously conscious of Jonas watching her as he put the car into gear and pulled away from the vacant lot. "You're a really good dog."

This time, the bleakness of his room didn't come as such a shock. And the place was considerably brightened by a huge jar of mauve and white lilacs in the center of the little metal table.

Laurel smiled at the fragrance wafting through the room. "What lovely flowers," she said. "Where did you get them?"

"Nellie brought them for me this morning when she came down to order her lawn fertilizer."

Laurel moved past him into the room, bending to sniff the flowers before she took the kettle from the stove and filled it with water.

"Nellie's such a darling," she said, trying to sound light and casual, as if being alone with Jonas in his room was nothing out of the ordinary. "I really love her."

"She loves you, too," Jonas said. "I'm afraid she's going to miss you when you leave." He leaned in the doorway, once again watching her with that sardonic look that always made her uncomfortable.

"Who says I'm leaving?" She opened a cupboard door and took out two coffee mugs.

"You did. I thought you were planning to move on as soon as you managed to save the bus fare."

Laurel turned away, unsettled by his intent gaze. "Well, I suppose I am," she said. "But with my salary, that could still take a while. Jonas, where do you keep the sugar?"

He crossed the kitchen and stood close to her, reaching over her head to open a cupboard door. Laurel gripped the edge of the counter, almost paralyzed by his nearness. His hard-muscled chest was touching her shoulder and she could feel the warmth of him, the controlled power of his body.

She moved away slightly and he dropped his hand from the cupboard door, then grasped her shoulder and drew her toward him.

"Jonas," she whispered, trying to pull away. "Jonas, I don't think . . ."

He slid his hands down over her back, onto her hips and buttocks and her bare thighs under the cutoff jeans, still gazing intently at her face. "You want this, too," he murmured. "I know you do. Why are you here, if you don't want it as much as I do?"

Laurel stared at him, searching for words. But there was nothing to say. He was right. She was a grown woman, and she'd known perfectly well what she was doing when she accepted his invitation.

She wanted him. In fact, her whole body ached with wanting.

He pulled her into a rough embrace and crushed her against his chest, bending to kiss her. But this time, his kiss wasn't gentle. It was hard and demanding, forcing her mouth open, making her gasp and strain in his arms.

After a moment, she yielded and began to respond. Her caution evaporated along with her inhibitions. She pressed herself against him, shameless with desire, grinding her hips into his and feeling the thrusting hardness of him.

"Oh, Laurel," he muttered against her mouth. "Oh, I want you. I want you . . ."

Laurel turned blindly and found his lips again, kissing him with hungry passion and a kind of abandonment she wouldn't have thought herself capable of. She ran her hands through his hair, kneaded his back and fondled the bulging muscles of his arms, pulling him closer and closer while he reached under her shirt to cup her breasts.

"Jonas," she whispered, lost and drowning in passion. "Please . . ."

He kissed her lips to silence her and began drawing her toward the couch, their mouths still joined, their arms entwined. She stumbled along with him, her body on fire and aching with desire. And through it all, she felt a rich, singing excitement.

This was really going to happen. She'd given in to her feelings, and she wouldn't fight them anymore. Soon she'd see his naked body, feel his strength and sweetness, lose herself in him . . .

Jonas pushed her gently onto the couch and sank down with her, tugging at her shirt. She reached up to help him, then tensed.

Something was happening, something that made him pull away and look up. Laurel blinked in confusion, then realized that the phone was ringing. Jonas got up and crossed the room in a couple of long strides, snatching up the receiver.

"Hello?" he said.

Laurel sat up and watched him, pulling her shirt nervously back into place and touching her hair.

"Look," he said tightly, "why are you calling me? I told you I don't . . ."

He listened again, his face hard.

"Because I'm busy," he said. "I have company. You understand?"

Suddenly, he glanced at Laurel, his eyes raking over her with a cold, intent look that chilled her.

"Yes," he muttered into the phone. "As a matter of fact, she's right here."

There was another silence while he listened, and she could see his knuckles turning white as he gripped the receiver.

"I don't think that's any of your business, is it?"

Another silence, and a grim smile from Jonas.

"Good," he said. "You remember that, okay? And don't call me here again. If I need to talk to you, I'll call you."

He hung up, glaring at the phone. Laurel slipped from the couch and stood up.

"I have to leave," she said, her cheeks hot with embarrassment. "I'm sorry, Jonas, but I really have to go home now."

"Why?" he asked. "It's not late."

"I know, but I have to—"

"And you told me you've got the day off tomorrow. You can sleep in for hours if you want to."

"I know," Laurel said again, looking down at the floor. "But having Saturday off is such a treat for me. I don't want to waste any of it."

She began to edge toward the door, while he stood watching her in silence.

"I'll...see you at the game tomorrow," Laurel whispered. "Good night, Jonas."

She pulled open the door and escaped, running down the rickety flight of stairs and out into the mellow spring night, alive with the sharp cries of nighthawks and the song of mating bullfrogs along the creek.

NEXT MORNING, Laurel opened her eyes to the warm glow of filtered sunlight and lay staring at the drapes, feeling drowsy and mellow.

Crystal had volunteered to work a double shift so Laurel could take her first Saturday off since arriving in Wolf Hill. The day stretched before her, endlessly rich and golden with promise.

Then she remembered the events of the previous evening and rolled over to bury her face in the pillow. All the memories came flooding back, the feeling of his hands and mouth, the wild anticipation she'd felt when she was ready to yield to him and the disturbing significance of that telephone call that had shattered the mood so abruptly.

Who was the person on the other end of the line? Was it some other woman?

Laurel remembered his clipped, angry tone, and the way he'd glanced over at her with such coldness, then returned to his call. She frowned and climbed out of bed, hurrying to dress in her ragged jeans and an old plaid shirt with a torn sleeve.

Downstairs, she ordered coffee and toast in the coffee shop, hoping Jonas wouldn't choose to come to the hotel for breakfast as he often did.

More than likely, she thought gloomily, he was just as anxious to avoid a meeting as she was. He probably wouldn't ever want to talk to her again, which would help considerably to ease all these complications.

Then she recalled their first baseball game, slated for that evening. She moaned softly, rubbing her temples.

"What?" Crystal asked, pausing by the table with a fresh pot of coffee. "What's the matter, Laurie?"

Laurel looked up, trying to smile. The young waitress looked better this morning than she had for a month. Her eyes were clear, her face calm and happy.

"Laurie?" she asked again. "Are you all right?"

Laurel nodded, looking down at her cup. "I'm fine. I just had...kind of an unhappy thought, that's all. You look really great," she added.

Crystal smiled. "Thanks to you."

"I didn't do anything."

"Oh, but you did. You took the time to show you cared about me, and you'll never know how much it helped."

"Well, I'm glad, Crystal."

The girl filled Laurel's cup and leaned closer. "I'm going to talk to Kate next week," she murmured. "Will you come with me?"

"What are you going to tell her?"

"The truth," Crystal said. "I'm going to tell her and Hilda about the baby, and ask if I can keep my job until I find something in the city that pays better, then give a month's notice."

"Of course you can do that. You don't need anybody's permission to change jobs."

"I know, but they've been good to me, and I'm tired of keeping secrets. I want to be straight with them. Will you come with me when I go to talk to them? Kate really likes you. She talks to you more than she does to anybody, except Hilda."

"Sure, I'll be happy to come along if you want." Laurel got to her feet. "Don't forget to put the toast and coffee on my tab, okay?"

Crystal patted her arm. "My treat. Have a good day."

Laurel smiled, then wandered outside and started walking downtown.

The morning sun lay in dusty pools on the sidewalk and filtered over lawns and hedges. Trees rustled in the gentle breeze and traffic moved slowly along the main street, mostly farm trucks loaded with livestock and supplies.

Laurel avoided the hardware store, going a couple of blocks out of her way to keep from passing its windows. She paused on the corner of Nellie's street, yearning to go in for a cup of coffee and a chat, but deciding to postpone the visit for a few hours.

She turned with sudden resolution and hurried down the street to the post office.

"Hi, Margie," she said, pushing open the door and going inside. The plump red-haired proprietor was behind her postal wicket, sorting mail and tossing it into numbered boxes.

"Hi, Laurie. You want the hotel mail?"

"Not this morning. I have the day off." Laurel took a deep breath. "Actually," she said, "I came down for a haircut, if you've got the time."

Margie brightened and pushed the mail aside, examining her with interest. "I've always got the time for a haircut. It's a lot more fun than sorting mail. Come on."

She emerged through the little wooden gate, pulling on a flowered smock. Laurel followed her past the china kittens and into the beauty parlor. With growing nervousness, she settled into one of the padded chairs, avoiding her reflection in the mirror.

"So," Margie said, tying a plastic shawl around Laurel's neck, "what kind of haircut, dearie? Just a trim?"

Laurel shook her head. "I want a real change," she said recklessly. "I want it chopped off short."

Margie whistled and pulled the dirty shoelace from Laurel's hair. Her eyes narrowed as she lifted the hair and let it fall around Laurel's face, examining it with keen professional interest.

"This here," she announced, "was a pretty good haircut."

Laurel shifted uncomfortably in the chair. "It's all growing out," she said. "It's getting hard to look after while I'm working."

"So you don't want it in a blunt cut again?"

"I don't think so. I'd like something kind of short and layered so I can wash and dry it without fussing. You know?"

Margie nodded, still examining Laurel's hair. "Is the color natural?" she asked.

"Yes, it is." Laurel hesitated. "Except for a few highlight streaks. I always used to keep my hair a couple of shades lighter, but I quit having it tinted more than two years ago and it's mostly grown out now."

Again, Margie gave her a shrewd, appraising glance. "Well, I'll be damned," she murmured, studying the soft mass of hair with its professional cut and highlighting. "I'll be damned. Exactly who are you, Laurie Atkins?"

"I'm a waitress." Laurie met the woman's eyes in the mirror above the chair, holding her gaze intently. "I'm a small-town waitress working for my keep and some pocket change."

Margie continued to study her thoughtfully. "Sure you are," she said at last, giving Laurel a meaningful wink. "And only your hairdresser knows for sure, right?"

Laurel felt another flash of that disturbing sense she'd had the night before while Jonas talked on the phone, a feeling of danger lurking beyond this peaceful sunny place, of other worlds pressing closer.

She shook her head to dispel the feeling and smiled at the other woman. "Yes, but hairdressers know how to keep secrets," she said. "They hear enough of them, after all."

"Now, *that*," Margie said cheerfully, "is the simple truth. You need a shampoo, kid?"

"I washed my hair last night."

"Okay." Margie took a spray bottle and dampened Laurel's hair. Then she picked up her scissors and began to clip. As she worked, the hairdresser chatted about the town, its history and inhabitants, while soft clumps of Laurel's hair drifted to the floor and piled up around the chair.

After the job was finished, Margie surveyed her handiwork with pursed lips and narrowed eyes and pronounced the whole effect a complete success. But Laurel wasn't at all convinced, after a quick glance at her image in the mirror.

She left the beauty parlor and ventured into the street with the stripped and defenseless feeling that often comes with a new haircut. All she wanted to do was hurry back to the hotel and the safety of her room.

But when she passed Baines's General Store, she decided to make a brief stop. She went inside and made her way to the back of the store, to stand in front of the wire rack crowded with Saturday newspapers from various cities.

"Please, please," she whispered aloud, "let there be a *Financial Post*. Even Harold Baines must know there's such a thing as the *Financial Post* . . ."

At last, she found a copy under a messy pile of tabloid newspapers with improbable headlines.

Laurel took her paper to the front where Harold was bent almost double, struggling to install a new tape in one of the computers.

"Damn stupid," he muttered, then stood up and gave Laurel an abashed smile. "Sorry, Miss Atkins. I just can't seem to get this damn . . . this darn thing working."

His eyes widened as he stared at her, then took the paper and her money. Laurel shifted nervously, taken aback by his look of frank admiration.

"Well, well," he murmured. "Now, ain't you the purtiest thing? You had Margie give you a haircut, I guess."

Laurel nodded, wishing a little frantically that she could find a mirror somewhere. The brief glimpse she'd had at Margie's hadn't really revealed much.

He wrapped her newspaper in a white cover sheet and gave her some change, then glared bitterly at the computer again.

"Is it an electronic feed?" Laurel asked.

Harold glanced at her in surprise.

"We used to..." Laurel's cheeks warmed and she shifted awkwardly on her feet. "In a place where I used to work, we...they had some computers that used backup tapes like these. You have to push the reset button if the tape's been rejected, before you can program your machine to accept the new tape."

"Reset button?"

"It should be a little red button on the back near the panel. Here it is."

She pressed the button, Harold struck some keys on the keyboard and the machine began to swallow the roll of tape.

Harold beamed at her as she left. "Thanks a whole bunch, Laurie. And watch out for those Saturday-night cowboys, you hear?" he called jovially as she went through the door. "There'll be a ton of guys chasin' after you when they see how cute you are with that new haircut."

She sat on a bench near the street, paging through the paper, paying only casual attention to the news stories from the fascinating world she'd left behind.

Mergers, hostile takeovers, new corporate alliances, stocks soaring and slipping, stocks splitting two for one... the news was interesting, but had somehow lost its urgency. Here in this sleepy, sun-washed town, the complexities of high finance seemed impossibly removed, as if they were happening on a different planet, or in some other dimension of time.

At last, Laurel reached the classified section and scanned the personal notices hungrily, then stopped.

Her breath caught in her throat and her heart began to pound. It read:

To My Best Girl.
Hope all is well with you and your chickens. Package arrived safely on Monday night. Everybody fine. More good news to follow soon. Love from all.

CHAPTER TEN

PACKAGE ARRIVED SAFELY on Monday night.

Laurel let the newspaper slip from her fingers and rested her head against the back of the bench. The sunlight fell warmly on her face, and soft blooms of color whirled behind her closed eyelids.

That message could only have one interpretation. Laurel had a baby brother or sister. Trust her father, she thought with wry amusement, to forget all the really important details—like whether the baby was a boy or a girl.

Tears filled her eyes and rolled slowly down her cheeks. For perhaps the hundredth time since her arrival in Wolf Hill, Laurel found herself fully, painfully, in the grip of homesickness.

She yearned for all of them. Her father and Marta with their new baby; loyal, funny Dennis and his endless procession of pretty girlfriends; the junior partners in the company and the competitors in the market; all the other people who made her life so interesting . . .

"I want to go home," she whispered aloud, her voice breaking. "Oh, God, I want to go home!"

She glanced around furtively at the empty street, then scrubbed the back of her hand across her eyes and studied the paper again.

"More good news to follow soon," her father's message said.

That, too, could only mean one thing. Laurel's homesickness was suddenly replaced by a surge of optimism. Stewart must be on the verge of proving his innocence. Any day now, there'd be a message telling her the investigation had been dropped and it was safe to come home. Probably it would be in next Saturday's issue of the *Post*.

Laurel felt a rising excitement.

She only had to endure one more week in Wolf Hill. Just seven more days of working in the hotel kitchen. Better, only a few more bouts of sparring with Jonas O'Neal and trying to resist him, when every treacherous part of her body screamed for more kisses, greater intimacy, nearer, nearer...

Laurel ripped out the page containing her father's message and folded it away in her pocket, then bundled the paper into a nearby recycle bin and started back toward the hotel.

But she paused when she reached Nellie's street, then hurried up the walk and knocked on the door.

Fluffy lay on the padded seat of the rocking chair, basking in the sun and regarding Laurel through the window with lofty disinterest. But Nellie, when she appeared in the doorway, was much more welcoming.

"Laurie!" she said, wiping her hands on her gingham apron. "I didn't expect you to drop by so early, dear. Oh, and look at your hair! Aren't you *pretty?*"

"I don't know," Laurel said dryly. "I just got it cut and I can't find a mirror."

Laughing with excitement, Nellie dragged her inside to the little pink bathroom and stood her in front of the mirror.

"Oh, my," Laurel breathed when she finally screwed up the courage to look fully at her own reflection. "My goodness," she said again. "I just...Nellie, I don't know what to say."

Margie had cut Laurel's hair in a fluffy, pixie cut, with long bangs and a shining cap of hair at her crown, softly layered for fullness, trailing into wispy strands around her ears and on the nape of her neck.

Both the style and the cut were gamine, flirtatious and very professional. The combined effect was enormously flattering.

"Oh, *no!*" Laurel wailed, putting her hands up to her cheeks, tugging frantically at the wispy strands of hair. "What am I going to do? I've never looked like this in my life."

Nellie met Laurel's eyes in the mirror, genuinely puzzled. "But...what's the matter, dear? It's so cute. You look wonderful."

"But it's not me. I look sort of like...I don't know. Like Liza Minnelli."

"I know. You look as sweet as a flower," Nellie told her soothingly. "Now stop fretting and come have some tea."

Laurel continued to brood over her reflection.

The woman in the mirror was attractive, all right. Jonas O'Neal would probably find her irresistible. But she looked hardly old enough to be an experienced financial analyst. She'd be completely out of place walking down Wall Street in a three-piece suit, carrying a briefcase full of stock listings and trading options.

"Nobody," she told Nellie grimly, "will take me seriously. I can't possibly do my job with a haircut like this. They'd laugh me off the trading floor."

"What floor?" Nellie asked.

Laurel looked down at the little woman's gentle face and wise blue eyes.

"Maybe it's time for you to tell me," Nellie said gently. "After all, dear, you've been trying to tell me for weeks, one way and another. Haven't you?"

Laurel smiled and hugged her. "You're far too smart for me, Nellie. How about if we go into the kitchen to eat whatever you're baking that smells so wonderful, and I'll make us a big pot of tea. And then I'll tell you a story."

"SO THAT'S WHY I came here," Laurel concluded, and selected another walnut cookie.

"Because you needed to hide, and some taxicab driver said a small town would be a good place?"

"That's right. And I'd just finished reading Ellen's diary, so I thought of Wolf Hill."

"My goodness." Nellie looked at her with wondering eyes. "Isn't life the strangest thing?"

Laurel smiled. "It's pretty strange, all right. If I hadn't come here, I never would have met you, Nellie. And now you're my best friend."

Nellie's cheeks turned pink. "Oh, pooh," she scoffed. "Back in the city, you must have lots of friends."

"Not really. I was...I'm busy all the time at my job, you know. I hardly ever go out anywhere, and lots of times I work twelve, fourteen hours a day."

"Why?" Nellie asked.

Laurel looked at her in surprise. "Just to...I don't know," she said. "Just to keep ahead of things, I guess. To keep from getting buried."

Nellie sniffed. "Sounds to me," she announced, "like it's a lot nicer to work in the hotel kitchen. No wonder you looked like a starved kitten when you first got here."

"You think so, Nellie? You really think I look better now?"

"Oh, much better," Nellie said. "You've had some fresh air and some good food, and a break from all that pressure. It shows, dear. It really does. You can't see how you've changed, but I can."

Laurel was silent, stirring her tea thoughtfully.

"Of course," Nellie went on, "good food and a cute haircut, those aren't the only reasons you've got stars in your eyes."

"What do you mean?"

Nellie looked at her steadily. "You know what I mean."

Laurel's cheeks warmed. "You're getting scary, Nellie. You can practically read my mind."

"I have eyes in my head," Nellie said serenely. "So," she added, changing the subject, "do you think your daddy's got this whole big mess straightened out now?"

"I'm sure of it. His message said good news would be coming soon."

Nellie shook her head. "All those weeks working so hard in that kitchen. Imagine a girl doing that for her father."

"I had no choice," Laurel said simply. "He's the nicest man in the world, Nellie. And he's completely innocent."

"Then why are you hiding?"

"I told you," Laurel said. "If I had to go before the committee and tell what I know under oath, my testimony would incriminate him."

"Why? I thought you said he didn't do anything wrong."

"He didn't." Laurel took a deep breath, reminding herself that Nellie was very old, and not accustomed to business matters. "But the orders he placed would look illegal to an investigating committee unless they understood that he'd done it on assurances from the government that he'd be protected."

"I see." Nellie added more boiling water to the teapot. "You and Kate Cameron," she murmured. "Both the same."

"Why?" Laurel asked, startled.

"Doing so much for your parents. You're out here on the prairie plucking chickens to protect your father, and poor Kate's been going through hell to keep from hurting her mother's feelings over that baby. Such loving daughters." Nellie gazed out the window at the pair of robins nesting in her apple tree. Her face was sad, her eyes faraway.

Laurel thought about Nellie's own daughter and granddaughter who lived so far away, and felt a wrench of sympathy. "Nellie," she said gently, "we'll still see each other, you know. I'll call all the time, and come out here to see you whenever I feel the need for a holiday and some fussing."

Nellie turned to smile at her. "No, you won't. You'll forget all about me when you get back to that high-powered job," she said. "But that's all right. Nobody can ever take away my memories."

"Oh, Nellie . . ." Laurel got up and hugged the little woman, holding her tenderly. "You're such a sweetheart. I'll never, never forget you. And you know what?" she added.

"What?"

"As soon as I get back to Vancouver, I'm going to make arrangements for you to have your trip to the city. You'll have a new dress and a lovely meal at a waterfront restaurant, and then we'll go to the theater. In a limousine," Laurel added. "You'll be just like visiting royalty."

Nellie sat down at the table and dropped her hands into her lap. "If something like that ever happened to me," she said simply, "I would feel like a princess, myself. Wouldn't that be wonderful?"

Laurel's eyes stung with tears. "You're wonderful, Nellie," she whispered. "And you're going to have your chance to be a princess, I promise."

Nellie collected herself and felt the sides of the teapot. "It's still nice and warm," she said briskly. "Stop talking nonsense and have another cookie. I baked them just for you."

LATER THAT EVENING, Laurel sat on the bench next to Jonas with a group of children huddled tensely around them.

"Okay," Jonas was saying. "This is the last inning, and we're up by two runs. We need to concentrate, guys. If we can hold them off while they're batting, we'll win the game. Laurie and I want to see some nice crisp fielding out there. Concentrate hard, look out for cactus and don't play with the gophers. Okay?"

They nodded solemnly, gazing up at him with eyes full of hero worship.

"Okay," Jonas said. "Hit the field and catch some fly balls. Let's get these guys out. Melanie, is your arm getting tired?"

Melanie shook her head.

"Good girl. Go out there and show 'em your best stuff."

Melanie trotted out to the pitcher's mound while Laurel stole a sidelong glance at Jonas. He looked almost irresistibly handsome in his yellow T-shirt. She found herself staring at his mouth and turned away quickly.

"Jonas," she murmured as the first batter stepped to the plate.

"What?" he asked, then shouted, "Tyler! Play this guy a little deeper. Back toward the fence."

"That phone call last night," Laurel said awkwardly. "When we were..."

"What about it?" he asked when she fell silent, her cheeks flaming.

"Who was it?"

He turned to her, lifting an eyebrow. "Why do you ask?"

"I don't know. I just... I sort of had the impression maybe you were... talking about me," she concluded lamely.

He grinned. "There are a few brief moments in my life, you know," he told her, "when I'm actually concerned with things other than you."

"Don't be like that," Laurel said, her embarrassment giving way to a surge of annoyance. "You know what I mean."

The batter got a walk and trotted to first base. Melanie scowled and stalked down to consult with the catcher. She took her position again and fired three strikes in rapid succession, then caught the runner leading off. Cheers went up in the outfield, and Jonas got to his feet, shouting encouragement.

"Two down," he called. "One more to go. Let's stay awake, everybody! Tyler, be on the lookout for a long ball."

The batter, a burly child who was taller and heavier than his teammates, strolled to the plate and leered at Melanie.

"Come on," he said. "Throw me a nice one, little girl. Give me one I can hit over the fence."

Melanie lobbed the pitch, a tight overhand slider that streaked with deadly accuracy toward the center of the plate. The boy swung and caught the ball full, lifting it high in the air.

Laurel watched as the ball arced and drifted down toward Tyler who stood frozen near the barbed-wire fence in left field, his glove outstretched.

"Catch it, Tyler!" she called, leaping to her feet along with the rest of the team. "Don't take your eyes off it!"

Tyler emerged from his trance and stumbled to his right, still holding his glove out rigidly. Laurel ached for the child, seeing the tension in his thin shoulders, the panic in his face.

The ball dropped closer, closer, and finally landed in his glove. Tyler looked down at it in blank astonishment, then started running toward the infield, his face breaking into a joyful grin.

The team shouted and Jonas turned to Laurel, hugging her with delight.

She nestled against him, silenced by a flood of emotion, loving the feel of his arms around her, his cheek pressed close to hers . . .

Abruptly, she pushed him away and knelt to congratulate the smaller team members while the opposing players collected their equipment and gathered to give the winners a good-natured cheer.

After the infield was cleaned up and the balls and bats packed away, Jonas approached her. "Come on, Laurie. I'm taking the team out for hamburgers to celebrate our first win."

Laurel shook her head, avoiding his eyes. "Not me, thanks. I'll just…I think I'll go home, Jonas. I still have to do my laundry tonight."

He looked at her keenly, but didn't argue. Laurel watched while he and the children set off toward town, still shouting with triumph and clapping Tyler on the shoulders.

"Laurel!" Jonas called.

"What?"

"Great haircut!" he said with a grin, then strode off into the sunset with his rowdy team. Soon, the last of them vanished and she was alone.

HOURS LATER, Laurel lay in bed trying to read. But the print kept blurring in front of her eyes, replaced by images of fields lit with gold by the fading sun and laughing children's faces, of her father and his new baby and the city life that seemed so far away.

She got up and wandered over to the window, standing in her nightgown and looking out at the moonlit street below. Faint sounds of merriment indicated that the Saturday-night darts tournament was apparently still going full swing in the hotel bar. But the rest of the town was empty and silent in the midnight calm. Even the wind seemed to have stilled.

Laurel smiled absently, thinking how surprised and scornful she would have been two months ago if somebody had told her she'd actually miss this place when she left. She recalled the grinding work of those first weeks in the hotel kitchen, and how lonely she'd felt all the time.

Now, except for an occasional bout of homesickness, like the one she'd suffered this morning after reading her father's message in the paper, she felt very much at home in Wolf Hill.

Partly it was because of the people, especially Nellie.

She looked up at the etching of stars on the soft black canvas of the sky, thinking about Nellie's trip to the city, and how much fun it was going to be to show her a wonderful time.

But Laurel had made other friends, too, people she was going to miss a great deal when she left. Crystal and Hilda, Kate with her baby, Luther and his model airplanes, the baseball team, Jonas....

Laurel rested her forehead against the cool glass, hastily pulling her thoughts away from that dangerous topic.

She was going to miss the prairie, too. There was something wonderful about the vastness of this land, the clean sweep of sky and grass, the breathtaking sunsets and the fresh sweetness of early mornings filled with meadowlark song.

A knock sounded on the door, startling her.

She turned and frowned, wondering if she'd imagined the noise. It was almost midnight, and nobody ever came to her door at night.

But the knock sounded again. Laurel moved across the room and looked through the peephole, her body suddenly rigid with alarm. Jonas O'Neal stood in the hallway, balancing a cardboard box under one arm.

Laurel opened the door and clutched the door frame, looking at him in astonishment.

"Jonas!" she said. "What are you...why on earth are you here?"

He reached into the box to remove a bottle of champagne and waved it at her. "A little celebration," he announced. "Our first win. Congratulations, coach."

He leaned forward and kissed her cheek, then stepped past her into the room, setting his box carefully on the dresser before he closed and locked the door.

Laurel hugged her arms, uncomfortably aware of her bare shoulders and breasts under the silky fabric of her nightgown. She watched as Jonas took out a couple of crystal goblets, setting them on the dresser with a flourish.

"You're drunk," she said coldly.

He shook his head, looking boyish and sincere. "Absolutely not. I had one beer with Luther, more than an hour ago."

"Go away," she said. "I mean it. I want you to leave right now."

"Or else what?"

"Or else I'll call the front desk and have you thrown out."

"There's nobody at the front desk." Jonas unwound the wire cage on his bottle and removed the plastic cork, trapping it skillfully in his hand. "Luther's still down in the bar playing darts. We've been celebrating together."

She picked up her terry-cloth robe, belting it firmly around her waist.

"A pity," he murmured sadly. "Such a beautiful body, and she covers it up."

"Jonas, I mean it. If you're not drunk, you're certainly behaving strangely, and I want you to leave."

He poured champagne into both glasses and offered her one with a courtly bow, ignoring her words. "To the team," he said.

She glared at him, then accepted the glass and took a reluctant sip.

"You know, maybe I should have gotten a little drunk," he told her.

"Why?"

"It probably would have helped a bit. Given me some Dutch courage."

"What do you mean?" she asked suspiciously.

"You're a formidable woman, sweetheart. When a man's planning to go to bed with a woman like you, he needs all the courage he can find."

Laurel set her glass on the dresser and tugged at the belt of her robe. "Jonas," she began, "I really don't think—"

"That's a terrific haircut," he said huskily. "You look so adorable."

"Jonas..."

He moved toward her, his eyes dark with purpose, and grasped her shoulders, looking down at her intently. Then he drew her into his arms and kissed her, his mouth moving hungrily on hers. Laurel found herself responding, yielding to him, pressing closer. He smelled faintly of smoke from the bar, along with the scent of clean masculinity that she always associated with him.

And his kisses were so sweet. In spite of her fears and doubts, her cautious reservations about the man, there was no denying that she loved the feel of him in her arms.

"I'm going to take you to bed tonight," he murmured against her cheek. "If you don't want me, you'd better tell me now while I can still leave."

"Will you go away if I ask you to?"

He kissed her again, then cuddled her in his arms. "Yes," he said quietly. "I will. Do you want me to leave, sweetheart?"

Laurel hesitated. If she said the word, he'd leave. She'd go back to the city with her life unchanged, free of troubling memories and regrets.

But then she'd never know what it would have been like to make love to him...

''Laurel?'' he whispered, running his hands over her body, tugging gently at the belt on her robe.

She shook her head and gave him a rueful smile, then reached up to undo his shirt buttons.

CHAPTER ELEVEN

JONAS BRUSHED her hands away and undressed her slowly, making a game of it. Occasionally, he paused to sip from the champagne glass, then offered it to her. Laurel was surprised by his gentle playfulness, and flattered by his awe as he finally stood gazing at her naked body.

"Beautiful," he murmured, moving his hands gently over her breasts and down to her waist, reaching up to cup her face and touch her hair. "You're such a beautiful woman."

Laurel trembled at his touch, feeling warmed and almost shy when he looked at her. Then she turned away and slipped into her bed.

"Come on," she whispered. "Come and hold me. I'm cold."

Jonas drained the wineglass and switched off the light. In the moonlit darkness, she could see his dim shape as he stripped off his clothes and joined her in bed under the hand-stitched quilt, reaching out to draw her close.

Laurel lay in his arms, delighting in the feel of his body. His naked maleness, warm and silky, hard with muscle and sinew, filled the bed.

"You feel so good," she said, running her hands over his shoulders.

He leaned above her, grinning. "How do you know how I'm feeling?"

She smiled and hugged him, then drew away in surprise and sat up, looking down at him while he reached to caress her breasts.

"What's this?" she asked.

"That's my stomach. And this..." He stroked her abdomen. "This is yours. And a lovely little tummy it is, too."

"Jonas, you know what I mean."

"See?" he went on, his voice light and teasing. "We have something in common, after all. We both have tummies."

"Come on, be serious," she said, running exploratory fingers across his waist. "I'm talking about this. What is it?"

"It's a scar."

She shivered, touching the hard ridges of skin. "What happened?"

"I had a little accident."

Laurel stared at his shadowed face. "What kind of accident leaves a scar like that?"

He pulled her down into his arms and kissed her neck, then trailed his lips onto her breast.

"Jonas," she said, drawing away, "what made that scar?"

"In medical terms, it's referred to as an exit wound," he said briefly.

"An *exit* wound? What's that?"

"It's what a bullet does to you when it leaves your body." Jonas rolled closer to her, turning on his side. "Feel this."

He directed her fingers to a small indentation low down on his back, about the size of a coin. Laurel touched it gingerly.

"That's the entry wound," he said. "A much nicer scar."

She leaned back on the pillow and looked up at him in horror. His hard features were etched with silver in the moonlight, and his expression was impossible to read.

"You mean, a bullet went right through your body?" she asked. "Somebody shot you in the back, and it came out here and didn't kill you?"

Again she touched the ridged mass on his abdomen.

"Guys like me are hard to kill," he said in that same casual tone. "But it made quite a mess, didn't it?"

"Tell me, Jonas O'Neal," she whispered. "Who are you?"

He chuckled and pulled her into his arms again. "I guess I could ask you the same question, couldn't I, darling? But," he added, nuzzling her cheek, "I don't want to ask any questions tonight, and I don't want to answer them, either. I'm just a poor guy who's too much in love to think straight, that's all. Come here and kiss me again."

Laurel moved closer to him and gave herself to his embrace, wondering if she'd imagined those final words.

The man in her arms was a mystery, a loner scarred by battles that she couldn't even imagine. And yet he was kissing her and talking about being in love.

His hands began to caress her, and soon her worry and speculation vanished in a tide of feeling so powerful, she lost all awareness of where she was and what she was doing. She was nothing but a bundle of sensation, a hungry ache that yearned to be soothed and filled.

"Jonas," she breathed, her lips moving on his shoulder as she arched against his hand. "Oh, that feels good. Don't ever stop."

He laughed softly, his hand drifting lower. "You like this?"

She kissed his lips and touched him with lingering passion, stroking his powerful chest and shoulders. "Yes, I like it."

"How about this?"

"Oh, Jonas..."

He laughed softly. "And I always thought you were cold."

"I'm not cold," she murmured. "I'm just really careful."

"You call this being careful, honey?"

Laurel nestled close to him, moving luxuriously in his arms. "It's so hard to be careful with a man like you," she said. "You seem to bring out the worst in me."

"Then I'm a lucky guy. I guess I'll have to be careful for both of us, right?"

"I think you probably will."

"Okay. Now stop talking and concentrate. I'm making love to you, and I want you to pay attention."

"I never thought...." She gasped as he moved above her. He lowered himself gently, settling his body into hers and filling all the hollow, aching places with richness and warmth.

"Is that all right?" he whispered in her ear. "Am I hurting you?"

"It's wonderful, Jonas. It feels absolutely wonderful."

"So do you." He moved in her body and she felt her passion rise to meet him, carrying her on a flood of emotion.

"Oh," she whispered, lost in sensation. "Oh, Jonas..."

A shuddering release swept over her, flooding her mind and body with molten sunshine. She moaned and bit his shoulder, clutching him in her arms.

"Oh, my goodness," she said when she was able to speak again. "That was so incredible."

She opened her eyes to see him leaning above her, smiling down at her.

Immediately, Laurel felt a stab of concern. "Are you...was it all right?" she asked cautiously. "You look so...so calm."

He chuckled and gripped her in his arms. "I plan to stay calm for quite a while longer, darling," he whispered. "I want to see that happening to you again before we're done."

"Oh." She sighed, closing her eyes. "Oh, my. I'm in heaven." She heard his delighted laugh, and smiled against his shoulder as he began to move gently again, building the rhythm that would carry her off into that rich golden flood.

Suddenly, Laurel remembered what she wanted to tell him.

"I never thought..."

"What, sweetheart?" he murmured, his face growing hard and intent as his own pleasure mounted.

"That you'd be so much fun," she whispered, and heard his soft chuckle from a distance as the warm tide of sunshine washed through her body once more.

THEY SAT against the mound of pillows, wrapped together in a careless tangle of arms and legs, sipping from their wineglasses and smiling mistily at each other in the glow of the chintz-covered lamp.

"To you," Jonas said, toasting her with his glass. "The most beautiful woman in the world."

She returned the gesture. "And you. The best lover I've ever met."

"Really?" he asked with a placid grin. "I'm the very best?"

She glanced at him severely. "Don't flatter yourself. I'm not all that experienced."

"What can I say?" He poured more champagne into her glass. "We all have our talents. I was obviously born to be your lover, because I'm so good at it."

"Jonas," she said, toying with the mat of curly hair on his chest. Unconsciously, her hand strayed lower to touch the ridge of scar tissue at his waist.

"Hmm?" he asked, bending to kiss her tousled hair. "Hey, quit tickling, woman, or I'll be forced to retaliate."

"What are you really doing in Wolf Hill?"

Laurel thought she felt a brief tension in his body, but his voice was casual.

"Working in the hardware store," he said. "Coaching baseball. Following you around like a lovesick puppy. What else would I be doing?"

"I don't know. It seems as if you..."

"What?"

"Don't belong," Laurel said, turning away so he wouldn't see her face. "It seems like a strange place for you to be."

"How about you?" he asked, giving her a thoughtful glance. "You may be able to fool almost everybody in this town, but Nellie and I knew you were a princess before we even met you."

"I'm not a princess," Laurel said quietly.

"So what are you?"

"I'm an investment broker."

He shouted with laughter and looked down at her, his eyebrows raised. "No kidding? I think I'd rather have a princess."

"I'm telling the truth, Jonas," she told him.

Suddenly, she was anxious to end all the lies and pretense. She'd told Nellie about herself, and now she wanted Jonas to know the whole story, too.

"Hey, you're not kidding, are you?" He leaned closer to peer at her face in the dim light. "So what's going on, honey?"

For the second time that day, Laurel found herself recounting the saga of her flight to Wolf Hill, including her father's well-meaning but disastrous financial dealings, the New York cabdriver's advice, her lonely bus trip to the prairie and the last straw—the disappearance of her money.

When she was finished, Laurel glanced up at him timidly, then turned away and took a hasty sip from her glass.

"Say something," she told him at last, hugging a pillow in her arms.

If she'd retained any lingering suspicions about Jonas O'Neal and his knowledge of her former life, they were dispelled forever by his expression.

The man was clearly astounded by her story, and visibly upset. He leaned back against the headboard, holding the wineglass forgotten in his hand as he stared at the opposite wall.

"Jonas," she said nervously.

He shook his head in wonder. "That's a truly incredible story, honey. Just amazing." He turned to look at her. "You're a poor little rich girl, out here plucking chickens so you won't have to testify against your father?"

Laurel nodded. "At first," she confessed, giving him a rueful smile, "I thought maybe you were an undercover policeman, following me."

"Me?" he asked. "Why?"

"I don't know. I guess I was just paranoid. I felt so out of place and conspicuous."

"But now you don't?"

Laurel shook her head. "I'm not afraid anymore. In fact, it's really surprising how comfortable this place is starting to feel. I've never had much to do with small-town life, you know. I'm actually enjoying the experience."

"Even your job?"

"Well, maybe not the job. After all, I'm trained and licensed in fairly complex financial matters. I'd rather be handling the hotel books and investments than washing the dishes. But I like the kids and their ball games, and visiting with Nellie, and getting my hair cut in the post office..."

"And going to bed with me," he supplied tranquilly, leaning over to kiss her.

"And going to bed with you," Laurel agreed. Her heart twisted with sudden pain. "I'm really going to miss everybody when I leave," she murmured. "Especially Nellie and you."

"Well, I don't know about Nellie, but maybe I'll just keep following you."

Laurel gave him a cautious glance. "Back to the city, you mean?"

"Maybe. Tell me, do they have any hardware stores in Vancouver?"

He drew her into his arms. Laurel nestled against him, sighing with pleasure. "I'm sure they do," she whispered. "But what's going to happen to our team? Who'll finish the season, if we both go away in a couple of weeks?"

He drew away and looked down at her. "You think you'll be going away that soon?"

She told him about her arrangement with her father to receive messages from the city, and the announcement she'd seen in the newspaper that morning.

"I'm sure he's close to having it resolved," she said. "Dad's never lied to me, Jonas. He said he'd have good news soon, so I expect to be going home before very long."

"I see. Are you happy about that?"

Laurel nodded. "In a way, I guess. I'm anxious to see the new baby, and find out what's been happening in the office, and talk to Dennis . . ."

He stiffened and drew away. "Who's Dennis?"

"He's my secretary. One of the nicest men in the whole world, along with you and my father." She leaned over and kissed him. "Jonas O'Neal," she said with delight, "I do believe you're jealous."

"Damn right I'm jealous. When a man finds a treasure like you, he's not all that anxious to share." Jonas pulled her down under the covers and began to kiss her with lusty energy, making her giggle.

But soon her giggles faded into silence, and her passion began to rise again. The lamp cast a soft, multi-colored glow over the room, and the prairie wind began to howl mournfully around the eaves of the old building.

But the man and woman in the bed weren't aware of their surroundings. Like all lovers since the beginning of time, they were oblivious to everything but each other, and the warm secret world that enclosed them.

"DID YOU clean this chicken?" Jonas asked lazily.

Laurel rolled onto her elbow and looked at the sandwich he held. "Probably," she said after a moment's thought. "I seem to be the designated chicken plucker in that kitchen."

He chuckled and went on eating. Laurel lay back on the blanket with a smile and raised an arm to shield her eyes from the sun.

It was Sunday afternoon, the day after their first lovemaking, and they were having a picnic on a sheltered, grassy slope near the creek. In fact, they'd hardly been apart since his arrival in her room, except for an hour or so while he hurried over to his apartment above the hardware store to change clothes and shave.

Even that hour had seemed impossibly long and lonely. Laurel could hardly bear to be separated from him. She loved to look at his face, touch him, listen to his voice...

"I can't believe how much I'm enjoying this." She sighed drowsily with pleasure as the sun poured warm showers of gold onto her closed eyelids.

He rolled nearer and kissed her. "Enjoying what?"

Laurel waved her arm. "The day. The outdoors. Being with you."

"About time you threw that last part in," he said dryly, then kissed her again and stretched out next to her. He took her hand tenderly and they lay side by side, wrapped in perfect contentment.

"I can't recall when I've ever felt so comfortable with anybody," she murmured. "It's heaven."

He smiled and kissed her again. "Want anything?"

"Like what?"

"A drink, maybe another sandwich? Some watermelon or something?"

She grinned. "Well...maybe something."

Jonas gave a sigh of mock weariness. "The woman is insatiable. I'm going to waste away to a shadow."

"Oh, sure," she scoffed. "I can tell how reluctant you are."

There was a brief silence while he lay with his eyes closed and she traced the strong line of his nose and chin, the softness of his mouth.

"Jonas," she began shyly.

"Hmm?"

"Has it ever been like this for you? I'm not talking about the sex," she said, "even though it's wonderful. I mean the friendship. Have you ever known anybody you could talk to like this?"

He turned and looked at her thoughtfully. "I don't think so. It seems so easy for us to talk, and that's not the usual thing for me. Normally, I'm a pretty quiet, private kind of guy."

"Why is this so different?"

Jonas stroked her arm, then lifted her hand to kiss her fingers. "I think it's because we agree about so many things," he said at last. "We share a lot of the same values and opinions. I've never felt so compatible with anybody."

"And safe," Laurel murmured.

"What's that, sweetheart?"

"I feel so safe with you, Jonas. I know you'll never hurt me or take advantage of me. It's wonderful to be able to trust somebody that way."

His hand fell away and he stared up at the sky. Laurel sensed a sudden tension in his long body.

"Jonas?" she asked. "Is something wrong?"

He gazed at her, his eyes bright with a teasing glint. "I was just thinking," he said lightly, "that you probably wouldn't trust me so much if you knew what was on my mind right now."

"Really? What's on your mind?"

"I'll give you a hint." He stroked her midriff with the flat of his hand, then leaned closer to whisper while his fingers began to creep higher, toward her breasts. "It isn't chicken sandwiches."

She laughed and moved into his arms, dazzled by the sun and the kisses that took her breath away.

"LAURIE? Are you busy?"

Laurel looked up from a table filled with piles of silverware waiting to be polished. She pushed the hair back from her forehead with a blackened hand, then smiled at Crystal who stood in the doorway, nervously wringing her hands in her apron.

It was Monday morning, in the brief lull between the breakfast crowd and the preparation of lunch plates. Laurel glanced down at the table and sighed.

"Nothing that can't keep," she said. "I'm sure this stuff isn't going anywhere. Are you ready to talk to Kate?"

Crystal nodded. "She and Hilda are in the office going over the coffee-shop accounts. I think it's probably a good time."

"Okay. Let me wash my hands and I'll be right with you."

Crystal leaned against the big refrigerator, while Laurel scrubbed her hands vigorously at the sink, then dried them on a gingham towel and rubbed them with lotion.

"My hands will never be the same again," she muttered gloomily, looking at her reddened, swollen fingers. "It'll take a whole year even to get them looking decent."

Crystal looked puzzled.

"Imagine," Laurel said lightly. "A dishwasher who's vain about her hands. Pretty silly, right, Crystal?"

Crystal gave her a nervous grimace that was probably intended to be a smile. Laurel paused next to the girl, dropping an arm around her shoulders.

"Buck up, kid," she whispered. "They can't hurt you. You only have to tell the truth."

"But I really need this job, Laurie. What if they fire me?"

"They won't fire you."

"But what if they do?" Crystal insisted. "I can't sleep at night, worrying what I'll do with a baby if I can't find another job."

Laurel drew away and looked at her. "Let's not assume the worst." She took Crystal's arm and held it in a comforting grip as they crossed the lobby and knocked on the manager's door.

"Come in," Hilda called.

The two women stepped inside and found Hilda alone, sitting on the near side of the desk with a pile of receipts and account books in front of her.

"Oh," Crystal said in disappointment, looking at the vacant chair across the desk. "I was hoping to talk with Kate, too. Where is she?"

"Back in a minute," Hilda said. "She just went upstairs to get the baby. She's almost ready to leave for home."

"Is it all right if we wait?"

Hilda gave them a curious glance, then nodded, her face inscrutable. She watched as they seated themselves in the hard-backed wooden chairs.

"Do either of you girls remember," she said after a moment, "which supplier we got that last shipment of napkins from?"

"Calgary Paper and Party," Crystal said promptly.

"You're sure?" Hilda frowned at the books. "How can you remember so clear?"

"The driver's cousin is a friend of mine," Crystal said. "He's really cute. The cousin, I mean, not the driver. *He's* old and potbellied."

Hilda grinned. "Okay, then have look at this invoice. What do you think we ordered from . . ."

Laurel sat with her hands folded quietly in her lap, enjoying this unexpected break from her morning routine. Beyond the mullioned window, the scent from Kate's little flower and herb garden wafted inside on the spring air, and there was a drowsy murmur of bees interspersed with bird song. Closing her eyes, she let her mind drift back to the picnic with Jonas. She thought of his wide mouth with its finely etched upper curve and the soft fullness of his lower lip. And his long dark eyelashes, so surprising against the hard blunt lines of his face. And his hands . . .

Laurel shivered and moved awkwardly in her chair, overcome by a sudden flood of sexual longing. She could hardly keep from moaning aloud.

Her need for the man was so intense, it caused an actual physical pain. She glanced restlessly at her watch, calculating how many hours would have to pass before she could finish work, change out of her workclothes and run across town to his little apartment.

She pictured herself climbing the stairs with Blackie at her heels, knocking on the door, waiting. Jonas would open the door and see her there, and then he'd say...

"What's going on? Is this a staff meeting or something?"

Laurel shook herself abruptly from her reverie, looking up to find Kate standing in the doorway.

"We... I just wanted to—" Crystal broke off nervously.

"Where's the baby?" Hilda asked.

Kate smiled. "Mom's taken him out in the stroller. I told her I wanted him kept awake this morning so he'd have a nice long nap after we went home."

Hilda looked up in surprise. "I was right there when you told Mamie that. She said she wanted to take him up to her room and put him down for a nap. She was practically insisting on it."

"I know. But she changed her mind," Kate said with another tranquil smile, moving over to her desk.

"You're up to something," Hilda said suspiciously. "I can always tell when you get that smug look."

Laurel and Kate exchanged a humorous glance. "I just decided it was time for me to take a really firm line with my mother," Kate said. "After all, Nathan and I are entitled to raise our baby the way we want to, right?

So last night, I had a little talk with my mother about things."

"Well, glory be," Hilda muttered. "How did Mamie take it?"

"She was pretty upset at first," Kate said, her smile fading. "But then, after we talked some more, she realized she's been awfully pushy about the baby and she needs to lighten up. As a matter of fact, Tom, my stepfather, is going to be in Paris later this month for his last furlough before the end of his mission, so Mom's flying out to spend a few weeks with him in Europe, then heading back to Vancouver to get their condo ready. She'll be leaving next week."

"And no hard feelings?" Hilda asked.

"None at all." Laurel and Kate exchanged another warm glance. "It feels wonderful. I should have done it months ago," Kate said.

"Well, well," Hilda murmured, smiling. "Good for you, honey. I'm real glad to hear it."

"Thanks to Laurie. She was my inspiration." Kate moved some papers around on her desk and assumed a businesslike air. "Now, can somebody remind me why I called this meeting?"

"I called it, sort of," Crystal murmured, gazing down at her hands, then raising her eyes bravely to look at Kate and Hilda. "I wanted to talk to both of you."

"What about, Crystal?"

"Well," Crystal began, taking a deep breath, "first, I want to apologize for the way I've acted the last couple of months, missing so much work and not doing my part. It wasn't fair to Laurie, because she had to do most of the work and she never complained."

The girl paused to give Laurel a shy, grateful smile, then clenched her hands into fists and went on.

"The fact is," she said, "I'm . . . pregnant, and I had a pretty bad case of morning sickness, but I'm better now."

Hilda nodded shrewdly. Laurel glanced from the cook's face to the hotel owner's, and realized that neither of them were surprised.

"Crystal wants to keep on working," Laurel said, "but she'll need a better job when the baby comes."

"What would you like to do, Crystal?" Kate asked quietly. "Can we help?"

Now that the agony of the announcement was over, Crystal relaxed and brightened, and began to talk more easily, outlining her dreams and plans. She was as beautiful as ever, with her glorious red hair and creamy skin. But now, Laurel thought, with the added glow of her pregnancy, the girl looked really spectacular.

Hilda and Kate were soon absorbed in a discussion of Crystal's future, searching their minds for contacts they might have in the city who could help her get established and obtain some training in the medical field while caring for her baby.

I'm a contact! Laurel wanted to tell them. I'll look after her, and she can stay with me in my condo. I have all kinds of room, and nobody lives there but me . . .

But it wasn't yet time to reveal those things. As soon as Laurel heard from her father, she'd be able to tell them exactly who she was, and that she was probably in a position to help Crystal get established in her new life.

For now, she needed to keep her secret a while longer.

Besides, she could hardly think beyond the coming evening, when she'd hurry through the sunset town to that apartment above the hardware store where Jonas would be waiting . . .

While Laurel daydreamed, the other women kept talking, finally agreeing that Crystal could keep her job as long as she found the work comfortable, and that in the meantime, everybody would put their best efforts into finding something more promising for her.

When they finally left the office, the girl was almost walking on air, so happy and relieved that her face shone.

"Thanks, Laurie," she whispered. "Thanks a million."

But Laurel was lost in her dreams again, and she could only smile absently as she drifted back to the dirty silverware.

As soon as the supper rush was over and the dishes were done, Laurel ran upstairs to tidy her hair and change into clean blue jeans.

She stood for a moment in the little flowered bathroom and gazed at her reflection in the mirror. The woman in front of her was a person she hardly recognized, as wide-eyed and glowing with excitement as a young girl.

"Like a kid on her first date," she said aloud, giving herself a gentle, mocking smile. "What on earth is happening to you?"

I'm falling in love, a voice whispered inside her mind. It's finally happening.

Laurel shook her head and turned away, suddenly distressed by that starry-eyed image. She grabbed her jacket from the door hook, picked up her knitting bag and let herself out into the hall, then ran lightly down the hotel stairs and out into the dusky twilight.

She could see the brick hardware store at the end of the street. Laurel looked up eagerly at its bulk against the sky as she drew nearer, but none of the lights were on in the little apartment on the second floor.

She felt a quick stab of disappointment, then wondered if Jonas was up there in the dark, waiting for her in the quiet, lilac-scented interior. She quickened her steps, running around to the backyard where Blackie sat by his water dish, looking disconsolate.

The dog's shaggy black ears perked up, and his long plume of a tail began to thump rhythmically on the grass as Laurel approached.

"Hi, boy," she said, bending to pat him. "How are you?"

He rolled his eyes eloquently and panted, showing all his teeth and the pinkish-gray interior of his mouth.

"Where's the boss?" she asked, running some water from the tap into his battered tin bowl. "Why hasn't he been looking after you?"

Blackie slurped from the dish, his tail rotating frantically with happiness. Laurel watched him for a moment, then began to climb the stairs.

She knocked on the door and waited, her heart pounding with excitement. After a brief interval, she knocked again and edged the door open.

"Jonas?" she called softly. "Jonas, are you in here? It's me."

But his room was silent and empty. Laurel paused uncertainly for a moment, then stepped inside and closed the door behind her. She flipped the light switch and stood on the threadbare carpet, wondering what to do. After a moment, she caught sight of a square of white paper lying neatly on the table, and moved nearer to read it.

Hi, coach,

Sorry, but I had to go out of town to make a rush delivery of some spraying equipment. Back as soon as I can. Relax and make yourself comfortable. There's fruit in the fridge.

Love,
Jonas

P.S. Give Blackie some water if he looks anxious, okay? Seems like that dog is always thirsty.

Love, Jonas.

Laurel looked at those words wedged in with such apparent casualness between the fruit and the dog. This situation was developing into something a lot more serious than a holiday romance. She was almost afraid to analyze her tumult of feelings.

Laurel touched the note, smiling at the blunt, vigorous strokes of his pen. She could have guessed his handwriting would look like this. Everything about the man radiated such strength and confidence.

Laurel lifted the paper and glanced furtively over her shoulder, then kissed the place where he'd signed his name, feeling more than ever like a lovestruck adolescent.

She wandered into the center of the room and settled herself on the little plaid couch, took her knitting from the bag and tried to concentrate.

"Knit one, slip one, pass slip stitch over," she muttered, glaring at the pattern. "I'm *doing* that. So why do I keep getting all these little holes?"

She considered running down the street to ask Nellie, but decided against it. Jonas might come back any time, and she wanted to be here when he arrived.

Finally, Laurel put the knitting aside, got up and wandered around the room, looking for something to give her a key to this enigmatic man she'd fallen in love with. But the place was as bare and impersonal as a cheap hotel room.

Laurel was strongly tempted to peek into drawers and cupboards, but honor forbade such an invasion of privacy. She hated having people snoop into her belongings, so she couldn't let herself do the same thing to anybody else, even though her curiosity about the private life of Jonas O'Neal was becoming almost unbearable.

She ventured into the bathroom and looked around. The place was neat and clean, not at all like the bachelor squalor she'd occasionally witnessed in other men's bathrooms. A couple of threadbare green towels hung over the rod, and a box of tissues sat on a rickety shelf under the mirror. Nothing of a personal nature was in evidence anywhere, except for a safety razor, a shaving brush in a porcelain cup and a can of shaving cream set out with geometric precision on the counter near the sink.

Laurel touched the gleaming wooden handle of the shaving brush, then looked at the medicine cabinet, fighting the urge to open the mirrored door and peer inside.

At last, she went back to the other room and opened the door of the fridge. By now, she wasn't surprised to see how tidy the interior was, but she hadn't expected it to be so well-stocked. Jonas had eggs, cold cuts, a few blocks of cheese, three bottles of salad dressing and quite a lot of fresh produce, along with some cuts of meat that showed he was cooking good meals for himself.

A bottle of imported white wine lay on its side near the back of the top shelf. Laurel smiled, thinking that Jonas was clearly expecting company. Her body thrilled at the memory of his lovemaking, and she leaned against the open door, almost faint with another thundering wave of sexual desire.

"Oh, Jonas," she whispered aloud. "Hurry back. Please hurry...."

She took an apple from the crisper, rinsed it at the sink and carried it to the couch, settling down next to her discarded knitting. She bit into the apple and munched hungrily, startled to remember that she hadn't eaten since noon.

Just as she took another huge bite, the phone began to ring.

Laurel stared at it, wondering if she should answer. It seemed terribly presumptuous to answer his phone when he was away. Jonas was such a private, mysterious person. Maybe he had a good reason for not wanting anybody to know there was a woman in his life.

On the other hand, it might well be Jonas himself calling, knowing she'd probably be there by now. What if he'd been delayed somewhere, and was calling to let her know?

Laurel struggled to swallow the mouthful of apple without choking. To her relief, the answering machine clicked on at that moment.

"Hi," she heard his voice say. "Jonas O'Neal speaking. At the sound of the beep, please leave your name and number."

Laurel smiled, delighted by the sound of his voice in the empty room. She moved closer and waited for the caller to speak, prepared to lift the receiver immediately if it turned out to be Jonas.

But it wasn't Jonas.

The caller sounded brusque and annoyed.

"Are you there?" he barked. "If you are, pick up the damned phone!"

Laurel gasped, her eyes wide with shock.

"Oh, dammit," the voice went on with obvious irritation. "All right, get back to me as soon as you can. Look, I got your message this morning and it's pretty damned upsetting. I don't know what's going on out there, but I don't want you to let that girl out of your sight! You hear me, O'Neal? I'm paying you a hell of a lot, and you'd better do your job!"

There was a harsh sound at the other end of the line, as if the caller had knocked something to the floor in his agitation. Laurel heard a click, then a beep as the machine switched off.

She stumbled backward against the wall and slid down to the floor, hiding her face on her knees and battling a cold wave of nausea. Whimpering, she pressed her hands to her aching head, trying to think. But the angry voice on the telephone kept ringing in her ears, drowning out all thought and reason. Laurel would have known that voice anywhere.

The caller was her father.

CHAPTER TWELVE

TEARS POURING DOWN her cheeks, Laurel fled through the empty streets, back to the hotel, barely conscious of her surroundings or of Kate at the front desk, looking at her in concern.

In the safety of her room, she huddled on the bed, staring blankly at the flowered wallpaper and twisting her hands together in her lap. Despite the warmth of the summer evening, her body was racked with deep shivers, and she felt a rising nausea.

In the space of a minute or two, her entire world had been turned upside down, leaving her with a dizzying sense of vertigo.

Nothing was what it seemed to be. Jonas was a liar, and her father . . .

She moaned softly, recalling that brusque, angry voice on the telephone.

Jonas had obviously come to Wolf Hill in pursuit of her. He'd been watching her right from the beginning, just as she'd suspected.

But he wasn't a policeman with a court order. He was a private thug in her father's employ, and the full implication of this knowledge was more than she could endure. Her mind drew away hastily, searching for some other explanation.

Maybe her father had simply been worried about her welfare during her enforced absence, so he'd sent

somebody along to make sure she was all right. Maybe
he . . .

Laurel rubbed her temples wearily and shook her
head, recognizing that she was grasping at straws. She
remembered telling her father on the telephone about
the mysterious stranger whose presence was so upsetting to her, and Stewart's breezy assurance that the man
couldn't possibly have any connection with her.

And all the time he'd known . . .

"You lied to me, Dad," Laurel murmured. "You've
never lied to me before."

But, of course, she wasn't convinced of that anymore.

Maybe he'd been lying to her for years, and she'd
been too gullible and trusting to realize it. All her secure foundations had been ripped away. She was floating in a terrifying black void with no idea how to right
herself, to find a place of safety or distinguish between
truth and falsehood.

At last she got up, hauled her battered duffel bags
from the closet and began to pack, moving around the
room in mechanical fashion, trying not to think about
the dreadful reality of that telephone call in Jonas's
apartment.

A knock sounded at the door. Her head jerked up
and she stared at the door in silence.

"Laurel?" a man's voice called. "Laurel, please open
the door."

She stood in the middle of the room, clutching an
armful of clothes and shoes.

"Laurel? I know you're in there," Jonas said. "Kate
told me you'd come back to the hotel, and that you
seemed really upset. I need to talk to you."

"Go away," she said.

"I'm not going away. Open the door."

"Go away," she repeated.

"If you won't open the door," he said calmly, "I'll go downstairs to the front desk, tell Kate you don't answer and I'm worried about you, and get her to come up here with the key."

Laurel knew the man well enough by now to recognize that he meant what he said. She pictured everybody in the hotel getting involved in her personal trauma, looking at her with curiosity and pity...

She crossed the room and flung open the door, then turned aside without looking at him.

Jonas came into the room, closed the door behind him and stood quietly by the dresser. "What are you doing?" he asked.

"What does it look like?" She went to the closet and hauled out another bundle of clothes.

"I thought we had a date tonight. When I got back to town, I went straight up to my room but you weren't there."

"Oh, I was there, all right," Laurel said bitterly. "I just left a few minutes ago."

"Why did you leave? Did something happen to upset you?"

"You might say that." She started to fold one of the shabby blouses, than abandoned the effort and stuffed it into the bag. "No need to bother, is there?" she said. "After all, I'm hardly going to need these clothes again. I'll drop them off at the first thrift store I run across."

"Laurel, I don't understand what's going on."

"Neither do I." She looked at him directly, forcing herself to hold back the tears of anger and pain. "Why don't you tell me what's going on, Jonas?"

"What's happened? Why are you so angry?"

The pain of meeting his eyes was too much to endure. In spite of his betrayal, her body still thrilled to his hard masculinity, still yearned to touch him and nestle in his arms.

She turned away blindly and continued jamming things into the bag.

"Did you check your phone messages, Jonas?"

He tensed. She could see his knuckles whitening in the hand that gripped the edge of the dresser. But when he replied, his voice was calm and level.

"No," he said. "I didn't think to check the phone when I got back and found you weren't there. Why, Laurel?" he went on. "Have you been listening to my machine?"

Laurel shook her head. "I don't snoop into other people's phone messages. Maybe that's my problem. I've always been so damned scrupulous and I expect everyone else to be the same."

Anger began to replace her confusion and misery, giving her the courage to face him directly.

"Pretty silly of me, isn't it, Jonas? Being so honest and fair, when nobody else is."

He met her gaze quietly. "If you didn't hear something upsetting on the phone messages, why are you so angry?"

"I was in your room when the call came, Jonas. I was eating an apple. The phone rang, and I didn't want to answer it so I let the machine come on. I heard your voice message, and I heard my..."

Her voice faltered briefly, then steadied.

"I heard my father telling you he was damned upset and that you'd better call him back right away."

"Oh, *hell,*" Jonas muttered, taking a step toward her and reaching out to touch her arm. "Laurel, I'm so sorry."

She shook his hand away angrily. "I haven't told you the whole message, Jonas. Don't you want to hear what he said?"

"No, I don't."

"Well, I'm telling you anyway," she said grimly. "He told you he was paying you good money, and you'd better do your job. He said he didn't want you to take your eyes off me."

Jonas dropped into an armchair and covered his face with his hands.

Laurel ignored him, furiously stuffing her clothes and belongings into the shabby luggage.

"Look," he said at last, "I know how all this must look to you. But I can tell you, sweetheart, that I never—"

Her composure deserted her. "Don't call me sweetheart!" she shouted at him. "And don't tell me any more lies, either. I'm really tired of being lied to, Jonas."

He watched in silence while she zipped up the last of the bags and turned to face him.

"I don't know what's worse," Laurel said in a low, bitter voice. "Being lied to by my father is horrible enough, when I've always loved him so much and done so much for him. I feel like such a fool, Jonas. But *you* . . . after we made love and you said . . ."

"Laurel," he pleaded. "Won't you even let me explain?"

"Oh, you don't need to explain," she said coldly. "I'm not stupid, you know, even though I've been so gullible. I understand perfectly. I know exactly what happened.''

"Okay. Suppose you tell me, then.''

Laurel studied his face for a moment, feeling another rush of misery when she thought how much pleasure they'd shared, how touched and surprised she'd been by his unexpected tenderness.

"He did it,'' she said at last. "His deal with Chet Landry, that was all just smoke to keep me confused, right? My father actually placed those illegal orders, hoping to profit from them. He knew I'd probably find out what he'd done, but that didn't matter because he could always trick me into covering for him.''

She gave Jonas an inquiring glance, but he said nothing.

"It's clear to me now,'' she went on. "There were all kinds of things about those orders that I should have recognized and questioned, but I didn't. I let him convince me because I wanted to be convinced. I couldn't bear to face the truth, that my father deliberately abused a position of trust for his own gain, and then lied to me about it.''

Jonas sat tensely in the chair, his strong, aquiline profile reflected in the darkening window.

"Didn't he?'' she asked.

"I don't know. Tell me the rest of the story, if you're so sure about what happened.''

"You know the rest of the story as well as I do. I believed his lies. I agreed to avoid the subpoena so he could dodge an investigation. But in order to protect himself, he needed to be sure I stayed safely out of the way, so he hired you to follow me.''

She looked at the handsome man across the room.

"What were your instructions, Jonas?" she asked bitterly. "If I showed any signs of heading back to Vancouver, were you supposed to break my legs or something? Is that what you are, a hired assassin? How far was my father prepared to go, looking out for his own interests?"

"God, don't say things like that! You're just upset, and you don't understand."

"Oh, I understand," she told him, her face grim. "All too well."

She paused, struck by a sudden thought. "How did you get here so quickly, Jonas?"

"When?"

"The very first morning I arrived in Wolf Hill, I saw you in the coffee shop. You must have been right behind me. How did you find me so fast?"

"I knew when you were leaving Vancouver," he told her, his face expressionless. "I was with your father when he called you that night and told you it was time to go."

"Of course you were," she said. "I didn't think of that. But still, he had no idea where I was going."

"I followed you down to the bus depot in Vancouver. When the ticket agent went out back to check some luggage, I flipped through the stubs on his desk, found the destination on your ticket and then drove straight out here."

"But when you arrived, you started looking for a job right away. How did you know I'd be staying here, not moving on somewhere after a day or so?"

He was silent, looking down at his hands. Another horrible suspicion dawned in her mind.

"My God," she breathed, moving closer and staring at him. "The *money*. Did you steal my money, Jonas?"

He stared out the window, his face hard and remote. "It wasn't too difficult," he said at last. "Just a few minutes in the baggage room, that's all. You should never carry so much cash in your luggage."

"You . . . you *bastard!*"

"I deposited it in the local bank in a holding account," he said tonelessly. "I'll give you a certified check in the morning."

"Don't bother. Keep it as payment for services rendered. After all, you really performed above and beyond the call of duty, didn't you? Sleeping with the enemy must have been a real hardship."

He shook his head and turned away, clearly stung by the bitterness in her voice.

But Laurel's anger was already fading into pain. "My father must have known that you stole my money. I'm sure it was all part of the plan, to make sure I was stuck out here for a while?"

She wrapped her arms around herself, trying not to cry.

"What a fool I've been," she whispered. "I've been a blind idiot for years, but I see everything clearly now. I just can't believe . . ." She grimaced with distaste. "I still can't believe he'd hire somebody like you to track my movements. And worst of all," she added with a shaking voice, "was the way I trusted you. I went to bed with you. I even imagined I was . . . falling in love with you."

She gave him a cold, mirthless smile while he watched in silence.

"I can hardly imagine how pitiful I must have looked to you, Jonas. You were being paid to keep track of me, and I fell into your arms like a lovestruck teenager. Did you and my father laugh about that when you called him to give your reports?''

His face hardened. "That's not fair," he said quietly.

"Fair!" She picked up a cushion from the bed and began kneading it in her hands. "I really don't think you have much concept of fairness, do you?"

"Why not?"

"Because you were working for a criminal. Don't tell me you weren't aware of what you were doing. He'd broken the law, and you were hired to protect him from getting his rightful punishment. You must have known that.''

"No," Jonas said. "I didn't know that."

"What did he tell you, then?"

"He said you did it."

She stared at him, her jaw dropping. *"What?"*

"He told me you'd cheated the shareholders by placing a series of illegal orders, and that you needed to stay out of sight while he tried to find a way to cover for you."

Her mind whirled. "And you were . . . what was your job supposed to be?"

"I'm a private investigator. That's my job."

"I see. So you follow people and spy on them, track down wandering spouses to get the dirt on them, that kind of thing?"

"Not usually. I don't like dealing with family conflicts. Mostly I work on causes like fraud or stolen goods, where people can't get satisfaction through the police or legal channels. I collect a finder's fee for recovering their valuables.''

"How noble," she said bitterly. "Like a modern-day Robin Hood, I suppose."

"It's a living."

"I'm sure it is. Why did you take on my father as a client, if you don't like family squabbles?"

"Because he seemed so concerned about you. He said you'd never done anything wrong before and you were so frightened of being caught..."

"*Me,* frightened of being caught," she echoed. "It's all such a ... Why did you care, Jonas? After all, I was a criminal in your eyes, right?"

"Yes, but I wasn't sure of your motives. Your father said you'd only stolen the money to help your company out of its financial bind. He wanted somebody to keep an eye on you and make sure you were safe while he tried to organize some way to cover your illegal trades."

"My illegal trades," she whispered. "What a liar the man is. I honestly can't believe it. And you were supposed to be my baby-sitter? It's all like some kind of lousy joke."

"Not a joke," he said quietly. "Your father convinced me that you might be in danger."

"What kind of danger?"

"From the other traders who helped you steal the money. He told me they were probably after you, so you had to stay hidden."

"My God," Laurel whispered, appalled. "Why would he tell such a *lie?*"

"I guess he realized I wouldn't agree to take on the job unless I believed you were really in danger." Jonas got up and crossed the room to take her arm. "Laurel, please listen to me."

She stared up at him. "Why should I listen? You've been lying to me from the minute we first met. And all the time, you believed I was a thief and a coward, running away to avoid the police."

"But I—"

"Didn't you?" she persisted. "You believed I'd stolen that money. Admit it, Jonas!"

"Yes," he said quietly. "I believed it."

"Get out," she said, aching with weariness. "Go away and leave me alone. I have a long, hard trip ahead of me."

"Not until you listen to me."

"I never want to listen to you again as long as I live."

She lifted the duffel bags from the bed and started toward the door.

"Goodbye, Jonas," she said.

The last she saw of him was his face against the black square of window. Then she was running down the hall, through the lobby and into the windswept street, heading for the bus depot.

SHE HAD just enough cash to pay the bus fare to Calgary. They rolled into the city an hour after midnight, and she called Dennis at his apartment.

"Laurel! Where are you?" he said sleepily. "What's going on?"

"Don't ask me, Dennis. Just send me enough money for a plane ticket to Vancouver, in care of the Calgary bus depot. Better make it a couple of thousand dollars, okay? I might need to charter a flight if there's nothing else available. And I need the cash before morning."

"Are you coming home right away? There's so much we need to do."

"I know. I'll see you tomorrow."

"Great," he said, beginning to sound more like his normal, cheerful self. "Hey, I can hardly wait to see you. And your money's on its way as soon as I can get some clothes on, but you've still got some heavy explaining to do when you get here, boss.''

"Oh, Dennis," she said miserably. "You don't know the half of it."

She hung up and stared at the telephone, struggling to hold back her tears. At last she trudged into a restaurant at the rear of the depot, to order a breakfast that she was too tired and unhappy to eat.

CHAPTER THIRTEEN

LAUREL MANAGED to grab a few hours of fitful sleep on a bench in the bus depot, and another hour on the plane to Vancouver. By the time she cleared the airport, hurried across town to her apartment to change clothes, then traveled back to the office, it was midafternoon and she was at a point beyond exhaustion.

In fact, she'd progressed to an eerie kind of calm. Her thoughts were icy and controlled, and she had a sense of quiet power, as if she could handle any crisis. She knew she'd probably collapse at the end of the day and sleep for twelve hours, but at the moment she felt prepared to deal with anything.

Even her father...

She rode upstairs in the elevator and entered her office, looking around with a sense of amazement. Had the windows always been this huge, the desk so impressive and the reception area so luxurious?

Somebody had even provided fresh flowers. They were arranged on one of the coffee tables, filling the room with color and fragrance. Laurel opened the envelope and took out a card.

"Welcome home, Ms. Atchison!" it read. "Love from Dennis and the girls."

She smiled absently and replaced the card, then stood rubbing her arms, trying to picture herself in this world. But the change had been too abrupt. Laurel felt lost and strangely detached, as if her soul had been left behind somewhere in that wide prairie sky over Calgary.

"Hi there," Dennis said, interrupting her thoughts. "It's about time you got back to work. I'm tired of running this office by myself."

"Well, thank you for the warmth of that greeting," Laurel said dryly. "I've missed you, too."

"Hey, I ordered flowers," he said with an injured air.

"I think I'd prefer a little tenderness," she said, her voice shaking, and began to fear that maybe she wasn't as calm and fully controlled as she'd thought.

Dennis crossed the room and gave her a thoughtful glance, then put an arm around her shoulders. "You look great," he said gently. "I love the haircut."

"Do you?"

"You look about sixteen. I think you've lost some weight, too."

"Really?" Laurel looked down at herself. She was wearing a lightweight suit of oatmeal-colored linen, and a brown silk blouse. "I just grabbed the first thing I saw in my closet. I can't believe all those clothes are mine," she added. "How could one woman possibly need so many clothes?"

He drew away and examined her carefully. "Hey, you're really different, aren't you?" he said. "Like a whole other person. That must have been quite a holiday you had."

She held up her hands, showing him the rough, reddened fingers, the cuts and burns and calluses.

Her secretary whistled. "I can't wait to hear this story."

"I'll tell you the whole thing," Laurel promised. "But," she added grimly, "not until I've had a little talk with my father."

She started toward the door while Dennis stood watching, his face strained with concern. "Laurel..."

"Yes?"

"We all know most of what's happened. The staff, I mean."

She stopped abruptly. "You know? How did you find out?"

"Stewart called a meeting yesterday and told us. Not that I hadn't suspected it before now."

"What did he tell you?" Laurel asked, her anger rising. "Did he say that I placed a lot of illegal orders and I was in hiding to escape being questioned?"

"Of course not," Dennis said, clearly astonished. "Who'd ever believe something like that?"

Her mind whirled in confusion. "Then what...what did he say?"

"He was very frank. He told us he'd been caught with his hand in the cookie jar, and that you'd been avoiding a subpoena so you wouldn't have to testify against him. He said he realized it's time to stop running, and he'd made arrangements to turn himself in and take his punishment."

Laurel closed her eyes and put her hands to her temples.

"He told us not to worry about our jobs," Dennis went on. "The two of you will probably be required to sell the company, but he's negotiating a deal to make sure we all retain the same level of employment. He was so apologetic, Laurel. He almost broke down. We all felt really bad for him, especially with the new baby and all."

Laurel stared at her secretary, appalled and silent, then turned and rushed through the carpeted halls to her father's office.

HE WAS in his usual place, practicing with his putting iron at the far side of the room. Laurel entered and stood watching, so distressed that she couldn't trust her voice.

Stewart glanced up and saw her. His face lighted with a smile of genuine happiness that faded when he saw her expression.

"Hello, Laurie," he said with unusual meekness. "I'm so glad to see you."

"Don't call me Laurie! I've been using that damned name for two months, and I'm sick of hearing it. My name is Laurel."

"Sorry, honey." Stewart crossed the room, avoiding her eyes. "Drink?" he asked, pausing by the console. "Maybe some fruit juice?"

"No, Dad," she said. "I don't want fruit juice. I want some explanations."

"There are no explanations. I did it." He looked up at her with disarming candor. "I placed those orders after getting an illegal inside tip, hoping I could get away with it and cover my tracks somehow. I should have known better."

Laurel stared at him, taken aback by this frank admission. "You certainly should have," she said. "Why did you do it?"

Stewart moved over to the windows, carrying a glass of tomato juice, and looked out at the sweeping view. "I was over my head, Laur...Laurel. When Marta and I were married, I wanted her to have everything, and I got far too extended. For the past year, I've been so worried about money, I hardly knew what to do with myself. I made some bad investments, hoping to recover, but you know what the market's been like. Things just kept getting worse. And then with the baby coming, I decided I needed to... I was so stupid," he concluded simply. "God, honey, I'm sorry."

"But I still don't understand... How did you think you were ever going to get away with it?"

Stewart shrugged. "I blamed it all on Chet Landry to throw you off the track. I thought if I could just buy myself enough time, maybe I could figure out a way to pay back what I owed and bury the accounts. But then the government investigators got wind of it somehow, and you know how relentless those guys are. They're like bulldogs if they catch a whiff of insider trading. I panicked when they started getting so close."

"And sent me off into the wilderness so I couldn't blow the whistle on you," Laurel said bitterly.

He looked at her with abject apology. "I never intended for it to take so long, honey. You've got to believe that. I thought a week or two at the most. But then you started settling into your life out there and seemed happy, and I kept hoping..."

He fell silent. "What, Dad?" Laurel moved closer to him. "Did you start hoping I'd just stay in that prairie town, working in a hotel kitchen for the rest of my life? Or did you care about me at all?"

"Of course I care! I love you, sweetheart."

"But that didn't keep you from telling Jonas O'Neal I was the one who placed the illegal orders."

Stewart's face drained of color and he gripped his glass tensely. "I had to," he said. "It was a rotten thing to do, but I had to tell him that."

"Why?"

"Because O'Neal seems to be a lot like you," her father said with a wry grimace. "That man's so bloody scrupulous, he never would have taken the job if he'd known I was the one in the wrong. I needed somebody to keep an eye on you and warn me if you were planning to come home unexpectedly."

But Laurel only heard part of this explanation. "You think he's *scrupulous?*" she asked in disbelief. "Jonas O'Neal?"

Stewart turned back to the window. "I'm sorry, Laurel," he said. "We're going to have to sell the company, you know."

Laurel found her fury and outrage slowly giving way to concern. Her father looked tired and old, not at all his usual jaunty self.

"I don't care about the company," she said at last. "I can always find work, Dad, and I can certainly do without the pressure of this partnership. But Dennis said the staff would be looked after...?"

"Mort Schall's taking over my shares, and incorporating the business into his own, along with most of the staff. I've stipulated that you get the option to sell out or stay on as partner."

"I don't want to be in a partnership with Mort Schall."

"I didn't think you would. Acquiring us will certainly give Mort a lot of power, won't it?" Stewart cast her a bleak smile. "I hope he's more trustworthy than I turned out to be."

Laurel sighed in exasperation, torn between the urge to punch him and the desire—almost as strong—to give him a comforting hug.

"How's the baby?" she asked at last.

Stewart's face lighted with pride. "He's fine. I keep forgetting you haven't even seen him. You should hear the lungs on that kid."

"What's his name?"

"Jeremiah."

Laurel's mouth twitched in spite of herself. "No kidding. That's a pretty big name for a little fellow. Will he be called Jerry?"

"Not if Marta has her way. It's Jeremiah or nothing, according to her."

"Poor Marta," Laurel said gently. "How's she taking all this?"

"She's not happy, of course, but she says it's actually kind of a relief. She's a smart girl, and she's suspected for a long time that something was wrong."

"Oh, Dad..." Laurel shook her head sadly. "Marta loves you. She would have been happy with anything you provided. You didn't need to break the law so you could lavish money on her."

"I realize that now. But, you know, I could never believe that a beautiful young woman like Marta would really want an old guy like me. It took a disaster like this for me to understand how much she loves me. So I guess," he added with a wistful smile, "it hasn't been all bad."

Laurel tried to remind herself that she was still furious with the man, but all her dark feelings seemed to be vanishing. She moved closer to him without speaking and put her arms around him. Stewart held her, patting her back with his free hand.

"What will they do to you, Dad?" she asked, taking a step back so she could see his face.

He gave her a debonair smile, looking more like his old self. "Not much. Probably a year or two in some nice upscale prison with saunas and tennis courts, and then a few years on probation. They'll lift my trading license, of course, but I can always get a job doing something else."

"Will Marta and the baby be all right?"

"We're selling the house, and the place in Palm Springs, and she's moving into a condo. That'll give her all the funds she needs to look after herself until I'm back."

"So everything's going to work out."

"As long as you don't stay mad at me. These past couple of months have been pretty terrible, kid. I can't stand it if you won't forgive me."

Laurel gave him a rueful glance and at last yielded to her other urge, punching him firmly on the arm.

"Nobody can ever stay mad at you," she said. "It's one of the most annoying things about you."

"How about Jonas O'Neal?" he asked as she turned to leave. "Are you going to stay mad at him?"

"I don't..." Laurel's voice broke, then steadied. "I don't want to talk about him, Dad. Ever again."

JONAS PAUSED by the gate in the lilac hedge outside Nellie Grossman's house, looking sadly up and down the street. It was early evening, a time of day in Wolf Hill that had been a favorite of his. But then, he told himself, he'd had lots of favorites.

The pearl-gray freshness of dawn, joyous with meadowlark songs had given him pleasure. And the drowsy stillness of noon when the fields were bathed in a flood of sunshine. Not to mention the hushed dark hour before midnight when the Northern Lights shimmered.

But since Laurel went away...

"Hello there," a voice said nearby, startling him. "What are you doing out there?"

Jonas moved through the gate and looked at Nellie. She stood in a flower bed at the corner of the yard, wearing her cotton housedress and a pair of sturdy black rubber boots. Nellie carried a flowered teapot in her hand, and was pouring its contents onto the damp ground among the geraniums.

"Never mind me," he said with a tired smile. "What are you doing, Nellie?"

"Getting rid of ants."

"By giving them tea?"

"Coffee," Nellie said briskly. "You run clear water over used coffee grounds and pour it onto the anthills in the evening, and the ants disappear in a day or two. I don't like using poison," she added, plying her teapot again. "Even if you and Clarence do sell tons of it at the hardware store."

"I don't like it, either," Jonas said. "I wish everybody used coffee grounds instead of chemicals."

Nellie straightened and looked up at him, studying his face with her wise blue eyes. "Come in for a cup of tea," she said gently. "I just baked some tollhouse cookies."

Jonas followed, watching as her rubber boots flopped along the path to the back door. "Do I really look so terrible, Nellie?" he asked ruefully.

"What do you mean?" She bent to remove her boots, stepped into a pair of sandals in the porch, then led the way to her kitchen.

"Like I'm so obviously in need of tea and sympathy?"

"Well, yes," she said. "I'm afraid you do."

She turned on the heat under the kettle, waving Jonas toward an antique china cabinet in the dining room, while Fluffy sat by the table and watched him with cold suspicion.

"You'll find cups and saucers in there," Nellie said, "and the place mats are in the second drawer. Get out a couple of salad plates, too. Have you eaten your supper?''

"I had something over at the hotel."

"But you could always eat something more, couldn't you?"

Jonas tried to smile. "I don't seem to have much of an appetite these days, Nellie. And we've got a baseball game in less than an hour."

"All right," she said. "We'll just have tea. But tomorrow evening you have to come by for a nice home-cooked meal."

"You shouldn't go to so much trouble over me," he protested.

Nellie waved a hand in dismissal and began to arrange cookies on a plate. "So, how are you doing?" she asked gently.

Jonas hesitated, his composure beginning to desert him in these cozy surroundings. "Not too well," he said at last.

"You really miss her, don't you?"

He sank into a chair and buried his face in his hands while Nellie paused behind him, resting a hand on his shoulder.

At last, Jonas turned and looked up at her, forcing a smile. "Sorry," he said. "I didn't mean to fall apart on you, Nellie."

She sat in the opposite chair. "Have you talked to her at all since she left?"

"I've tried. She won't take my calls at the office or at home."

Nellie shook her head, looking troubled, and got up to pour boiling water over the tea leaves.

Jonas stood up. "I think I'll go out of my mind if she won't talk to me soon," he said simply.

"You hurt her so much," the little woman said. "It's going to be real hard for her to forgive you."

"Have you talked to her?" he said.

"She called last night."

"How is she?" he asked hungrily. "God, I wish I could just hear her voice..."

"She's not very good, either," Nellie said. "Everything's still up in the air about their business affairs. And it's been such a terrible shock to the poor girl, finding out about her father. She adored that man, you know. She still does."

"But why is she taking it out on me? I'm not the one who made her father lie and cheat. He did that all by himself."

Nellie carried the teapot and cookies into the dining room, while Jonas followed with a tray containing sugar, cream and napkins. Fluffy stalked at his side, keeping a watchful eye on him.

"But you must understand," Nellie said, "that she trusted you. She fell in love with you, Jonas. And when it turned out that you were lying to her, it was just too much to bear. On top of her disappointment over her father, she couldn't stand it."

"I didn't lie to her. In fact, I was careful not to tell her any lies. I know I didn't tell the whole truth, but I never deliberately lied."

"That's not the point." Nellie poured tea and looked at him sadly. "You still don't understand, do you?"

He shook his head. "I keep thinking that if I could only get her to talk to me, everything would be all right. I could explain, and make her see that I didn't intend to hurt her. I was only doing my job, working for her father. If she—"

"It wasn't the business with her father that hurt the most," Nellie interrupted. "It was that you believed she'd done something wrong. That's what she couldn't stand."

"But her father told me that whole story, and he's a very convincing man. Nellie, how could I have known it was a lie?"

"You should have known it from meeting her," Nellie said gently. "That first time you looked in her face, you must have realized it was all a lie. And," the little woman went on, her eyes gentle but relentless, "you certainly shouldn't have made love to her without telling her the truth. She's a woman who demands complete honesty, you know."

He gazed into his cup in brooding silence. "I know, Nellie," he said wearily. "I know you're right. Actually, I began to doubt her father's story as soon as I got to know her, because she didn't seem capable of the kind of deceit her father described. But I know I should have told her the truth before we got so..." He broke off, looking out the window.

"Why didn't you?" Nellie asked after a brief silence.

Jonas shook his head. "I've been fooled before," he said bitterly. "I've been lied to by a person I trusted, and it caused me a lot of pain. When something like that happens to you, it makes you really cautious about trusting people again."

"But being too careful can cost you a lot more," Nellie said simply. "There can't be love unless there's trust."

"I know that now," Jonas said. "I realize how much this has cost me."

Nellie looked at him thoughtfully. "The first time I saw you, I could tell that you'd been hurt by life. Do you want to talk about it?"

He shook his head. "Not now, Nellie. Maybe sometime, but not now."

"You love that girl a lot, don't you?" the old woman said.

Jonas nodded and rubbed his temples. "Yes, I do." He looked at Nellie in despair. "I never thought I'd love someone the way I love her. Even now, when I can't see her or talk to her, she fills my life."

Nellie's eyes looked faraway and sad. "I know what it's like," she murmured, "to love somebody that way. I know how much it hurts."

"I need her the way I need air to breathe, Nellie. I feel like I'm going to suffocate if I can't be with her again."

"So what are you going to do?"

"What can I do?" Jonas looked at her in quiet appeal. "If she won't take my calls, what can I do?"

"I'm going to be seeing her quite soon," Nellie said. "Next week, actually."

Jonas felt a wild surge of hope. "She's coming back here?"

Nellie shook her head. "I'm going to Vancouver." Her face lighted briefly with anticipation. "Laurel arranged everything, and Crystal's coming along to take care of me. Laurel's sending a car to pick us up and take us to Calgary. Then we're flying to Vancouver to stay a few days and see *Showboat.*"

Nellie sighed and bent down to stroke her cat, then looked up again at Jonas.

"I can't believe this is really happening to me," she said. "It's going to be so wonderful."

"Nellie, do you think you can get her to call me? Can you tell her that I—"

Nellie shook her head and squeezed his hand gently. "You have to find a way to tell her yourself, son. You have to go to the city and talk to her."

"You know, I still have an apartment there," Jonas said. "You're right, Nellie. I guess it's time for me to go back and see what's happening with the rest of my life."

"I'm surprised you're still in Wolf Hill. I thought you'd leave right away, after your..." Nellie hesitated awkwardly. "After your job was finished."

Jonas gave her a bleak smile. "So did I. But it seems awfully hard to leave this place. If Laurel were here, Wolf Hill would be perfect. I don't think I'd ever leave."

"She's not here, though," Nellie said. "She's in the city, and she's going to stay there. She's already had two job offers that she's considering, and both of them sound mighty impressive."

"I'm not surprised," Jonas said quietly. "After all, she's an impressive woman." He got to his feet and stood looking down at his hostess. "When I think of what she did, coming out here and working in that kitchen, trying to protect her father..."

"The girl is a princess. I told you the first time I met you that she was a princess."

"I should have listened to you," Jonas said. "I always knew she was rich, but I believed she was a thief. God, how could I have been so blind?"

Nellie watched as he moved toward the door. "Can't you stay and have another cup of tea?"

Jonas shook his head. "I have a ball game in a half hour. Those little kids don't care about my problems,

Nellie. They just want their coach to turn up and be full of energy."

"You're a good man, Jonas," she said quietly.

"I wish I could believe you," Jonas said. "But I'm afraid Laurel's probably right about me."

"THAT'S A NICE OUTFIT. Understated but very sexy. Is it new?"

Laurel glanced down at her dark green silk jump-suit, then at her secretary who stood in the doorway balancing an armful of file folders.

"No, it's not," she said. "I bought it about three years ago when I was in Spain, but it was always a little too tight in the hips until now."

"Well, you look great. That outfit goes with your new hairdo."

Laurel gave him a thoughtful glance. "How can you stay so cheerful when the whole world's been turned upside down?"

"What's upside down?" Dennis asked calmly. "There's going to be a different nameplate on the door, and some new people in the major office suites. Apart from that, things will go on pretty much as usual, won't they?"

"Except for the fact that I won't be here, and you'll have a new boss," Laurel said, brooding over the messy stacks of moving boxes around her desk.

"That's a definite drawback, all right. But we'll still be friends, you know. In fact," he added, "after you've left the firm, you can pressure me to escort you to boring cocktail parties without fear of a sexual harassment lawsuit."

She laughed, cheered as always by his good humor. "I'm going to remember that, Dennis. And I fully intend to hold you to it."

"Good." He sat on the corner of her desk and lifted a little executive toy from a box, placing it on the polished teak and setting the metal balls swinging.

"So," he said, "how does it feel to be moving up in the world?"

"Am I moving up?"

"Of course you are," Dennis said in surprise. "Your new job's going to make you one of the most powerful women in the financial community. Lots of people would give their eyeteeth for the opportunity you're getting."

"I wish you'd reconsider and come with me," Laurel said.

Dennis shook his head, looking out the window with a wistful expression. "You know how much I'd love to do that. But keeping the staff intact was part of the deal your father made with Mort, and I feel some loyalty to the old company. Besides," he added, "I'm getting a promotion, too, you know. Under the restructuring plan, I'll actually have two people working under me."

"Have you finished interviewing for the new receptionist?"

Dennis grinned. "Not yet. I'm finding the interview process a little difficult," he admitted. "It's so hard for me to shift gears and react to these people as employees instead of women."

"Dennis, you're such a chauvinist. I don't know why I even bother to talk to you."

"Because you love me," he said tranquilly. "Speaking of love," he added, concentrating on the swinging metal balls, "exactly what happened to you out there in the wilderness, kiddo?"

Laurel tensed. "What do you mean?"

"Just what I said. Why do you look so sad and far-away all the time? Who's the guy with the deep voice who keeps calling and you keep refusing to speak to? What's going on?"

"Nothing's going on. Have you seen my framed certificates, Dennis? I thought I packed them in this box, but I can't—"

"I sent them all downstairs to be wrapped in bubble-pack. Answer the question."

"You're still the employee, remember?" Laurel said, trying to smile. "And I'm your boss until the end of the month. You can't push me around like this."

"He says his name is Jonas O'Neal. Who is he, and why won't you talk to him?"

"Because he's a liar and a cheat. He even stole money from me." Laurel began to grab books from the shelves and jam them furiously into boxes. "Why on earth should I talk to a man like that?"

"Well, for one thing, you go as white as a sheet and look unhappy for hours after he calls," Dennis said quietly. "It seems to me this is something you need to get settled."

Laurel was dismayed by a sudden flood of emotion. "It's already settled," she said. "I don't want to talk about it, Dennis."

"Well, I'm afraid you're probably going to have to."

Laurel looked at him sharply. "Why?"

"Because the man's here in the city."

"Jonas is *here?* How do you know?"

"He told me the last time he called. Said he'd be dropping by to see you, and asked when I expected you to be in."

"I hope you didn't tell him anything. I can't... Dennis, I can't possibly see him! I don't—"

"No need to get worried," Dennis's voice was soothing. "I told him you'd be in and out, and it was hard to say when he might find you. I said you weren't making any appointments until after your move to the new job."

"Oh, good." Laurel sagged into a chair. "Thanks, Dennis."

"No problem. So, how's the other big guy?" Dennis put away the toy and lounged in one of the leather chairs opposite her desk.

Laurel's face clouded. "It's been hard on everybody else, but he seems to be bearing up pretty well. He's even cheerful, strange as it sounds."

"Probably just from the relief of having it all out in the open."

"I'm sure you're right. Dad will be heading off to prison in a few days, but he's been cooperating fully and they expect the sentence to be commuted to less than two years."

"Good. And how's your little brother?"

"Jeremiah?" Laurel said with a wistful smile. "He's such a darling. You should see him, Dennis. He's growing so fast, getting all round and pink, and he sleeps almost all the way through the night..." Her voice broke and she went back to stuffing books in cartons.

Dennis gave her a thoughtful glance. "You should have one, too," he said.

Laurel looked up at him, startled. "One of what?"

"One of those babies." Dennis hoisted himself from the chair and strode across the room. "I think it's time for you to settle down and start getting domestic, Ms. Atchison."

"I see. And what if I said the same thing to you?"

"I'd agree in a flash," Dennis said calmly. "In fact, if I could find the right girl, I'd... My God," he whispered, looking beyond Laurel, his eyes widening in shock.

Laurel followed his glance and forgot her troubles briefly in a warm surge of happiness.

Crystal stood by the door to the office suite, looking shy and astonishingly beautiful. She wore loafers, loose khaki trousers and an olive green pullover that highlighted her red hair and delicate complexion.

Dennis gaped at the newcomer, openmouthed. "Are you... are you here for a job interview?" he asked, finding his voice at last.

Laurel laughed and hurried across the room to pull the girl inside. "No, she's a friend of mine. Dennis, this is Crystal. She and I worked together for a couple of months."

Dennis shook the girl's hand, beaming at her. "Hello, Crystal," he said, beginning to recover his aplomb. "Are you sure you don't want a job?"

"As a matter of fact, I *am* looking for a job." Crystal gave him a warm smile that obviously jolted his composure badly. "But right now, I'm here to see Laurel. Wow!" she added, looking around at the luxurious office. "Imagine you leaving all this to work in the Wolf Hill Hotel."

Laurel hugged the girl. "Crystal, I'm so happy to see you! I wish I could have met you at the airport, but I had a meeting this morning that I just couldn't avoid."

"That's okay. It's really fun to ride around in that limousine you hired. Nellie loved it."

"How have you been feeling?"

"Oh . . . I'm fine, I guess," Crystal said, flicking a nervous glance at Dennis. "Nellie's back at the hotel, resting."

Laurel felt a quick surge of anxiety. "Is she all right? Was the trip too hard on her?"

Crystal chuckled. "She's a little tired, but only because she got so excited. Neither of us has ever ridden in a plane before, you know. Nellie sat by the window and spent the whole time telling me every time she saw a mountain or a lake. She was bouncing up and down like a little kid."

"But she's really all right? You're absolutely sure?"

"Absolutely. In fact, I told her she had to lie down and take a nap, but I think she was planning to go down and sit by the pool. She said she could sleep for a week after she gets back home, but while she's in the city she wants to enjoy every minute of it."

Laurel smiled fondly. "The darling," she murmured. "I can hardly wait to see her. Did she like the dress I sent?"

"*Like* it!" Crystal rolled her eyes eloquently. "There was a full dress rehearsal the other night, with her shoes and little beaded handbag and everything. Jonas and I both went over for supper to see her outfit. And Margie gave her a perm yesterday in honor of the trip. She really looks terrific."

Laurel was momentarily silent, distressed by the unexpected image of Jonas sitting in Nellie's cozy living room with Crystal and the big gray tomcat. She felt a stab of pain, then a fierce hunger that almost took her breath away.

"Who's Nellie?" Dennis asked, still gazing at Crystal as if she'd dropped out of a rainbow.

"She's a friend of ours," Laurel said. "She's eighty-three years old, Dennis, and her fantasy has always been to spend a glamorous night on the town."

"So that's why I bought you those three tickets to *Showboat?*"

Laurel nodded. "And afterward, we're going to the dining room at the Four Seasons."

Dennis whistled, then winked at Crystal. "A pretty classy evening. Don't you ladies need an escort?"

Crystal smiled back at him. "That'd be nice. Would you still be able to get a ticket to the show?"

"Oh, yes. Dennis has all kinds of connections," Laurel said dryly.

"I'll make some calls," Dennis said happily. "The Four Seasons, right? I'd better find my tux."

"What's going on?" Laurel asked her secretary. "You're usually so reluctant to take me out anywhere. Now you're all excited, just because my eighty-three-year-old friend is going along?"

Dennis turned away from Crystal long enough to give his employer a placid smile. "I'm very, very fond of grandmothers."

"Oh, I'm sure you are," Laurel said, but her gentle sarcasm was lost on the two young people who were smiling at each other again, clearly oblivious to everything else in the world.

CHAPTER FOURTEEN

THE THEATER FOYER was crowded with people dressed in their best, gesturing with fluted champagne glasses and talking animatedly over the strains of Vivaldi that drifted on the flower-scented air.

At Laurel's side, Nellie gripped a small beaded handbag and stared at the crowd with rapt attention, as if trying to commit the entire scene to memory.

Laurel and Marta had gone shopping together and chosen a dress for Nellie of midnight-blue silk with a delicate spray of rhinestones on one shoulder. The dress was cocktail length, simply cut so it didn't overpower her tiny figure.

With it, Nellie carried her beaded dinner bag and wore silver low-heeled shoes. Her freshly styled hair glistened in dainty curls, and Dennis had even thoughtfully provided her with a white orchid corsage.

"You look so lovely," Laurel murmured, giving her a fond smile. "I think you're the very best-looking woman in the room."

Nellie chuckled. "Now, that's surely proof that beauty is in the eyes of the beholder," she said. "Look at some of these ladies, and the way they're fixed up. They must all be famous movie stars."

"Is it all you hoped it would be, Nellie?" Laurel asked.

Nellie smiled. "It's pure heaven. I feel like Cinderella," she said. "In a couple of days, the magic will be gone and I'll be home in my rubber boots, killing ants and slugs in the garden, but I don't mind at all. This has been the most wonderful adventure I could ever imagine."

Laurel sank onto a velvet banquette and gestured for Nellie to sit next to her. "I've been meaning to ask you about that. It's so hard for you, Nellie, looking after that house all by yourself. Wouldn't you rather move to the city where you could do things like this all the time?"

As she spoke, Laurel imagined having Nellie come to live somewhere nearby. They could visit regularly, go shopping together, talk on the telephone every day. And there were so many things that Laurel could show her, wonderful things...

But Nellie dashed these wistful hopes before Laurel could even express them.

"Of course not!" she said, laughing and extending a small foot to admire one of her slippers. "This is surely the most fun I've ever had. But soon I'll be getting anxious to see my little house again, and Fluffy and my garden. That's where I belong."

"I know you're right. It's just that it's going to be so hard for me to see you as often as I'd like. This new job is going to take most of my time."

Nellie gave her a shrewd glance. "Aren't you happy about the new job, dear?"

"I don't know." Laurel sipped from her champagne glass. "I know it's a wonderful opportunity. But something feels different now, Nellie. It seems like..."

"There's no zing anymore," Nellie concluded. "The new job doesn't seem nearly as exciting as it would have a year or two ago."

"That's exactly right." Laurel looked at her in surprise. "How did you know?"

Nellie smiled. "Instead of trying to move me to the city, you should come back and work for Hilda again. I hear she's having a real hard time replacing you."

"I called her as soon as I got back," Laurel said, "to apologize for running off without telling her. She said Luther was filling in for a few days, and that she'd been interviewing people for Crystal's job, so she just hired two of them instead of one. She didn't seem all that upset."

"Well, she's upset now," Nellie said cheerfully. "I guess the new girls haven't turned out that well. You know what Hilda's like. She's a pretty hard woman to work for."

"I really liked her." Laurel gazed absently at the well-dressed crowd. "Hilda's an honest woman. You always know exactly where you are with her. There aren't enough people like that in the world."

Nellie gave her a keen glance, then patted her hand and turned away. "Where did those children get to? We'll miss the first act if they don't hurry."

"There's still a lot of time," Laurel said, checking her watch. "In fact, I'd like to get us one more drink before we're seated, but I'm waiting for Dennis to come back so I don't leave you all alone in this crowd."

"There they are," Nellie said suddenly. "And looking very pleased with themselves, too," she added.

Crystal and Dennis approached through the crowd, returning from a trip backstage where one of Dennis's many friends worked in the lighting booth.

As Nellie said, they seemed to be positively glowing with pleasure in the occasion and each other's company. Dennis was debonair and handsome in his black tux. In typical Dennis fashion, he also sported a jaunty red tartan bow tie and cummerbund.

Laurel had wondered how she could tactfully send Crystal some money to buy a new outfit for this occasion. The last thing she wanted to do was insult the girl. She'd solved the problem by sending a generous amount of money to cover their trip to Vancouver, with a note saying that whatever was left over should be considered Crystal's reward for looking after Nellie, and could be used to buy a new dress for the theater if Crystal chose.

And Crystal had obviously chosen well. She wore a plain, tailored sheath of ice-green silk with gold and pearl buttons, and dainty high-heeled sandals. Her red hair was gathered up in a casual knot, with a few tendrils escaping onto her shoulders, and her face glowed. She moved gracefully at Dennis's side, calmly ignoring the warm glances of admiration that followed them wherever they went.

"That boy looks like he's died and gone to heaven," Nellie observed.

Laurel felt a stab of uneasiness as she looked at Dennis and saw the dazed, wondering expression that seemed so unlike his usual self.

"What's the matter?" Nellie asked.

"He's falling in love with her," Laurel said. "Anybody can see it."

Nellie gave her a thoughtful glance.

"Nellie, do you think he knows?" Laurel whispered.

"About the baby?"

Laurel nodded, feeling miserable.

"It's their business, dear," Nellie said gently. "That's one of the things you learn when you get old. How to mind your own business and let folks work things out by themselves."

"But Dennis looks so...smitten. I'm afraid that when he finds out about the baby, he's going to be badly hurt, and I don't—"

She stopped speaking abruptly. Dennis and Crystal were beside them, smiling.

"We saw Bryan Adams backstage," Crystal said, her eyes wide with awe. "He was visiting a friend who's in the show."

"My goodness!" Laurel said. "Are you sure it was him?"

"Dennis said it was," Crystal said simply, as if that were the only proof required. Dennis beamed and dropped a casual arm around her shoulders.

"You should see the way people look at this woman," he told Laurel. "They all think she's either a model or a movie star."

"You're so silly," Crystal told him placidly. "I'm just a waitress in a nice dress. It's Nellie who's the real knockout."

Nellie beamed. "I'm real pretty tonight," she agreed, "but Laurel looks a bit different than last time we saw her, too. Doesn't she?"

"What did she wear out there on the prairie?" Dennis asked with interest.

"Torn blue jeans," Crystal said. "Stained T-shirts and old blouses with holes in them. Baggy plaid jackets without buttons."

He chuckled. "I sure hope somebody got pictures of her. I'd pay a whole lot to see them."

"Not a chance," Laurel said dryly. "That period of my life has definitely not been saved for posterity."

Dennis glanced at his watch and took Crystal's arm again, then reached for Nellie and tucked her in cozily at his other side. "Come on, girls," he said. "Time for you to meet a few more of the local celebrities. Hey, Laurel," he added, looking over his shoulder, "could you wait here for us? We'll be back in a minute, and I'll bring you a drink."

Laurel nodded, then watched as the three of them moved off into the crowd. She got to her feet and stood looking around, listening to the eager flow of conversation and the soothing violin music.

In honor of Nellie, Laurel had chosen to wear the most glamorous dress she owned, a designer creation bought in Paris during a business trip the previous autumn. It was a halter style in bronze silk with a softly draped tulip skirt that opened in the front to display her legs.

Her accessories were golden-brown, and her jewelry was a necklace and long earrings of topaz set in heavy antique gold, heirlooms that she'd inherited from her mother.

Laurel had wondered how the boyish haircut she'd brought back from the prairie would go with the sophisticated outfit but it didn't seem to detract at all from the look. In fact, the contrast accentuated the glamour of her dress and made a number of heads turn as she lingered quietly at the edge of the crowd.

But Laurel ignored everyone. She gazed absently at a mural on the opposite wall depicting the Nine Muses, and waited for her friends to come back.

Suddenly, a tall figure caught her eye. She gasped and her knees felt weak, as if they might crumple under her.

Jonas O'Neal was approaching through the crowd, almost a head taller than most of the men around him, his strange golden eyes fixed steadily on her face.

Laurel watched him, silent and breathless at this unexpected meeting, gazing at him as if she couldn't get enough of his face and body.

He wore a beautifully fitted black tux and bow tie, and managed to look completely at ease in the formal wear. His brown hair gleamed softly under the crystal lights overhead. Even his shirt studs were impeccable, fine black jet in an understated setting of gold.

Only his face looked the same, that combination of good looks and remoteness that had attracted her interest the first time she saw the man.

Laurel bit her lip and glanced behind her automatically, searching for a place to hide, but flight was impossible. He'd already seen her.

She wondered if this meeting had somehow been organized by her friends. It was certainly suspicious, the way they'd all vanished at once and then Jonas had appeared a moment later....

"Is this a trap?" she asked when he drew near enough to speak.

"Maybe," he admitted, gazing down at her hungrily. "But I couldn't think of any other way to see you. How have you been?"

"Fine," she said curtly.

"God, you're so beautiful," he whispered. "The most beautiful woman..."

He reached out as if to touch her, then let his hand drop when she stiffened and moved away slightly to avoid the gesture.

The nearness of him was almost more than Laurel could endure. Her heart pounded, and her entire body clamored to touch him, to move closer and kiss his mouth, touch his face, run her fingers over his broad white-shirted chest...

"I haven't spoken to your father for a long time," Jonas went on, his eyes still fixed on her. "What's happening with your business?"

"Nothing that I care to discuss with you," Laurel said calmly. She sipped her drink and turned away from him to watch the streams of people who walked by, laughing and chatting.

"I sent the three thousand dollars to your secretary, along with the interest it's earned, and told him to deposit it to your account."

"I know," Laurel said tonelessly. "He told me."

"And our baseball team made it into the playoffs. The preliminary series starts this weekend."

Laurel felt a treacherous stirring of interest, thinking about Melanie's cheerful freckled face and little Tyler with his shy, eager smile.

But she suppressed the urge to question him.

"That's good," she said neutrally. "I'm sure they're all very happy about it."

Jonas leaned toward her, his face hard and intent. "Is this the way it's going to be, Laurel? Answers in monosyllables while you wait for me to go away... Is that all I can expect from you?"

"At least it's honest," she told him, meeting his eyes directly for the first time. "That's better than anything you ever gave me."

His face hardened. "You really mean that?" he asked. "You think I didn't give you anything honest? Even after the way we—"

"Don't talk about it!" Laurel said abruptly. "I don't want to... to remember any of that."

He looked at her in silence while she sipped the last of her drink and struggled to compose herself.

"Why are you in the city?" she asked at last.

"I've been living here for years," he said. "In fact, I have an apartment not far from yours."

"Oh, that's right. I keep forgetting," she said grimly, "that you aren't a country boy at all. You were just out in Wolf Hill on assignment. This is your home base, right?"

"Yes, it is. But lately I've been thinking I might—"

"Well, look who's here," a voice said nearby.

Jonas smiled, though his face still looked tired and strained. "Hi, Nellie," he murmured. "Aren't you a pretty sight?"

"Quit flirting with Nellie and have a look at Crystal," Dennis said proudly.

Jonas obeyed, then gave the two ladies a courtly bow while they giggled in delight.

"Did you get the ticket?" Dennis asked. "I know it's up in the balcony, but it was the best I could do on short notice."

Jonas nodded. "It's great. Thanks, Dennis."

"Apparently, you two have already met," Laurel said, looking from one man to the other. "In fact, everybody seems to have become well acquainted on fairly short notice."

"That's because we all have something in common," Dennis told her, his eyes sparkling.

"Really," she said. "What?"

"We all love you."

Laurel felt the warmth flood her cheeks. She dared not look at Jonas. "Let's go in and find our seats," she said to the others. Jonas reached out and grasped her bare arm. She shivered at the feel of his hand on her skin.

"Laurel," he said urgently. "Please, can't we..."

"Let me go," she said. "We have nothing to talk about, Jonas. Nothing at all."

Determined not to let him see how much her words cost her, she pulled away from him and swept toward the theater doors, with her head high and her golden dress rustling as she moved.

ABOUT TWO WEEKS after their evening at the theater, Dennis came into the office to find Laurel sitting quietly behind the desk.

A warm summer rain was falling, splattering against the windows and flowing down the glass in long rivulets. In the street below, passing cars sent up streams of water, and the trees along the boulevard swayed and rustled in the downpour.

"Wow," he muttered, looking at the empty walls. "This place has sure been plucked clean."

"The last of my stuff was moved this morning," Laurel told him. "It's so empty it practically echoes in here."

He perched in his customary spot on the edge of the desk and looked down at her soberly. "So this is goodbye, right?"

She felt her eyes stinging with tears.

"Don't be ridiculous," she said, as much to herself as to her secretary. "My new office is just down the street. We'll be seeing each other all the time. Besides," she added, "I haven't given up hope of luring you away to work for me again."

"That salary offer you made was pretty tempting," Dennis agreed. "But I have an even stronger incentive to stay with the old company these days."

"Really? What's that?"

He beamed happily. "They've agreed to give Crystal the job of running the lunch counter downstairs, earning about three times what she's making back there on the prairie. She's planning to move out here at the end of the month."

"Dennis!" Laurel said, delighted. "That's wonderful news! I talked to Nellie just last night, and she didn't say a word about it."

"Nobody knows yet," Dennis said. "We've been waiting to hear. I just got the word from personnel yesterday and called Crys. She wants me to start looking for an apartment for her right away. I can hardly wait till she gets here," he added. "There are so many things I want to show her."

Laurel got to her feet and began to gather up her handbag and umbrella.

"I really have to thank you for introducing me to that girl, Laurel," he added, looking serious for once. "She's different from anybody I've ever met. I'm sort of... actually, I'm crazy about her."

Laurel paused by the door, looking at his pleasant face and engaging smile, and came back to give him a hug.

"Dennis..."

"Yeah, boss?"

"You can't call me that anymore," Laurel said, trying to smile. "From now on, we're just friends, remember?"

"And as friends," he said gently, "there's something you want to tell me, right?"

She pulled away and looked at him. "How did you know?"

He grinned. "Call it a sixth sense. After all, we've known each other for a long time. So come on," he added. "Tell me."

"It's..." Laurel played with the strap on her umbrella, fastening and unfastening it to avoid his eyes. "It's about Crystal. I just wondered if you... if you knew about..."

"The baby," Dennis said calmly. "That's what you're wondering about, right? You want to know if she's told me about the baby."

Laurel's cheeks warmed. "I'm sorry, Dennis," she murmured. "I know it's none of my business."

"Well, she told me right away, as soon as I started showing an interest in her. She said there was no point in being dishonest, and she wanted me to know the truth right up front."

"She was wise," Laurel said with a sudden twist of pain. "That's certainly the only way to begin a relationship."

A silence fell, broken only by the gentle hissing of rain and the muffled traffic noises in the wet street below.

"So," Laurel ventured at last, "everything's all right? Her pregnancy doesn't... bother you?"

"Why should it?" he asked in surprise. "I like babies, and I really like Crystal. So why should I be upset if Crystal has a baby?"

Laurel patted his arm. "You're a treasure, Dennis," she murmured. "Have I ever mentioned that?"

"Occasionally," he said with a grin, then sobered. "I'm not pretending it'll all be a stroll in the park, you know. Crystal's pretty young to be raising a baby, but she's grown-up in a lot of the ways that really count. I think she's got what it takes to handle this, and eventually get her nurse's training, too, if that's what she really wants."

"And where do you fit into the picture?"

"As a friend," he said quietly. "We both know better than to force the issue too early. I'm crazy about the girl, and I've been getting to know her pretty well over the past couple of weeks. I've got the long-distance bills to prove it. But we still plan to start off as friends and let things develop on their own."

"That's the best way," Laurel agreed, looking down at the umbrella in her hands.

Her mind was flooded with memories of long walks in the prairie dusk, a meadowlark's nest and a blanket on a grassy creek bank, of sunsets and lilacs and children's baseball, of tea and cookies in a sparse kitchen above a hardware store.

And so much emotion that her heart couldn't begin to contain it all...

"As a matter of fact," Dennis went on, interrupting her sad thoughts, "Crys and I have already talked about natural childbirth classes. I'm going to be her breathing coach."

Laurel smiled. "No kidding?"

"Absolutely," he said gravely. "The old playboy Dennis is a man of the past. I'm ready to get serious about life. It makes a big difference," he added, "when you meet the right person."

"I suppose it does," she said, keeping her voice light. "At least, that's what I've been told."

"But it doesn't help to meet the right person," Dennis went on, "if you're going to run away as soon as you find her. Or him."

Laurel glanced at him sharply, then began to fumble with her umbrella again. "I don't know," she said in a low voice, "why everybody keeps doing this."

"Doing what?"

"Forcing that man on me. Dennis, I've told you enough of the story that you have a pretty good idea what he did to me."

"Tell me again," Dennis said calmly.

"He lied to me and deceived me. He even stole money from me."

"All of which has been returned with interest."

"Why are you taking his side like this?"

"Because I like him," Dennis said. "I happen to think he's a good man."

"Even after what he did to me?"

"He was only doing his job."

"But that's the whole point!" Laurel said furiously. "He was only doing his job, and all the time I thought..."

She fell silent and turned away, not trusting her voice, while Dennis watched her in silence. At last, he came forward and dropped a hand on her shoulder.

"This has been a really hard time for you, hasn't it?" he asked gently. "Especially with all your dad's problems."

Laurel bit her lip and nodded. "My father was always so... he loomed so large in my life. He was everything to me after my mother died. To find out that he's capable of dishonesty and cowardice just like everybody else...it's been pretty tough for me to deal with."

"And you feel that Jonas participated in your father's dishonesty, right?"

"Of course he did. Even when we were... when we got really close, and I told Jonas the whole story about those illegal orders and how I was in hiding while my father worked to clear his name..."

She gave Dennis a questioning glance and he nodded thoughtfully.

"Even then," Laurel went on, taking a deep breath, "Jonas didn't tell me the truth. He kept on pretending to care about me, and all the time he believed I was the one who lied and cheated. He kept reporting back to my father."

Her head started to ache and she rubbed her temples wearily.

"So," Dennis said at last, "have you seen your dad yet?"

Laurel shook her head. "Marta and I are taking the baby up there this weekend for a visit. Not something I'm looking forward to," she added with a bleak smile. "Visiting your father in prison isn't exactly a favorite weekend pastime."

Dennis gave her a hug and reached for her umbrella. "Quit fiddling with that thing," he said gruffly. "Come on, I'll be a gentleman for once and escort you down the street to your new office. I have to go out and pick up some sandwiches, anyway."

Laurel smiled and moved with him to the door, pausing to take one final look at the empty office before she left.

"Do you think he's too warm?"

Marta leaned anxiously over the front seat to examine her son as he howled and squirmed in the baby carrier.

Laurel glanced in the rearview mirror at her brother's unhappy red face. He wore a blue terry-cloth romper suit and little white socks, which waved indignantly in the air as he yelled.

"I don't know much about babies, Marta," she said. "Could he be hungry again?"

"But I fed him less than an hour ago." Marta reached into the back seat. "And he's not wet, either," she reported.

"Then maybe he's just exercising his lungs. Should we let him cry for a while and see what happens?"

Marta nodded dubiously and settled back in the front seat of Laurel's car, closing her eyes. Laurel cast a fond glance at her youthful stepmother, happy to see that apart from her present concern over little Jeremiah's welfare, Marta looked calm and rested.

"Have you . . ." She trailed off, then raised her voice to be heard over the baby's lusty howls. "Have you adjusted to all this?" Laurel asked. "I mean, with Dad being where he is, and the fact that you've had to sell the house, and everything?"

Marta opened her eyes and smiled. "Actually," she confessed, "it's all been sort of a relief to me."

"That's what Dad said, but I can't understand how you'd be relieved to have your husband in prison."

"You see, I was so worried before I found out the truth about what Stewie was doing with those shares. I was as big as a house, covered with heat rash, and he was so quiet and tense all the time, not even wanting to talk to me. I thought. . ." Marta laughed. "I thought he was having an affair. When I found out it was all just about money, I was so happy."

"Even though you knew he'd been concealing a crime?"

"He never meant to hurt anybody. And everything's been paid back since the company was sold. But it wasn't fair to you," Marta added. "That was the only thing that bothered me. Your father should never have treated you that way."

"It was pretty awful, all right. But, you know, I have to take some responsibility for what happened. After all, people can't take advantage of us unless we allow them to. Even our parents."

Marta nodded, then glanced over at her baby son, whose roars had now subsided to a monotonous humming sound.

"You were right," she whispered. "I think he's going to drop off."

"Good," Laurel murmured, glancing in the mirror again.

Jeremiah's eyelids were drooping, and his round face had returned to its normal shade of pink. His little stockinged feet lay still against the padded footrest, and his hands were curled like flower petals.

"He's such a darling," she whispered. "Especially when he's asleep."

Marta laughed and reached back to pull a blanket over the baby.

"Do they let you take him inside?" Laurel asked. "Can Dad hold him?"

"Oh, yes. It's all very casual. After all, this is a minimum-security prison. Nobody's in there for doing anything violent. It's what they call white-collar crime."

"Just nice, clean, nonviolent fraud and embezzlement," Laurel said dryly, then regretted her words when she saw the pain in Marta's eyes.

"He's not a bad man, Laurel. In fact, most of his problems have come from trying too hard to make everybody happy."

"I know." Laurel frowned at the highway and turned onto a tree-shaded lane that wound up a hill to a spot overlooking the ocean. "I guess it's just really hard for me to get used to, that's all. Where do we park?"

Marta gave directions. Laurel parked and got out, then watched while her father's young wife lifted the sleeping baby from the back seat.

"Do you need help with him?"

"Thanks." Marta pulled the blanket up around the baby's face and dropped a kiss on his cheek. "Can you bring the diaper bag for me?"

Laurel shouldered the bag and followed Marta toward the central building, which looked like the main hall at some rustic guest ranch. She walked up onto the ivy-covered veranda, battling a flood of reluctance and uneasiness.

But Marta's description had been accurate. The place was surprisingly casual, without any of the iron bars, screens or two-way telephones that Laurel had envisaged. A group of people, mostly women and children, sat around a large shabby lounge filled with Naugahyde couches and armchairs.

The prisoners were all men, mostly middle-aged, distinguishable from the rest of the group only by their standard garb of khaki trousers and faded blue denim shirts.

"Well, here's the whole group," a hearty voice said behind her. "And look at my boy! He's growing like a weed."

Laurel turned to see her father standing next to the couch, smiling down at them. Stewart Atchison looked as handsome as ever, even more striking with a dark tan that set off his silver hair and vivid blue eyes.

Marta got up and hugged him, then handed him the sleeping baby. Stewart came around the end of the couch, holding his son, and sat next to Laurel.

"Hi, honey," he said. "It's good to see you."

"Hi, Dad." Laurel met his gaze briefly, then looked away.

Stewart hugged the baby, who opened his eyes and examined his father's face gravely.

"Sorry, Marta," Stewart said. "I didn't mean to wake him."

"Oh, that's all right. He can sleep any time," Marta said. "He only gets to see his daddy once a week."

Jeremiah beamed and waved his fists.

"Look," Stewart exclaimed in delight. "He smiled at me!"

"He's been smiling like that for almost a week," Marta said proudly. "I thought he smiled at me right after he was born, but that was probably just gas pains."

"Well, isn't he the handsome fellow," Stewart crooned, kissing the baby's plump cheek. "Isn't he Daddy's big handsome fellow?"

Jeremiah smiled again and wriggled, then began to look distressed. He whimpered, screwing his eyes shut, and his face reddened alarmingly. Stewart handed him back to Marta, who looked down at her son.

"I think I'd better slip away and feed him," she said to the others. "I don't want him crying all the time we're here. I'll be back in ten or fifteen minutes, okay?"

Laurel felt a stirring of panic. She watched helplessly as Marta gathered up the diaper bag and vanished down a hallway with the baby.

Finally, she turned to her father, who sat quietly on the couch next to her.

"You're looking well, Dad," she ventured after an awkward silence.

Stewart leaned back on the couch, stretching his legs. "I've been working," he said. "It's good for me. Up till now, the most strenuous activity I've had was playing eighteen holes of golf."

"What kind of work are you doing?"

"We're using shovels and pickaxes, clearing brush out of one of the upper meadows and getting ready to put in a garden. It's more physical work than most of us have ever done."

"It seems to agree with you," Laurel said.

"Well, it's tough and monotonous. I've had lots of time to think about what's important, and what really matters in life."

"What conclusions have you reached?"

"I've learned a lot," Stewart said thoughtfully. He fixed his eyes on a framed picture that adorned the opposite wall, a cheap print of a sailing schooner battling high seas. "I've realized that money doesn't matter at all. The only important things in life are the people you love, and the kind of relationship you have with them."

Laurel twisted the straps of her handbag, avoiding his eyes.

"I honestly can't believe I treated you that way," he went on with quiet sincerity. "From this perspective, it's really hard to grasp the fact that saving my own skin seemed important enough to lie to you and put you through the kind of misery you went through. I hope you know how sorry I am, sweetheart."

"Dad..."

"All my life," he went on, "I tried so hard to be a tycoon. You know why?"

Laurel shook her head.

"I wanted to show everybody that I wasn't just a guy who'd married a rich wife and then inherited her money after she died. I wanted to be successful and important all on my own, and I went too far. I was such a fool."

"Dad," Laurel whispered, her heart aching. "You don't have to be so hard on yourself. It's bad enough that you have to stay here for a whole year."

Stewart glanced at her in surprise. "I'm not being hard on myself. I'm just being honest. Besides, staying here for a year is probably going to do me a lot of good, as long as it doesn't get to be too hard for Marta and the baby. I'll be a different man when I leave, and a better one, too."

"What will you do?" Laurel asked curiously. "Will you go back into the financial business?"

He shook his head. "Not a chance. I never liked it, you know. I'm going to take whatever money's left when Marta and I have settled our debts, and I plan to do something I've always wanted to do."

"What's that?"

"I'm going to open a gardening shop. Bedding plants, nursery stock, houseplants...all kinds of growing things."

"A gardening shop? That's what you've always wanted to do?" Laurel thought she'd reached a point where nothing could surprise her anymore, but this announcement made her stare at her father in amazement.

He nodded. "It's a good investment, you know. With all the baby boomers reaching retirement age, gardening's becoming a major growth industry. Maybe I can still build something really worthwhile for you and Jerry to take over someday."

"Call him Jeremiah," Laurel said automatically. "Don't shorten his name, Dad. Marta doesn't like it."

"Sorry, honey." Stewart gave her a rueful smile. "I guess I have to stop being so arrogant, don't I? But old habits are hard to break."

Laurel was uncertain what to say. The man beside her seemed so different, she hardly knew how to address him. And yet, she realized, this quiet man in the ill-fitting khaki trousers was genuine and appealing, even more likable than the old Stewart.

"Is it...what's it like in here?" she ventured. "Do they feed you well?"

"Nothing fancy. When we have the garden established, we'll have a more varied diet. Anyhow, most of us can stand to lose a few pounds."

"Can you watch television, and read whatever you want?"

"There are some scheduled hours of leisure activities in the evening, but we're usually too weary by the end of the day to take much advantage of them. Still, there's a fair amount of personal freedom. I can make a couple of phone calls every day, for instance, and receive incoming calls one evening a week."

Laurel glanced up at him. "People can call you?"

He nodded, meeting her eyes steadily. "Yes, honey. People can call me."

She flushed and dropped her eyes, concentrating on the strap of her handbag.

"As a matter of fact," he went on, still watching her with that intent look, "I had an interesting phone call on Wednesday night. It was from a friend of yours."

Laurel's heart began to pound, and she kept her eyes carefully averted. "A friend of mine?"

But when he spoke, she was astounded once more by his answer.

"An incredible lady by the name of Nellie Grossman," Stewart said. "She tells me she's eighty-three years old, and she's lived all her life in that little town."

"*Nellie* called you? How on earth...where did she get the number of this place?"

"I don't know. Obviously, she has some interesting contacts."

"But..." Laurel faltered, "I don't understand, Dad. What did Nellie want to talk to you about?"

Stewart smiled. "She was pretty firm with me. That lady loves you a whole lot. She practically ordered me to tell you a few things she felt you should know."

"What kind of things?"

"Some facts," Stewart said quietly, "about the life and times of Jonas O'Neal."

CHAPTER FIFTEEN

"JONAS?" Laurel whispered. "Nellie told you something about Jonas?"

"Most of it I already knew before I hired him. He was recommended by a friend of mine in the security business who knew his story. But Nellie added a few details I hadn't been aware of. I guess Jonas has been confiding in her, and she thought some of these details were important for you to hear."

"Like what?"

"Well, to start with, do you know anything about the man's personal history?"

Laurel shook her head. "Almost nothing. Jonas never wanted to talk about the past, even after we got to be... after we'd become quite close."

Suddenly, like fragments of rainbows, the images filled her memory, moments of intimacy and shared laughter, sweet interludes of lovemaking that still took her breath away. When she'd last seen Jonas, it had been early summer. Now the leaves were falling and the October mornings were chilly with frost. She looked up to find Stewart watching her quietly.

"Tell me about him, Dad. Was he a policeman before he became a private investigator?"

"I thought he didn't tell you anything about his past."

"He didn't, but he always had that look. Sort of authoritative, you know? Besides, I was so afraid of being tracked by the police, I guess it sharpened my instincts."

"Well, your instincts were right. Apparently, the man grew up on a farm in Ontario, and joined the Toronto police force. He worked for a few years as an undercover cop in the narcotics division."

Laurel shivered, forgetting for a moment that she was still furious with Jonas O'Neal.

"That must be...such a terribly hard job," she whispered.

"It is, but apparently the man had nerves of steel. He also had a partner and best friend on the force, a cop he'd worked with and trusted for years. The guy turned on him."

"What do you mean, Dad? What guy?"

"O'Neal's partner. There's a lot of temptation in the drug trade, I suppose. Just like high finance," Stewart said dryly. "Lots of big money floating around. After a while, if you're weak, you start thinking some of it should be yours. Apparently, Jonas caught his friend dealing on the wrong side, and threatened to turn him in."

"Oh, poor Jonas," Laurel said softly. "His best friend?"

"A pretty nasty situation," Stewart agreed quietly. "Much like yours, actually, when you caught your daddy with his hand in the till."

"Don't joke about it!" Laurel said. "It's not...not the same thing at all."

Her father watched her in silence while she struggled to compose herself.

"Go on," she said tensely. "Tell me more about Jonas and this other policeman."

"I guess the story ended like a Hollywood movie. Jonas confronted his partner in an old warehouse down by the lake, on a cold winter night. He told the guy to make a choice, come in and confess what he was doing or leave that night and start running. Then Jonas walked away, after telling his friend that he was going down to the station to report the whole thing."

Laurel listened, hardly daring to breathe.

"What happened?" she said at last.

"His best friend shot him in the back while he was walking away."

"Oh, God," she moaned, hugging herself and rocking on the couch.

She remembered their first time in bed together, her discovery of the cruel scar on his abdomen and his quiet voice telling her about bullet wounds.

Her father watched intently. "I suppose an injury like that would leave a pretty nasty scar," he observed with deliberate casualness.

"I can't believe it," Laurel murmured. "Jonas was shot in the back by his best friend...."

Stewart nodded. "The guy disappeared after that. The other cop, I mean. He ended up dead in an alley after a drug war in Montreal."

"What happened to Jonas?"

"He was in the hospital for a long time, getting all his vital organs stitched up and stabilized. When he finally came out, he was awarded a huge cash settlement from the city, probably enough to keep him in comfort for the rest of his life. But he still wanted to work."

"So he moved to the West Coast and started being a private investigator?"

"That's what I heard. When I was looking for..."
Stewart hesitated, giving his daughter an awkward
smile. "When I needed somebody to do a discreet little
surveillance job for me, I heard about this injured cop
who has a Robin Hood complex and only takes cases
where somebody's been cheated or robbed. He helps
them get their money back and keeps a small finder's
fee."

"Is that why you made up the whole story about me
being guilty?"

"O'Neal wouldn't have taken the job if he didn't believe you'd absconded with a whole lot of money that
belonged to other people. I had to convince him of that,
Laurel. And I had to convince him that I was working
on a way to return the money. All I needed was for him
to keep an eye on you."

"Why?" she asked bitterly. "Couldn't you just find
yourself a less scrupulous investigator, and not bother
with all the lies?"

"I wanted Jonas O'Neal. I knew he was an honest
guy who'd watch and protect you, no matter what his
motivation was, and I didn't want you to be in any
danger."

"Just up to my elbows in chicken grease."

"I never wanted to hurt you, sweetheart." Stewart
smiled apologetically. "I love you more than anything."

"I know you do, Dad," she said, smiling back at him.
"I'm not angry anymore," she said after a pause. "I
can understand what happened, and why both of you
did what you did. The thing I can't bear is how he..."

"What?" Stewart prompted gently.

"We fell in love, Dad," she said, looking directly at
her father. "At least I did. And Jonas pretended to feel

the same way. He was so sweet to me, and it felt just...just wonderful..." Her voice broke, then steadied. "But all the time, he believed I was a thief. He was making love to me and then calling you later to report on my actions. I feel so lousy about it, Dad. I've been cheated and betrayed by a man I really cared about."

"But you've got it all wrong, honey. That's what your friend Nellie wants me to tell you."

"Wrong? What do you mean?"

"Well, toward the end, I started having some real problems with my man in the field," Stewart said with a fleeting grin. "Jonas turned on me, and started to question the whole assignment. Scared me half to death."

"He turned on you? Does that mean..."

"Let me finish the story. Apparently, you told him about the whole sorry mess one night, and he obviously believed your version, not mine. He called next day but I was out of town on business. Jonas left a message on my voice mail saying that he thought me beneath contempt, considering what I was doing to my daughter, and that he was officially resigning from the job of baby-sitting you."

Laurel's eyes widened in shock. "Jonas did?" she breathed, staring at her father. "He said that?"

Stewart grinned. "And a few more things besides. The man was furious, that's for sure. When I listened to that voice message and recalled what he looked like, I was damned glad he was a thousand miles away."

"So what did you do?" Laurel asked.

"I sat down and thought things over. I knew I couldn't hold on much longer, but the investigators hadn't found anything irregular in the books and they were starting to lose interest. If I could just keep you away from them for another few weeks, I might still wriggle out from under. Finally, I decided the best defense was a good offense."

"So you called him," Laurel said in a flat, unemotional tone.

"That's right. I called his number in Wolf Hill, or whatever godforsaken place you were all living in. He wasn't home, but I left a tough-sounding message on his machine, ordering him to toe the line and get back to work or he'd be in big trouble. I said—"

"I know what you said, Dad. I was there." Laurel felt tears burning in her throat, and swallowed hard. "What...what was his response?" she asked, hardly trusting her voice.

"I never heard from him again. I still owe him quite a lot of money for services rendered up to that point, but I can't find him."

"What do you mean? Surely you must have an address for him."

Stewart shook his head. "He had an apartment here in the city, but last time I called that number, the phone was disconnected. I checked with the leasing firm, and they said the place was vacant."

"What about...what about Wolf Hill?" she whispered. "Maybe he's gone back there."

Stewart shook his head. "Nellie says he's disappeared completely. There's another young fellow working at the hardware store, and living in the room upstairs where Jonas used to stay. Nellie says the boss's wife even had to take over your baseball team for the last few games."

"Oh, well," Laurel said, forcing a smile. "That's not all bad. If anybody can force those kids to be winners, Aggie Krantz can probably do it."

She got to her feet and moved restlessly around the room.

"What will you do, honey?"

She stood by the window, hugging her arms. "What can I do?"

"Maybe," he suggested awkwardly, "you could hire somebody to..."

"Track him down?" Laurel asked with a bitter smile. "Follow him and tell me what he's doing? I don't think so, Dad."

"But if you..."

"He knows where I live," Laurel said, returning to the couch. "If he wants to see me, he'll come back and find me. But it's never going to happen," she added. "He's gone, Dad, and he's not coming back."

She lifted a shabby pillow and cradled it in her lap, fingering the tufted corners while her father sat nearby in silence.

Marta returned with the baby, who now looked drowsy and content after his feeding. Laurel watched for a while as Stewart played with his son.

Finally, she got up and wandered outside onto the prison grounds to allow the others a little time alone.

She crossed a field and stood alone on the high bluff overlooking the ocean, near the ragged field where Stewart and his fellow prisoners were planning to install their garden. Far out across the bay, lush green islands glimmered in the silvery distance, and the dying sun cast long streaks of pink across the sky. The wind whipped at her hair and dried her tears before they could begin to fall.

ABOUT A MONTH LATER, Laurel drove toward the town of Wolf Hill early in the afternoon. Summer was over and the faded warmth of late autumn lay across the rolling countryside. The fields, rich and green when she'd first arrived in the spring, had now been harvested. They lay shorn and quiet in their blankets of pale golden stubble. Cattle grazed in the fields, fat and glossy, ready for market. The town itself, as she drew nearer, seemed hardly to have changed at all. The grain elevators still pointed rigidly toward the sky, and the houses lined the streets behind brown lawns and limp shrubbery.

She looked around with pleasure, happier than she'd been in months, delighting in the peace and tranquillity of the little town. Harold Baines's general store advertised summer sandals and beachwear at half price, and Margie's Beauty Shop, next to the post office, was running a special on permanent waves.

Laurel touched her hair, wondering whether to let it grow out again or ask Margie to give her another haircut.

The Wolf Hill Hotel still dominated the town. A couple of retired farmers lounged on the shaded veranda, rocking comfortably as they exchanged gossip.

Laurel parked her car under their admiring gaze and mounted the steps.

"That there's a Cadillac," one told the other, adjusting the wad of tobacco in his cheek.

"I guess I know what a Cadillac is," his companion said, looking annoyed. "Hi, Laurie," he added casually. "Came back from the city for a visit, did you?"

Laurel looked at him puzzled, then realized that everybody in the little town must have heard her story by now.

"It's just a rental car," she told the farmer, then strolled inside, leaving the two men exchanging glances.

She paused in the lobby, noticing that everything looked exactly the same. The only thing different, Laurel thought, was herself.

She wore a pair of tan linen slacks and a loose silk shirt of burnt orange, with a woven leather belt. But the difference in her went far beyond a sophisticated wardrobe. It was something that came from the core of her being, a new strength and understanding that she'd never possessed before.

Hilda bustled out from the coffee shop and stood gaping in astonishment.

"Well, look who's here!" she said. "What a surprise. And don't you look spiffy?"

She hurried over to hug Laurel, beaming in delight.

"Hilda, it's so nice to see you," Laurel said. "You wouldn't believe how much I've missed this place."

"No," Hilda said cheerfully, "I don't s'pose I would. We worked you pretty hard, didn't we?"

"Pretty hard," Laurel agreed. "But in a lot of ways, you know, it was the best time in my whole life. I didn't even know how much I loved Wolf Hill until after I left."

Hilda held her at arm's length and looked at Laurel's stylish clothes. "I don't imagine you want your old job back, do you?"

Laurel laughed. "I don't think so, Hilda. Although," she added, her smile fading, "come to think of it, I'm not all that happy with the job I've got. Maybe I should consider your offer."

"What are you doing?"

"I'm running the commodities section of one of the biggest brokerage houses in Vancouver. A year or two ago, it would have been my dream job."

Hilda looked at her shrewdly. "But not anymore?"

"Nowadays, nothing seems very exciting," Laurel said. "It's all kind of…empty." She glanced at the other woman, who nodded thoughtfully. "Are you really short-staffed, Hilda?"

"It's been pretty tough." Hilda led the way into the kitchen and filled coffee mugs for both of them while Laurel sat at the table. "First you left, then Crystal, and the new girls never stay more than a week, it seems. Poor Luther, he's working for me almost full-time. He never gets to play with that toy airplane of his anymore."

"Can't you hire somebody else?"

"I'm trying," Hilda said. "In fact, I've got two new girls starting on Monday. But I really loved you and Crystal. It's hard to get used to somebody else in my kitchen."

"Don't be that way," Laurel said with a smile. "They'll be just fine."

"Well, Luther sure hopes so."

They sipped coffee for a few moments in companionable silence, while Laurel looked around the room and thought about the mountains of dishes she'd washed, the piles of wet chicken feathers and French fries, the talk and laughter…

"Everything's different," Hilda said, breaking the silence. "There's been a lot of changes since you left."

"Like what?"

"Well, Crystal's gone to the city, and Kate's mother left for Paris and finally gave that poor girl a chance to raise her own baby."

"That's good. I think poor Kate was almost at her wit's end."

Hilda nodded. "And Aggie and Clarence are leaving town, too."

"They are?" Laurel said in surprise. "I can't imagine this town without them. Aggie practically runs the whole place, doesn't she?"

"They're only going to Calgary," Hilda said dryly. "She'll probably still have a finger in every pie in town."

"Why are they moving?"

"They finally got a buyer for the hardware store, after years of trying to sell it. Aggie wants to live in a condo like Nathan's parents. She's always been a great one for trying to keep up with the Camerons."

Laurel smiled. "I see. Any other news? Is Nellie all right?"

"She's fine. I saw her yesterday at the grocery store, and she told me you were coming for a visit. She was as excited as a little kid, practically buying out the whole place."

"I can imagine," Laurel said fondly. "It'll be so nice to see her again."

But when Laurel finally left the hotel and wandered outside, she didn't go straight over to Nellie's house. Instead, she got into her car and drove slowly down the street, past the grocery store and the post office. She parked near the hardware store, looking up at the windows of the room where Jonas had once lived.

A stranger was working there now, a wiry young man with a ponytail who could be seen unloading cartons at the back of the store. There was no sign of Blackie, the mongrel dog that Jonas had adopted. The place seemed desolate without the two of them.

But her memories made it too painful for her to linger. Laurel put the car in gear and drove out of town toward the west, gazing at the mellow autumn prairie and the soaring arch of turquoise sky.

She passed the grove of willows along the creek where she and Jonas had once spread their picnic blanket and made love under the gentle noonday sun. Her throat tightened, and tears burned in her eyes.

Finally, she came to a field of bleached grass that rippled in the wind, sweeping away to the horizon. She parked and got out, walking slowly up toward a ragged fence line, concentrating on the ground.

A few yards to her right she saw a pile of stones and went over to look down, then knelt to peer into the grass. The meadowlark nest was still there, hidden within the shadows, empty and silent.

Laurel touched the woven circle of grass, remembering the first night Jonas brought her to see the tiny oval eggs nestled cozily in their bed of grass and feathers. And later when they'd come back, arm in arm, to see the newly hatched chicks, then the little fledglings ready to take flight...

"Oh, Jonas," she whispered, tears rolling down her cheeks. "My darling, I love you so much. I can't bear it..."

A long shadow fell across the grass. She looked up, startled, her eyes dazzled by the sunlight.

"They're all gone," a voice said. "I think they've flown away to a warmer place."

"Jonas?" she whispered in disbelief, scrambling to her feet.

He stood nearby, looking at her intently. Laurel gazed at him, unable to speak, drinking in the lean power of his body, the clean, hard lines of his face. He wore jeans and a casual plaid shirt, open at the neck, and his thick hair lifted gently in the afternoon breeze.

"Where . . . where did you come from?" she asked, shading her eyes with her hand.

"Home," he said casually, extending his arms to show her a smear of white on his sleeves. "I've been painting the veranda railings."

"Home? You *live* here?"

"I bought the Krantz house. Clarence and Aggie are moving to Calgary."

"I know." Laurel gazed at him, stunned. "You bought their place? That beautiful old house with all the dormers? Hilda never said a word about it."

He smiled. "Nobody knows yet. We just signed the papers yesterday morning. And that house may be beautiful, but it sure needs work. I've got a lot of plans for the place."

"I don't understand," she said, aching to touch his hand but afraid to make any kind of move toward him. "You're going to live here in Wolf Hill?"

"I have to," he said calmly. "I've become a local businessman."

Sunlight glimmered on his face and neck, highlighting a small pulse beating in his tanned throat. Laurel reached up toward it, then let her hand drop again.

"Aren't you interested in my business venture?" he asked, still looking at her intently.

"Of course," she whispered. "I'm . . . interested in everything about you, Jonas. Everything that's ever happened to you."

He smiled briefly and moved a few steps closer to her. "I bought the hardware store," he told her. "I liked this place so much, I couldn't stand to leave. And Clarence was prepared to give me a really good price, so I decided to take the plunge.''

"Why?"

He shrugged. "I'm tired of the life I've been living. And even though I'd lost you, being with you for a little while was enough to convince me that I was finally ready to stop running away from happiness."

Laurel struggled to understand what he was saying. But he was near enough by now to set all her senses reeling, and she couldn't think clearly.

"Oh, Jonas," she whispered, yielding at last to the impulse to touch him. "Darling, I've missed you so much." She reached out and put her hands on his broad chest, sighing with pleasure, loving the warmth and hardness of him.

He covered her hands with his own and stood looking down at her. "I'll need a bookkeeper," he said huskily.

Laurel moved closer to him and rested her cheek against his shoulder. "A bookkeeper?"

He kissed her cheek and held her tenderly. "Do you know anybody who's good with figures? Reliable and honest? Experienced in financial matters?"

"I might." Lost in happiness, she nestled in his arms and reached up to stroke his hair. "Any other qualifications?"

"Maybe a couple."

"Like what?"

"Well, she has to be a good ball player, and terrific in bed," he whispered. "Also willing to bear our children and grow old with me."

"I think," Laurel murmured, "that I know just the woman for you. Somebody who..."

But she couldn't say anything else, because his mouth was on hers and his kisses were carrying her to a place full of sweet sun-warmed ecstasy, where there was no need for words.

Through mists of happiness, she heard a distant warbling, a soft trill of music on the prairie wind that sounded like a meadowlark's song.

EPILOGUE

Two years later

THE DAY AFTER Christmas dawned silent and clear, with a pale sun that glistened on a desert of white. By mid-afternoon, shadows gathered across the upper dormers of an old house near the edge of town, now beautifully restored and festooned with colored lights and pine branches.

In the master bedroom, Laurel fastened her long tartan skirt, pulled on a red sweater and attached a holly-shaped brooch at the neck, then went in search of her husband.

She found him in the bathroom, kneeling on the floor next to the tub giving a bath to baby Ellen, now almost nine months old. Bath time with Ellen was a messy, riotous affair, and Jonas had removed his shirt as a safeguard against flying water and bubbles.

Laurel leaned in the doorway, looking at the cruel pucker of scars on his abdomen and the utter contentment on his face as he lathered his daughter's small body. She smiled mistily, offering up a silent prayer of thanks to whatever Christmas angels hovered nearby.

"One little toe," Jonas muttered, not seeing Laurel in the doorway, "and another little toe... Ellie, don't kick. Look, poor Daddy's getting all wet."

The baby squealed when she caught sight of her mother, and waved a rubber duck.

Jonas turned and grinned. "What a pretty lady," he said approvingly as he lifted his daughter's little pink body from the tub and wrapped her in a towel.

"Mum," the baby said happily over his shoulder, her voice somewhat muffled because she was chewing on the rubber duck. "Mum-mum-mum."

"Mummy's busy." Jonas nuzzled Ellen's fat neck, making her squeal and kick with delight. "Daddy's going to dress you. Is her outfit ready?" he asked Laurel.

"It's all laid out on the chest in her room." Laurel kissed both of them, then hurried downstairs to prepare for their guests.

Her father and stepmother were already there, having come out to Wolf Hill for the holiday a few days earlier. They sat in the living room near the holly-draped fireplace, watching their little son Jeremiah build a shaky tower out of plastic blocks.

Blackie drowsed in his basket near the fireplace, a jaunty tartan bow attached to his collar, and opened one eye occasionally to check on the little boy's welfare.

Laurel came into the room in time to catch Stewart and Marta holding hands and exchanging a hasty kiss.

"What a pair of lovebirds," she teased. "You'd think by now the honeymoon would be over."

"It isn't." Stewart hugged his wife placidly. "And I hope it never ends. In fact, I feel like my life is just beginning."

Her father looked strong and hearty, and more at peace than Laurel had ever seen him. She exchanged a smile with Marta, then went to answer the doorbell.

"Nellie," she exclaimed in delight. "Merry Christmas! I'm so happy to see you. Did you have a nice time?"

Nellie's son William was with her, a genial, florid man in his late fifties, wearing a festive bow tie. "We drove to Calgary and saw all the Christmas lights," he said. "Mom loved it."

"And guess what?" Nellie hopped from one foot to the other in excitement while Laurel was removing her coat and hanging it away in the closet. "Guess what William gave me for Christmas?"

Laurel looked from Nellie's bright face to William's expansive grin. "I couldn't imagine."

"I'll give you a hint," Nellie said. "It's absolutely wonderful, and it arrives on Thursday."

"I give up. What is it, Nellie?"

"My whole family, Karen and Stacy, and the babies!" Nellie threw her arms around Laurel and hugged her fiercely. "They're all staying for a week, and then Karen's taking me back to Ottawa with her to visit for another month."

Laurel held her friend and smiled over Nellie's curly white head at William Grossman.

William winked and Laurel patted his arm, then brought Nellie and her son into the living room to meet Stewart and Marta.

The doorbell rang again, admitting Kate and Nathan Cameron, along with Mamie and Tom. Little Joshua was now a shy, winsome child of three, clutching his grandmother's hand. Nathan carried a baby seat containing the Camerons' newborn son, Thomas.

Joshua edged his way into the room, his eyes brightening when he saw Jeremiah playing with the mound of blocks.

"Hi," Jeremiah said, waving a hand expansively at the other child and moving over to make room. "Wanna play?"

Joshua glanced up at his mother for approval, then joined the little boy near the Christmas tree. The adults settled in chairs and sofas around the fireplace and watched the children.

Luther and Hilda arrived next, along with Clarence and Aggie Krantz.

At the sound of Aggie's strident voice, Blackie looked up alertly, then slipped from his basket and vanished into a cubbyhole under the stairs, where an anxious dark eye could be seen peeping around the corner.

Jonas came downstairs, wearing the cashmere pullover Laurel had given him for Christmas. He carried little Ellen who was resplendent in bright red shoes, lacy tights and a red velvet dress lovingly hand-sewn by Nellie.

Jonas set the baby near the coffee table. She gripped the edge to hold herself upright, watching the two little boys as they played.

Jonas strolled into the kitchen and paused to drop a kiss on the back of Laurel's neck as she filled trays with Christmas cookies.

"I love you," he murmured. "You always look sexy in red."

She turned to nestle in his arms. "Oh, Jonas," she whispered. "I'm so happy. If only..."

The doorbell rang again, startling her.

"Now, who could that be?" Jonas said in mock surprise, peering through the curtains at the street. "I thought all our guests were already here."

Laurel cast him a suspicious glance and went to answer the door, then stared in amazement.

Dennis stood in the colored glow of the outdoor lights, looking prosperous and handsome in a long woolen topcoat, holding a small boy in his arms. Crystal was just behind them, composed and beautiful, though her eyes glistened with tears of happiness.

"Merry Christmas, Laurel," she whispered.

"But...I never dreamed... Oh my goodness," Laurel said, laughing and crying at the same time. "Where on earth did you come from?"

"Jonas and I made some last minute arrangements." Dennis held up the little boy, warmly muffled in a coat and scarf. "Denny, say hello to your fairy godmother."

Laurel reached out and took the child. "He's so sweet," she murmured. "Hello, Denny."

"He's almost two," Dennis said cheerfully as they removed their coats in the foyer, "and hell on wheels. Aren't you, son?"

Dennis knelt to take off the little boy's coat, revealing a tiny pair of dress pants, a white shirt and a natty plaid vest. The child had Crystal's red hair surrounding his face in a halo of curls, and blue eyes full of laughter.

"Dennis, I can't believe it. He actually looks like you." Laurel watched as the redheaded child toddled into the living room and approached the Christmas tree.

"Why not? He's my boy," Dennis said proudly, one arm around his wife. The couple entered the living room amid happy shouts of greeting.

Laurel found her father alone in the kitchen, refilling a tray of cheese and crackers. Stewart dropped a kiss on top of her head, then moved toward the doorway and looked out at the group in the living room. He leaned quietly against the door frame, sipping a glass of ginger ale.

Laurel came over, carrying a mug of eggnog for Dennis, and slipped an arm around her father's waist. "What are you thinking, Dad?"

"I'm looking at these people. All the babies, and happy faces and warm friendships . . . and I'm thinking that I've been given a second chance at happiness, Laurel, and I intend to make the most of it."

"I'm glad, Dad." Laurel hugged her father and turned to watch her husband, who was lifting his daughter high enough to see the angel at the top of the Christmas tree. Ellen reached out a chubby finger, puffing with excitement, and touched the angel's white satin skirt.

"A year ago, I was in prison, and now . . . Isn't life strange?" Stewart said softly.

"Strange and wonderful," Laurel murmured, as Jonas smiled at her across the room and cuddled their child in his arms.

Fall in love all over again with

This Time...
MARRIAGE

In this collection of original short stories, three brides get a unique chance for a return engagement!

- Being kidnapped from your bridal shower by a one-time love can really put a crimp in your wedding plans! *The Borrowed Bride*— by **Susan Wiggs**, *Romantic Times* Career Achievement Award-winning author.

- After fifteen years a couple reunites for the sake of their child—this time will it end in marriage? *The Forgotten Bride*—by **Janice Kaiser.**

- It's tough to make a good divorce stick—especially when you're thrown together with your ex in a magazine wedding shoot! *The Bygone Bride*— by **Muriel Jensen.**

Don't miss THIS TIME...MARRIAGE, available in April wherever Harlequin books are sold.

HARLEQUIN ®

HARLEQUIN SUPERROMANCE®

Emotional, daring, adventurous—a stunning new novel from the award-winning author of *The Third Christmas* and *The Keeper*. **Margot Early** has been called "an author whose talent will carry her to the top" and "one of the brightest rising stars of contemporary romance." This book proves it!

Waiting For You

According to family legend, golden-haired Christopher was born with a mission—to break a family curse. Only he, it is said, can end the history of miscarriages, stillbirths and maternal deaths.

Christopher, a doctor living and working in Colorado, isn't sure he believes all this. But now Dulcinea—the first and only woman he ever loved—is pregnant. With his brother's baby.

She comes back to Christopher, begging him to take the risk, to break the curse. *How can he refuse?*

Waiting For You will be available in June wherever Harlequin books are sold. Don't miss it!

HARLEQUIN SUPERROMANCE®

Showcase

Not Without My Child
by
Rebecca Winters

A very contemporary and deeply emotional story of love, family and second chances. By the award-winning author of *The Wrong Twin*.

Tessa Marsden. Her marriage was a mistake; her son, Scotty, was not. She loves her child with all her heart and soul. She's tried hard to make the marriage work, but this is a marriage that can't be saved. She knows now that she has to get out—before it completely destroys her *and* her husband, Grant.

But when she files for divorce, Grant—for reasons of his own, reasons she doesn't understand—demands full custody of Scotty. Tessa can't live with that. *She can't live without her child.*

Alex Sommerfield. He's the lawyer handling her divorce. He defies all the rules by falling in love with his client. But he's determined not to put her custody case or her happiness at risk....

Watch for *Not Without My Child* in June wherever Harlequin books are sold.

UNLOCK THE DOOR TO GREAT ROMANCE
AT BRIDE'S BAY RESORT

Join Harlequin's new across-the-lines series, set
in an exclusive hotel on an island off the coast of
South Carolina.

Seven of your favorite authors will bring you exciting stories
about fascinating heroes and heroines discovering love at
Bride's Bay Resort.

Look for these fabulous stories coming to a store near you
beginning in January 1996.

Harlequin American Romance #613 in January
Matchmaking Baby by Cathy Gillen Thacker

Harlequin Presents #1794 in February
Indiscretions by Robyn Donald

Harlequin Intrigue #362 in March
Love and Lies by Dawn Stewardson

Harlequin Romance #3404 in April
Make Believe Engagement by Day Leclaire

Harlequin Temptation #588 in May
Stranger in the Night by Roseanne Williams

Harlequin Superromance #695 in June
Married to a Stranger by Connie Bennett

Harlequin Historicals #324 in July
Dulcie's Gift by Ruth Langan

Visit Bride's Bay Resort each month wherever
Harlequin books are sold.

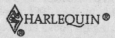

BBAYG